Praise for Mistress of the Wind

"Diener's adaptation retains the familiar elements of the original, echoing both the structure and spirit of the classic, but true to form, she puts her own spin both the plot and the narrative, crafting an intricately alluring tale of self-sacrifice, steadfast devotion and enduring love."
Flashlight Commentary

"The story is fast-paced and never boring, the world a beauty and Michelle's writing so wonderfully detailed that I felt I was with Bjorn and Astrid on their journey."
Book Bird Reviews

"Author Michelle Diener takes this re-telling to another level. She doesn't restrict herself to an East of the Sun, West of the moon retelling. Instead we are also given parts reminiscent of Psyche's quest. Which just allowed for a much richer story."
Paperback Wonderland

D1617026

Mistress of the Wind

MICHELLE DIENER

ACKNOWLEDGMENTS

A big thank you to everyone who helped make this story the best it could be. To beta readers Fee, Julia, Jo, Stephanie, Mel and Laura, thank you for your great feedback! To my critique partners Edie, Liz and Kim, your suggestions were much appreciated. Thanks to Amy at AEMS for the technical side, and Laura Morrigan for the amazing cover.

Fairy tales are stories for the soul, and delving into the mysteries of East of the Sun, West of the Moon to write this book was pure pleasure.

Chapter One

Bjorn ran along a path of his own making, between the thinning trees at the top of the mountain. Sometimes, when he was so exhausted he lost himself, his existence *was* running. Was watching the ground flash beneath him, hypnotized by it.

Tonight, though, he looked forward and up. Time was running out for him. He could feel it slipping like snow off pine branches. It held, and it held, and then suddenly, in a hiss, it gave.

He could no longer afford the luxury of weariness. There would be no rest until this was over, and if he didn't find the girl, there would never be any rest.

Unless he was dead.

He reached the pass, his legs quivering with exertion, and sank shoulder deep into the snow drifts. He noticed, in the detached way he'd adopted over this last year that he'd been a bear instead of a man, that his fur looked dirty white against the snow's purity.

He started forcing his way through, every step slower than the last, until, just for a moment, he leaned into the cushioning white and rested.

"Do you give up yet?"

Had he dreamed Norga's voice? He lifted his heavy head, saw her standing a few feet from where he'd fallen in the snow.

He was too weak to fight her, and besides, it was against the rules they'd set between them. He let his head flop back down.

"You've been looking how long now? Isn't it time to give in to the inevitable?" Her voice was spun sugar in the frosty air. Sweet and brittle.

Strange, he thought she'd enjoy waiting out the full year. Enjoy seeing him return defeated. The chances of his success were so low, it was why she had agreed to this in the first place, rather than risk an open war between her people and his.

It seemed out of character for her to want to hurry him up.

"I have a month left."

"And what can you do in one month you haven't been able to do in the last eleven?" A freezing wind lifted her dark hair and tugged at the gossamer dress she wore and she did not so much as shiver.

You can't feel the cold when your heart is a sliver of stone.

"The woman doesn't exist, you fool." Spun sugar gave way to daggers of ice. "You were always a dreamer, but now you're letting your dreams rule your life."

Bjorn ignored her. Stretched out. Tried to ease

some feeling into his weary limbs.

How had Norga found him? She was powerful, but to have tracked him down to this mountain top, at his lowest hour? Just wondering how she'd accomplished it put a spark of energy back into his body.

"You do not answer because you know I have it right. Put yourself out of your misery."

Though she spoke with confidence, with a gleeful relish at his condition, deep within him, hope bloomed. He was careful not to move, to give even the smallest twitch of reaction to alert her she'd given herself away.

"My misery starts the moment I give up. I'll spend my month searching, as our bargain allows, whether I find her or not."

"You've thought about your fate, have you? Thought about your life once you fail and have to marry my daughter as we agreed?" She smiled, then dropped her magical appearance, allowed her true colors to show. As big as he was when he stood on his hind legs, her back was twisted and bent, like a gnarled old tree. Her nose was sharp below two gleaming black eyes, alight with cunning.

She loomed over him, a trollish nightmare.

His father had thought her the most beautiful creature alive. Bjorn wondered bitterly what he would think of his beautiful bride now. She had never revealed herself to her husband before his death, only to her stepson. Out of necessity the first time, and thereafter to frighten and intimidate him.

And then she'd turned him into a bear.

"I might not fail." He turned away from her, curled up on himself and closed his eyes. "I have one month left. I'm taking it."

"Suffer a bit longer, then. I'll see you soon enough."

He didn't answer, and after a moment of silence, looked round to find her gone.

He had never given up, but he had been flagging. Had begun to doubt his memory. Doubt that a small girl had once reached out her hand to him in a clearing long ago and whispered: 'I will love you forever.' The strange connection he'd felt with her since that day had been frayed and stretched almost to breaking-point.

He forced himself up and started moving again.

He was close. Close enough to scare Norga into a little visit. Close enough that she thought there was a chance he might win.

He found a new rhythm as he loped across the snow. The rhythm of hope renewed.

———◄✐►———

Someone was watching her.

Astrid scanned the edge of the forest, clutching her hoe defensively.

There was a stillness in the trees. The birds were

gone, the branches did not move as the wind held its breath. It no longer whispered to her as usual, with words she could almost hear and understand.

She forced herself to lift the hoe and pretend to work. She was imagining things, surely?

But no. She knew, *knew* someone . . . some*thing* was there. Every nerve in her body screamed at her to run. As she slammed the blunt blade of the hoe into the cold, wet earth, her arms shook.

There were many dangers in the forest, and there was every reason to fear them.

But this felt different.

This felt personal.

And absolutely terrifying.

It would be a long time before anyone returned home. Father, Eric and Tomas would only come in when the light started to fail and they couldn't see to cut wood any more. Her mother and older sisters would be back even later from market.

She was alone.

She shivered as the wind started up again, a chill breeze off the snow-topped mountains that ruffled over the treetops and blew through the thin, scratchy wool of her dress. Tugging her toward the house.

There was no reprieve from the invisible eyes. They were still on her. And she had come to trust what the wind told her, even if she no longer mentioned the strange kinship she felt to it.

She wanted to be indoors. Now.

Her eyes jerked to the trees again, and she made up her mind. She couldn't stand being out here any longer.

She took a calming breath. What could it be, anyway? A wolf? A bear? She was close to the house. Neither would be quick enough to get her before she reached the safety of the front door.

But this isn't one of those things.

She knew it with bone-deep certainty.

Ridiculous, she told herself.

Then she threw down her hoe and ran.

Chapter Two

S he sensed him.

Interesting.

Less gratifying was her reaction—unmitigated terror was not a good start. Especially given the rules between his stepmother and himself.

If Bjorn were to beat Norga, he would require this woman's cooperation.

As he'd watched her working, his heart had beat faster and faster, his excitement stirring in tandem with the wind.

The bond that he'd felt so strongly after he first met her snapped back into place at the sight of her, as if it had never been tested to its limits. His worries of how he would know her, now a woman rather than a small child, were blasted away by the cold wind that pummeled him.

Hope surged in his chest. He had found her, now he had to find a way to have her. Time was running out.

He peered through the thicket and across the fields to the small cottage, trying to see movement at the window. As he stood in the deep shadow of the trees, the wind changed direction, swirling around him and blasting his eyes with grit and leaves. He shivered and blinked.

His lady must come willingly, no matter what the cost to others or himself. Forcing her was against everything he stood for.

The deal he'd struck with Norga was more than just finding the right one, though. It was keeping her with him for a whole year, while never allowing her to see him. And keeping the deal he had made with Norga a secret, as well.

And that was where she'd had the good instinct to run. Before Norga got hold of him, he'd have been the first to tell her how wise she was to barricade herself safe against his ilk.

The sons of demi-gods were hard work at the best of times and came with more baggage that they were most likely worth.

There was no help for that now.

He would have to find a way for her to accept him or this last year of searching, this last chance for them all, would be for nothing.

He eyed the small cottage, old and frayed at the edges. There was a helpless look to the clumps of thatch falling from the roof, to the smokeless chimney.

It huddled in desperation. A stench of poverty pervaded the place, with an overlay of fear.

He concentrated for a moment, and a sack of gold appeared, then another. It was a massive sum, but the vault he'd magically whisked it from was full, and in truth, he'd give every one of his sacks for her. With a touch of his paw, the sacks shimmered out of sight, hidden until he needed them.

Gold was a powerful motivator.

He would lay out his case first without resorting to bribery, but he was not his father. He was a realist.

Her family needed gold, he had plenty of it. They had *her*. He needed her.

He took one final, long look at the door barred against him and turned back into the deep forest.

That door would be open to him soon enough.

Astrid faced the forest again. The blue grey of the mountains behind the trees had almost disappeared into the black grey of a threatening sky. She was rooted to the spot as she stood in the field, mud caked around her shoes, the cold catching her throat and making her eyes water.

"What is it?" Freja snapped, impatient. Eager to be within.

Was it Astrid's imagination or had the forest stilled again?

"I don't want to go."

"You should have thought of that while you sat like a princess inside and neglected your duties." Her father slammed the hoe into the earth, and Astrid shivered at his tone.

"I told you . . ."

"And I told *you*. Fetch the mushrooms your mother needs for her stew. Now."

She looked from her father's closed face to her sister's more forgiving one. But everyone was angry with her, even Tomas. They were tired and hungry, and there she'd been, huddling indoors, babbling about being watched. She was the youngest, but she had never been treated like a baby. There wasn't enough of a gap between them for her to feel very much younger, anyway.

"We didn't sell enough at the market to buy meat," Freja whispered. "There's not much to put in the pot tonight."

Astrid nodded. Looked at the forest again.

She was angry with herself.

It wasn't even as if she'd seen anything. It had just been a feeling.

"Are you still here, Astrid?"

Her father's shout made her jerk, made her body tense for a blow. Before her father got round to it, she grabbed the basket from Freja.

"I'm going."

She headed for the forest, determined there would be no falter in her stride. In defiance of her father and whatever waited for her within.

Never let them see the fear.

Even if it meant going straight into the jaws of unseen danger.

As she stepped through the first line of trees, she looked back and saw the flicker of light as Freja opened the door and went in, saw the glimmer from a gap in the shutters at the window. She could just make out the smudged outline of her father finishing up her work.

If she didn't hurry, she'd have to feel her way back in the pitch dark.

She knew the best places to look for mushrooms, and with the rain they'd had recently, there was sure to be a good crop. This didn't need to take long.

So hurry.

Within minutes she found a tree whose lower trunk was covered in her mother's favorite mushroom. Dark brown skin on the top, the underbelly tender and white, almost luminous. Her hands shook as she pulled them off the bark and threw them into the basket.

Calm down, calm down, there is nothing here.

She stood, straightening her shoulders. Lifted her head high. She forced herself to walk slowly back down the path despite her inclination to run.

She couldn't give in to this irrational fear. The forest was her back garden. She needed to come here often and she couldn't let anything scare her away.

The icy grip in her gut lessened as she neared the tree-line. The only sounds around her were the familiar swish of the trees and the rustle of small animals, the crunch of dead pine needles under her feet.

The light was almost gone, and she could just see the path in front of her. She kept her eyes on it, watching where she stepped, no longer looking for mushrooms.

An imprint in the soil of the path caught her eye and she frowned. She crouched down to look, sure she must be mistaken.

If only she had a light to see properly.

The ground was soft, claylike with the rains. Perfect for recording footprints.

She placed her hand down, fingers spread wide, and they did not cover the impression on the path by a quarter. Something big had been here.

It had been standing just here, looking out at her hoeing the fields.

She'd say it was a bear print, but if so, it was like no bear she'd ever seen. A giant bear.

There was a rustle in the trees behind her, and a sudden flurry of wind in the branches, whispering *run, run, run*. Astrid's heart stopped in her chest.

She grabbed up her basket and took a first, flying step.

"Stop."

She froze, and as she stood motionless, she frantically tried to work out if it was magic or fear that held her in place.

"Do not look around yet," the voice said from

behind her. "I would talk with you first, before you see me."

Could she turn around? Astrid thought not. Tried it.

"I cannot turn my head, as you well know, so why ask me not to?" Fear sparked a fury within her at being so obviously at his mercy. She could hear herself panting like a rabbit caught in a snare.

When he spoke again, he sounded bemused. "I do not wish you to turn around, so I have made sure you cannot."

"How are you keeping me frozen like this?" Even as she asked, Astrid realized how stupid the question was. There could only be one way.

"I have cast a spell upon you."

"What are you?"

"I would leave that to later."

But she knew, didn't she? Unless two creatures had been watching from the path since the rains of yesterday.

"Were you watching me today?" She was sure of it, but would he admit it?

"You know I was. You ran from my gaze. Why was that, beauty?"

"I ran because I was afraid. I could feel your eyes on my very soul, and I did not trust you." As she said it, she knew it was true.

"There is no need to fear me." He spoke softly.

"How can I not?"

He was silent for a long moment.

"Very well, I will release you, but do not turn around. I would like to talk to you more before you see me."

"You have my word." She had no intention of turning around. None whatsoever.

"Then you are released."

She felt as if she'd been pulled out of deep water. That she was back in the free-flowing air. She swung her arm to test whether it was so.

"Keep your word," he said, his voice deepening.

"I never break my word," Astrid answered, then ran as fast as she could down the path.

She didn't look back.

Chapter Three

"What story should we have?" Bets asked, moving over as Astrid sat down beside her at the hearth, the kitchen at last neat and clean.

"We could have one about a giant bear," Eric smirked. Astrid saw he was carving the image of a bear into the small piece of hardwood in his hands. "Perhaps you were visited by a Jotun today, Astrid, a bear from the land of trolls and giants."

"Do not joke about these things," their mother said sharply, lifting her eyes from her sewing. "I met a troll once, deep in the forest. It was hideous."

Astrid twisted her head to look at her mother in surprise. She had never heard this story before.

"When was this? What happened, Mother?"

Her mother slid a furtive glance at her father, and then stiffened her spine.

"You were with me, Astrid, but you won't remember it, you were too little. The troll had killed an old hag, and there was a young boy, the hag's grandson, perhaps, and—"

"Gerda." Father looked up from his own carving.

"I saw what I saw. And even you say the weather has been colder since that day," Mother said defensively.

"Gerda." Father's voice was heavy with warning, his eyes narrow, and her mother closed her mouth in a thin line.

For an uncomfortable beat no one spoke and the only sound was the rain, smacking against the wooden shutters, and the wind rattling them, trying to get in. It kept Astrid constantly on edge.

"I believe Astrid saw bear tracks. Bears are everywhere now, getting in their last feed before winter sets in." Tomas spoke mildly, as always coming to her defense. "Some of them can be huge."

There was a moment of silence, and Astrid did not dare look at Tomas. Sometimes just the exchange of a look between them could set Father off.

"Bah." Father shifted in his pride of place, right in front of the fire, his mood darkened by her mother's disobedience, but not too much. Astrid relaxed muscles she hadn't realized she'd tensed.

"Fine, a bear, but do you have to always exaggerate, Astrid? Does it have to be a giant bear? A talking bear who casts spells?" Father's tone dared Mother to contradict him. Dared her to remind them again there were such things as giant bears, and trolls, and strange magical creatures in the world.

He knew they were just a turn in the path away— hadn't Astrid seen him paint Thor's hammer over the barn door himself, to shield their home from such things?

"It's just like when you were younger, those stories you used to tell us about the wind talking to you."

"It's what I saw and heard." She didn't push it any further. What did it matter anyway? The tracks would be gone by morning in this weather, and it was only her word that the conversation she'd had in the woods took place.

"The mushrooms were good." Mother tried to smile.

Astrid could see the fatigue on her face, the way she let her head rest on the high chair back, closing her eyes for a moment. Her pale beauty was scrubbed away, almost to nothing. Her hair was once golden as Astrid's, but now, it was a dull mix of grey and yellow. Her eyes were a shade lighter than they had been, as if faded by too many tears. Too many years of living too close to the edge of survival.

A terrible pit gaped open inside Astrid, and she fought the helplessness that rose up every time she saw her mother this close to despair.

Fought the logic that said this would always be her life. That one day she would be the mother in the chair, sick with worry over how they would get through the winter.

"Thank you, Mother."

"Took her long enough to get them," her father muttered, unable to let go of his anger at her.

She bent to her needlework and kept her mouth closed. Fighting with her father again would not make her mother's life any easier.

Instead, she turned to Bets and Freja, sitting beside her on the mat near Mother's chair, darning. "How was market—"

The blow against the shutters silenced her.

Silenced all of them.

Eric stood, his eyes never leaving the window.

The bang came again, making the shutter hinges screech in protest, making Astrid jump and Bets scream.

"Who is there?" Father's voice sounded too loud. Afraid.

Bang. The knock sounded again.

"Three times," her mother murmured, and Astrid felt a chill in her heart.

Her father went to the door, hesitated a moment, and lifted his hand to the lock. Eric joined him, exchanging a look with Tomas as he crossed the room.

Tomas reached for the ax leaning against the fireplace, hefted it in his hand. Then he went to stand between Astrid, and her sisters and mother, and the door.

Her father wrenched the door open, and he and Eric stepped into the driving rain. As they were swallowed by the darkness, the wind took the door and slammed it shut behind them, as if protecting Astrid from whatever stood outside.

She could feel the eyes again.

She should have known running from him wouldn't make him go away. Whoever the mysterious watcher was, he wasn't skulking in the woods anymore.

———◄✍►———

There was no way to make himself smaller, so Bjorn bowed as well and as low as his inconvenient shape allowed.

"Good evening to you, sirs." The wind shrieked louder, ruffling his white fur and trying to unbalance him, taunting him with his words. It was not a good evening.

Her father stared at him, mouth open, eyes so filled with terror he looked ready to faint. The brother was calmer, braver, but his face was white, all the same.

"I apologize for my poor timing, and for disturbing you, sir, but I come to ask for your daughter." He kept his eyes on the father. The decision-maker.

The man seemed incapable of speech.

"Your daughter. I wish to take her with me, to my home. I promise to take care of her, and that she will want for nothing."

"Which daughter?" The son's voice quavered, but his eyes held Bjorn's steadily.

"The one I spied today, working the fields. The one I spoke to in the wood earlier."

"My youngest. Astrid." The father found his voice

at last.

Ah. Of course that was her name. The fair and beautiful one. "Yes. Astrid." He savored saying it.

"Why do you want her?" The brother's suspicion made him forget his fear for a moment.

Bjorn should have anticipated the question, and now that he was faced with it, he considered answering it truthfully. But it would only be a half-truth, because he was bound by the deal of secrecy he'd struck with Norga, and it may be dangerous for them to know too much.

"I find myself in need of a companion." His words were glib, and never before had he lied so blatantly. It felt like a betrayal of her, of her worth. "She caught my eye, and I would have her."

"Have her?" There was no mistaking the suggestion the brother was making. And crude though he was being, he had the right of it. Bjorn hesitated, but they would not believe him if he said he did not want her in that way, and he was afraid they would imagine worse things.

"Yes. Have her."

"You would marry her?" The father frowned in confusion.

"Alas, I cannot. Perhaps one day . . ." He thought of the circumstances which would free him to marry her. It would mean he'd have won. He'd have beaten Norga for good and there would be no wedding between him and Norga's daughter. "When my enchantment is over."

"Why would I give you my daughter, then? If you don't intend to make a respectable woman of her."

Was that a considering look he'd seen in the woodsman's eyes? A glint of greed? A look passed between father and son, and Bjorn felt a stir of disgust. And he was as soiled at they were, horse-trading a woman's innocence.

It could not be helped and he had no time to play coy. And enough gold to dazzle Astrid's father.

"If you can persuade your daughter to come with me, I will make you wealthy beyond your wildest dreams."

"How would you do that?"

"I have two sacks of gold right here." Bjorn shuffled back and revealed the bulging bags beside him.

Both men's eyes widened at the sight of them.

"I will *make* her go—"

"No!" It came out as a roar, and the woodsman cringed back. The brother stood his ground, but Bjorn saw his whole body trembled with fear.

Bjorn shook his head. "She must come willingly or not at all."

The father looked back at the house. Hesitated.

It would not be easy, Bjorn realized. His Astrid was not one to blindly obey. She had spirit and courage, as he'd found out in the woods. It gave him a moment's pause, and a flare of admiration.

"Father?" Someone fought the door open, and

Bjorn saw a second, younger son step into the rain and raise a lantern. "Who is there?"

The father and the first son shared a quick look.

Ah, Bjorn thought, here is Astrid's champion. The one who will stand in my way.

He bowed even lower than he had before. "Good evening, sir."

"Give me a moment to speak with her," the father said.

He turned and went past the gaping younger son, through the door. The older son followed him, and after a moment of staring, the younger one stepped back within. As the door closed in his face, Bjorn wondered if Astrid would be persuaded tonight.

The shrieking wind laughed at his hopes.

Chapter Four

"Who is there?" Astrid took in Tomas's white face, the suppressed excitement in Father's stance, and twisted the embroidery in her hands.

"Do you know who was watching you earlier?" Her father stepped closer to her, and for the first time since this afternoon there was no edge to his tone.

Astrid shook her head, felt her heart trying to escape from her ribcage.

"It was a bear. A giant bear, you were quite right," Eric said, the words bursting out of him, earning him a dark look from Father. "A magical white bear."

Freja gasped, and her mother made a choking noise, her eyes going wildly to the door. Bets said nothing, hugging her knees tighter to her body as she sat on the floor.

Astrid looked at Tomas. "A giant, magical, white bear?"

Tomas nodded, and there was something in the way his eyes slid to Father and Eric that made Astrid's every nerve tingle with warning.

"He wants you for his own, Astrid. As a

companion." Eric opened his arms, pleadingly. "And if you will willingly go with him, he promises to take care of your every need."

"And the two bags of gold?" Tomas asked, and it was as if the night's cold autumn rain had seeped into his voice.

"If you become his, he wants to see to the well-being of your family, too. He will give us the gold, so we have no more worries." Father spoke quickly, but there were patches of high color on his cheeks.

"What kind of companion?" Her mother leaned forward on her chair, her eyes on Father.

Her father looked at the ground, the flush creeping down his neck. "I do not know." He seemed to struggle with himself for a moment. "He said he cannot marry her."

There was an extended silence at her father's words.

"Why not?" Tomas's question cut through the shock. "Why can't he marry her if he wants her in that . . . way?"

"Perhaps his enchantment forbids it." Eric tried to shrug with nonchalance. But for once, even he was thoughtful.

"And what is the nature of his enchantment?" Astrid asked, feeling as if both bags of gold were lying in the pit of her stomach.

"Ask him." Tomas stepped toward the door, and

opened it.

"No—" Father spun, tried to grab the door, but Tomas swung it wider, and Astrid took her courage in both hands and walked toward it. Toward the eyes.

She felt Tomas at her side as she stood just within the threshold and stared up at her suitor.

"Astrid."

He spoke her name as if it were a jewel he was holding to the light. She only came to his shoulder, he was so huge. A hulking mass of white fur, his black eyes looking out at her, not with the wild canniness of an animal, but with the cool intelligence of a man.

"Sir." She forced herself into a curtsey, then shivered as the rain needled her, and fear shook her core. "We meet again."

"Indeed." He bowed to her, managing to look threatening and polite at the same time. "I don't give up, as you can see."

She ignored that. "My father says you wish to have me. As a companion." Her tone leaned heavily on the word *companion*.

The bear gave a huff of surprise, but did not deny it.

"I wish to know why you want me, and why I should go with you."

"As to why I want you," his voice was a deep growl, "it is because you are like a ray of sunshine to me. You will grace my life and bring me happiness." He shuffled his huge body. "As to why you should go with me . . . I will care for you, and give you everything you could desire. I will give you a new world."

A new world? Astrid started. Had she not wished for just such a thing, only minutes ago? Had she not looked at her mother and longed for something else?

Be careful what you wish for.

She swallowed. "Who enchanted you and why?"

Again he huffed, looked at her more closely. "I cannot tell you."

"Then I cannot go with you." She lifted her chin. "Good evening to you, sir."

Then she stepped back and closed the door.

Bjorn blinked away the rain as he stood, stunned, outside the house.

Whatever he'd imagined her to be, the fierce, intelligent woman at the door had not been it. From her countenance he'd thought she'd be biddable, shy.

The wind howled with glee at his mistake.

The door swung open again, and her father stepped out to join him, wincing as the wind slammed the door shut behind him.

"Give me three days, Bear. Come again with the gold and ask for her one more time."

Her father's eyes slid to the two sacks.

"You think her answer will have changed?"

"We are a poor family," her father forced his eyes up to Bjorn's own. "The weather has grown colder with each passing year, our crops have not done well and we are going to have a hard winter." He looked at the gold again. "Astrid is headstrong, but she loves her family, and she will sacrifice a great deal to see her mother happy."

Even her father thought going with him would be a sacrifice.

"Do you love your daughter?" he asked the woodsman. The question shamed him the moment he spoke it.

The woodsman's face twisted at his words. "Do you want her or not?"

"I do."

"Then come in three days."

Bjorn scooped the sacks up and turned to go.

"Don't forget the gold," the woodsman called, and Bjorn could hear the defiance in his voice.

Maybe the woodsman loved his daughter, maybe he didn't, but he was willing to sell her to a monster for enough gold.

You deserve better, Astrid, he thought as he reached the trees.

But you're getting me, instead.

Chapter Five

She was worn down smooth as a stone in a fast-moving stream by the pressure. Or rather, ground into tiny chips of rock like a boulder in the wake of a glacier. Astrid shook a few vegetables onto the table and sat down wearily.

She ignored Freja and Eric, busy with their own chores on the other end of the kitchen table. Tomas and Bets were her only safe havens, the only two who did not try to urge her to go with the bear.

Mother said nothing to her, but Astrid had only to think of the lines on her face to ask herself why she wasn't giving anything to ease them. Even her very life.

She knew the answer.

She'd never taken well to commands.

And they wanted her to go not just with a stranger, but with a stranger who wasn't even a *man*. With a bear who could talk, and who stood twice her height and looked at her with eyes as black and keen as an eagle's. And who could enchant her with a word, make her freeze in place whenever he wished.

Though she was prepared to sacrifice herself for

the survival of the others, she'd like to do it voluntarily. She knew it was small of her, but she hated the thought of Father and Eric thinking they had won.

"It's not as if you have such a wonderful life here anyway," Freja suddenly spoke out while she kneaded dough. Eric stood beside her at the table, and Astrid ignored them both and shaved the skin off a carrot.

"She's right. Father picks on you all the time. You always get the worst jobs. What have you got to lose?" Eric leaned forward, so earnest he surely could not hear what he was saying.

Astrid put down the paring knife and folded her arms.

"Thinking about the two bulging bags of gold into the bargain, as well as getting rid of me?"

At that, Freja's eyes jerked up from her work and she looked, for the first time, stricken.

"Yes." Eric slammed his fist into the table and shouted in her face.

She flinched, and for a long moment they stared at each other, finally seeing who the other had become.

Astrid barely heard Mother, Father, Tomas and Bets come into the room. Summoned by Eric's shout.

"Yes, you ungrateful cow." Eric lifted an arm and wiped the spittle from his lips with the back of his hand. "That's exactly what I'm thinking about. Two bulging, lovely bags of gold, and one less mouth to feed."

"What have you against me, Eric? I have never

harmed you."

"You take up space and food, and you are fey. You talk to the wind and you talk back."

"Eric." Father's soft call was like a whip crack through the tension in the room.

"No," Astrid spoke slowly. "He's being honest for the first time." She rose up and took a step toward Mother. "I will talk with the bear when he comes. I may choose to go with him, I may not."

"That is all you have to say? With the sun almost set?" Her father shook with a wild anger that came close to violence. The kind of anger that had earned every one of them bruises from him in the past.

"That is all I have to say," she replied, refusing to move back, or look away.

"That is all we can ask of you, Astrid," her mother said quietly. "If we should be asking you at all."

"He is not a troll, Gerda. For the last time, he is not a troll." Father clenched his fists, close to snapping.

"How do you know?" her mother cried, reaching out to grab Astrid, to pull her into her arms. "And what does it matter? He is enchanted. He could be a troll. He could be anything. As it is, he is a *bear*."

"Mother." Astrid hugged her close. Loving her more at that moment than she had for a long time. Finding respect for her after thinking she'd lost it forever.

"Do not go," her mother whispered to her. "This will only lead to unhappiness."

Astrid put her mouth to her mother's ear. "I will make him swear an oath before I go with him. I will not be harmed, I promise you."

Her mother gasped a breath between her sobs. "No one can stop a heart breaking."

"Rather my heart than my spirit."

Her mother stilled. Slowly drew back.

"What are you whispering?" Father asked, his eyes narrow, but for once, her mother did not keep quiet.

"Things that concern mothers and daughters, and no one else," she said. "Astrid, go and tidy yourself. Whether you say yes or no, I would have you looking neat."

Astrid nodded, and began climbing the stairs. While she was up in the room she shared with her sisters, she could pack her few things together.

For she knew in her heart, she was going.

--------◄❦►--------

Bjorn moved toward the cottage. He had not been near it all day, afraid she would sense him and fear him too much to agree to come.

But he knew to the minute when the three days were up, and he came exactly on time, dragging the bags of gold in his mouth.

The woodsman stood at the door, waiting for him, and he bowed nervously to Bjorn. It was an ominous sign.

"She has not agreed," Bjorn said flatly, and a yawning pit of despair opened within him.

"No!" The woodsman shouted. "She would talk with you one last time, before she decides."

It was as if an ax coming down on his neck somehow slipped from the executioner's hand, and fell harmlessly to the ground.

"Then we shall talk," Bjorn said. He kept his voice steady. He would not betray his desperation to this man.

The night was clear and cold. No taunting wind or icy rain as Astrid stepped over the threshold to speak with him.

As his eyes fell upon her, the night lit up as she stood in her ragged dress, her hair brighter than a lantern.

"Alone, Father," she said, coldly, to the woodsman, and Bjorn saw the flash of temper on her father's face as he closed the door, and left them be.

Astrid walked a little way away from the cottage, and he followed her, intrigued at her bravery in seeing him alone.

The shutters were not closed across the windows tonight, and light spilled from them. "Stand in the light a little, Bear, I would see you properly," she said, turning to him, and Bjorn obeyed. He had made sure to see her properly, after all.

He felt her eyes on him and then she reached out

and touched his fur, rubbing the soft white between her fingers.

He suppressed a shiver.

"I will go with you, Bear, on two conditions," she said, and he could see from the way she spoke, and the way she stood, arms crossed over her chest, that she had thought this through.

"What are they?" He held his breath, wondering if they were at all in his power to grant. So close . . .

"I need your word that you will treat me always with respect and never let me come to harm."

"You have my word, on my life." The words were the most heartfelt he'd ever spoken.

She stared at him a moment, then nodded, satisfied, and Bjorn felt the first fizz of joy in his blood.

"Then, I wish you to give the gold to my family in such a way that my father and brother Eric are not the sole controllers of it."

That gave him pause. He flopped to the ground and rested his head on his paws as he thought it through. Then he stood again, stretched, and grinned. "That I can promise you, also."

"Then, Bear, I will go with you."

He let the words swirl on the crisp autumn air for a moment, then he stood on his hind legs and bellowed out his triumph.

You are half-defeated, Norga.

The door of the house slammed open, and the

youngest brother came running out. "Astrid."

Bjorn dropped to the ground, and bowed. "Your sister is safe. She comes with me."

"Astrid?" The brother said again, ignoring him and looked at Astrid, *his* Astrid.

She nodded.

"I will go with the bear, Tomas. But he has a promise to fulfil, first." She looked pointedly at the bags of gold.

"Woodsman," Bjorn called, and one by one, Astrid's family filed out of the cottage. "Your daughter is willing to come with me. And as agreed, I give you two bags of gold to see you settled."

Bjorn placed a massive paw on top of the bags. "The gold is enchanted, and should be used for each person in this family equally. If any one takes more for him or herself out of greed, the gold will call to me, and I will come and hold that person to account."

Astrid's father looked longingly at the bags, and then moved his gaze to Astrid. "That was your doing."

"It was," she said calmly, and came to stand by Bjorn's side.

"Would you go and fetch your things?" Bjorn asked her, and she held up a small rag, made into a bundle.

"I have everything with me, already."

"Then say your farewells, we have far to travel tonight."

He watched her embrace her mother, the youngest brother and the younger of her two sisters, who had begun to weep from the moment Bjorn had announced Astrid's choice.

More cautiously, she put her arms around the older sister. To her father and older brother, she bowed. He saw the older brother pass something small to her, and the surprise on her face as she looked down at what was in her hand. She slipped the small gift into her bundle.

"Climb onto my back," Bjorn told her, crouching down so she could do so, and she clambered up and hung on to his neck.

"Goodbye," she called back as he began to lumber away, but he hardly heard her, and thought not at all of her family. He could go home at last. Rest at last.

"Where are we going," she asked him as he ran into the forest, a catch in her voice.

"To my palace," he answered, and sped up.

Chapter Six

The time for second thoughts had come and gone. The bear ran with long, ground-eating strides, his massive paws as sure-footed on the rocky mountain paths as on the soft forest floors.

Astrid's arms felt numb from holding tight, and she wondered if the night would ever end. If they would ever rest. But she kept quiet. He was doing most of the work, after all.

But at last they came to a quiet clearing, deep in a forest far from home, and the bear sank down in the lee of a massive tree trunk, his breath coming in short, sharp pants, little white puffs in the cold darkness.

"I can go no further tonight," he said, and waited for her to slide off his back before he stretched out on the leafy ground and groaned.

Astrid stood next to him, unsure what to do, what was expected of her.

"Come lie with me for warmth, Astrid, the nights are bitter."

She hesitated.

"Are you afraid?" He spoke with his eyes closed,

without even looking her way.

"No. I wonder where I might lie that you will not roll on me and crush me by mistake."

One eye opened. "Did I not swear mere hours ago that I would never let you come to harm?"

"You did."

"Well then." He shuffled closer to the tree, and she sat next to him, then gingerly lay her head on his extended paw and tucked her hands into the deep fur of his chest.

He rumbled his approval, the sound vibrating against her fingers, and she closed her eyes, so tired now they had stopped, she could barely remember her own name, let alone any danger she might be in.

"You really aren't afraid, are you?"

"No," she whispered. "I am not."

And as she fell heavily, deeply into sleep, she realized she was telling the truth.

When Astrid had slid down his back, he'd felt a lurch of conscience when he saw her pale face, the way her arms shook with fatigue.

He'd forgotten that she would have had to hold fast to him so as not to fall, and yet she had not made a single complaint.

It felt so good to lie with her close, her golden hair

spread across the white of his massive paws, her hands fisted deep into his fur. He was so tired, and yet having her lying against him, the first touch of anyone for so long, he found he was not able to fall asleep just yet.

And when they got to the palace . . . He closed his eyes, thought what that would mean.

Every day when the sun set, after eleven long months, he would be a man again.

He looked down at Astrid, and his heart squeezed inside him. The rules of the bargain were that Astrid could never look upon him in his human form and he could never explain why to her. Norga's last, vicious twist of a condition in case, by some sliver of chance, he ever did find the the girl from the clearing long ago.

Norga thought she'd been clever but he had had long months to think this through. Endless nights and empty days. Searching, searching and thinking of what might happen when his searching was over.

And he knew there was a way she could be his wife in all but name. And he would risk it despite what he stood to lose. Because he found as the months wore by, he'd begun to care less and less about the burden he carried not just for himself but for many others. His father's people—his people—who counted on him.

He'd grown cold as the places he was forced to sleep, cold almost as Norga's own heart.

And since he'd first laid eyes on Astrid, he felt a thaw. It was agony, this warming up. Every new emotion stabbed him through the heart. And he knew if he abandoned her in his palace, never held her, he would freeze up again. Become even colder than before.

He was playing with fire if he implemented his plan, but he'd rather get burned by such a fire than freeze, cold and alone and with nothing to show for it.

With a final huff, he closed his eyes, and let sleep take him under.

It seemed to Astrid the wind hushed as they emerged from the forest. The trees, almost alive while they'd been among them, stilled. The rock-strewn foot of a gray-stoned mountain was before them, the sheer cliff-faces soaring up to an ice-blue sky.

The bear paused just out of reach of the trees' shadows.

"Where are we?" Astrid asked from her perch on his back, her voice sounding too loud in the quiet air.

"My home. Before us lies my palace."

Astrid said nothing. She saw no palace, but didn't like to say so in case she offended her . . . what was he? Not her master, no one was that but she.

But by letting him carry her off, she'd agreed to be his companion, and over the three days it had taken them to get here, they had formed a bond, a camaraderie that came from her riding his back each day and sleeping tucked up against him at night.

Now they were at their destination, though, and she knew things would be different.

A tremor of fear ran through her, and she had to breathe deeply, twining her fingers more tightly into his fur. She needed to keep her wits about her.

"What is wrong?" His words were soft.

"I see a mountain before me, not a palace."

"Fair enough."

She heard laughter in his voice and trained her eyes on the cold gray stones, wondering what sort of life she would have amongst them.

With a decided spring in his step, the bear ran forward, up the grassy slopes and into the rocky beginnings of the mountain. They stopped in front of a sheer cliff face.

The bear lifted a paw, placed it against the stone. "I am at my journey's end, let me in." He spoke quietly, with a low rumble in his voice.

Nothing happened.

Astrid felt him tremble beneath her. He suddenly reared up, taking Astrid by surprise. She cried out and slid down his back as he roared out:

"Let me in. Part of my quest is fulfilled."

The stone began to shake, and then the faint outline of an arched doorway appeared. It parted, grinding and protesting as it made a gateway straight into the mountain.

The bear dropped down on all fours and looked

back at her. "I never doubted you were the one." He turned his full attention on the entrance. "Follow me. We are home at last."

Astrid looked up at the blue sky and then at the dark, shadowed entrance to the mountain palace. This was not her home, no matter what bargain she'd struck. No matter what her strange new companion said.

She looked longingly at the green slopes down to the forest, and thought for a moment of running.

A gentle breeze brushed her face with fingers so solid she felt she could reach out and touch it back. A tear slid down her cheek and the wind flicked it away.

She turned back to the door. She had agreed to this, and as she'd told the bear once before, she never broke her word.

With head high, Astrid stepped over the dark threshold. If it were not home, she would have to make it so.

Chapter Seven

He was back.

The halls seemed more beautiful than he remembered them, the hundreds of torches suffusing everything with a warm glow that welcomed him again.

He shivered, the after-effects of the panic he'd felt outside the door when it had not yielded to him. He'd lied to Astrid when he said he'd never doubted she was the one. For a terrible moment he'd thought he'd made a mistake. Taken the wrong woman.

He looked down and saw a distorted reflection of himself in the gold-flecked granite floor, its warm brown polished to a mirror-like sheen. The black granite walls glimmered with silver sparkles in the fire-glow.

Behind him, the entrance ground and screeched closed, and he realized he'd forgotten Astrid.

He turned, and there she stood, rag bundle in hand, gaping at the hall, at the room of silver and gold flashing in the torch light.

"What is this place?" she whispered.

"I told you, my home. Built into the solid granite of the mountain."

"And the torches? Who lit them?"

"No one. They burn on their own."

She dragged her eyes away from the wonders and looked directly at him. "Who else lives here?"

"There is just you and me, although once this was full of my father's servants and followers."

He thought back to that time, the bustle and hum of this place when it was thriving and happy. When the balance was kept.

"We are alone?" Her voice sounded thin and frightened, bouncing and echoing in the empty chamber.

"Perhaps not forever." If he could only outwit the troll queen who sought to end the balance for good.

Astrid nodded, but he could see she hardly heard him, her eyes bright with tears, and he felt a stab of shame for bringing her here, for taking her from her family and making her live alone.

But she was the one for him, and it was just for a year, if he could walk the thin tightrope of Norga's conditions and his own desires.

Yes, she'd be alone during the day. But through the night—why, he'd make sure the loneliness melted away.

———◄⟡►———

The palace was the most beautiful place she'd ever seen, and the most daunting.

She didn't fit in here, in the rooms of gold and

silver, decorated with furniture her father and brothers would weep to see, so beautifully did they respect the wood and celebrate it.

She ran her fingers along the polished stone walls, smooth as glass, the silver like fish scales on black velvet, enriched with a hint of blue and green.

"Your room is this way," the bear called her from the stairway in the center of the main hall, and she lifted her hand from the wall slowly, unwilling to see what now lay in store for her.

"Night is nearly falling," he said urgently, and there was something in the way he spoke, a suppressed excitement, that slowed her steps still further.

"Astrid, please hurry." His voice came in a shout, and the huge arches bounced his plea around her, amplifying it, making her jerk.

"All right." She walked toward him, not running, not lagging either, cradling her bundle of things in her arms. Uncowed.

"I am sorry, but we must make haste. And when I ask you to do something, you need to listen, for your own safety." His voice was quieter, but no less urgent.

She quickened her steps, her only acknowledgment of his order. It was too similar to her father's constant demands that she go faster, work harder, be more obedient. Although, to be fair to the bear, he had said please. And sorry.

He waited until she was level with him, gave her a

fierce look, and led the way up the deep stone stairs.

Astrid bowed her head, though it was not in acquiescence. She did not want him to see the defiance in her eyes, or the willful set of her jaw.

She was not a dog, nor a bought thing. She had come of her own free will.

"How do you know night is falling?" she asked him.

His stride faltered. "I feel it, soul-deep."

His answered surprised her, and she looked away from him. "I will find it hard, without windows."

"For your protection, I must keep you within, but the magic my father infused into this place should more than make up for it." He spoke as if his mind were on other things, and he increased his pace as they reached the floor above.

"The magic?"

"Ask what you want, and it will appear. Whatever dish, whatever drink you desire. Whatever clothes you need." He was almost loping along now, down the wide passageway, and Astrid had to jog to keep up.

Why was it so important to find her chamber before nightfall? And with all the rooms in this palace, why was there one special room for her?

"Here. Your chamber." He was panting slightly as he pushed open a door. "This is the only room you may sleep in."

Astrid stepped into the room. Like the rest of the

palace, the floors were brown granite bright with gold, the walls black and silver. A massive bed stood in the middle of it, with a canopy of dark blue velvet drawn up in pretty folds, waiting to be let down to enclose the bed in a tent of luxury.

The walls were hung with silk hangings, portraying beautiful scenes from the outdoors. Waterfalls, forests, mountains and fjords.

And there was something odd.

Astrid frowned as she tried to work it out, and then she realized. Of all the rooms she'd seen, this one alone was not lit by torches hanging from sconces. Instead, the light came from cleverly cut skylights in the side of the mountain, slanting down into the room.

Natural light. And perhaps this was why he was in such a hurry to show her the room before the sun set.

She had misjudged him.

"Oh, thank you." Her voice caught at his kindness. "It is beautiful."

He seemed pleased at her words, and bowed low. "The light is fading and I must go. Ask for a hot bath, dinner, whatever you wish." He backed out of the room.

Surprised, she lifted a hand in goodbye. But the way he hunched, a small furtiveness in his eyes, made her check the farewell, her hand half-raised. Then he closed the door. Closed her in.

Unsure, Astrid took a tentative step toward the pale wooden door and then another. Lifted her hand to the handle and pulled.

Locked.

He had locked her in.

And for the first time she saw, while she had natural light from her skylights, it was the only light she did have. There was no fireplace here, or wall sconces. Within a few minutes, she'd be in darkness.

"I want a hot bath. And towels. And a beautiful white nightdress. And dinner fit for a king," she called out, fear and anger mingling at being tricked, at being imprisoned. She closed her mouth abruptly as the things appeared. The bath in one corner, the nightdress and towels hanging from a wooden stand next to it. The dinner laid out on a table with a white linen cloth.

"Oh." She breathed the word out, sniffed the tantalizing smell of roast lamb with mint and rosemary. The rose scent of bath oil.

A solution to her problem occurred to her and she grinned suddenly. "I want a candle," she called.

Nothing appeared.

"A fire."

Still nothing.

"A torch."

Nothing moved in the room except the perfumed steam from her bath and the fragrant steam of her meal, drifting upwards, swirling in the fading beams of light from her ceiling.

Cool air flowed in from the sky lights and Astrid

shivered. Hugged herself. "Why do you want me in the dark, bear?" she whispered.

As if she wasn't in the dark enough already.

Chapter Eight

He never made it to his chamber. He wasn't sure afterward why he thought he needed to. As it was, halfway there pain struck him like a bolt of lightning and ripped him to the core, like a tree split and charred in a thunderstorm.

He slammed against the wall and slid to the floor, sure somehow Norga had not honored the deal. That he was dying.

He lay there, flaying like a fish out of water, and for a moment, as the pain increased beyond the imaginable, beyond what he could take, he knew he was dead.

Astrid was imprisoned in her room and she'd be stuck there, while his body rotted in the passageway outside, was all he could think. Until he couldn't think anymore. Of anything. Except the stabbing, slashing knives of pain.

As he curled up, almost gave up, the pain just stopped.

It was as shocking as running into a door.

He shuddered, reeling at the absence of pain

where once pain was all he had.

He looked down at his paws . . . hands.

He was free.

Until the sun rose, he was free.

He lay shaking for a minute more, unable to move, unable to trust it wasn't a terrible joke.

But nothing happened and he pushed up on his knees, held his arms in front of him, twisting them this way and that. He stuck out a leg, wriggled his toes. Then used the wall to pull himself to a stand.

Elation expanded his chest. He would give every miserable second of the last eleven months three times over for this. Every soul-destroying, happiness-leeching day had been worth it to find Astrid, without whom he could never have set foot inside these walls again.

He glanced back the way he'd come, to her chamber at the far end of the corridor. Looked toward his own rooms.

He needed to get used to himself again. And the thought of a bath, of food like stew and bread after too long on raw fish and berries, decided him.

He used the wall to steady himself as he moved toward his wing of the palace, but when he reached his door, he couldn't help a last look down the passage.

He would walk this corridor again before the sun rose.

The snick of the stone shutters closing over the skylights jerked her out of her doze. Astrid held her breath, her heart thundering.

She'd closed those shutters herself earlier, then, frightened by the absolute darkness they created, opened them again. She preferred to pull down the velvet drapes of her bed to cut off the cool air from the outside than entomb herself in her chamber.

Another shutter clicked closed. Someone was in the room.

Now she was aware of it, she heard footsteps, bare feet padding across the granite floor.

A man. Not Bear.

He blundered into the table she'd wished up earlier, clean of dishes and leftovers, and she heard a curse.

"Who is there?" she called out, sitting straight up and looking wildly around for a weapon. What could she use . . . of course! "I want an ax," she whispered to the room, and one suddenly weighed in her hand.

She could have asked for any number of sharp objects, but she knew how to handle an ax.

"I don't mean to frighten you," a voice called, a deep voice, a bit like Bear would sound if he were human.

"Well, you have." Astrid scrambled to her knees on the bed and held the ax double-handed. "I am armed, do not come any closer."

She wished she could draw back the velvet drapes, although with the shutters closed, she'd be just as blind as she was now, the starlight shut off.

"Armed?" He sounded amused.

"With an ax."

"Astrid, where would you have gotten an ax?" The way he said it made her cock her head to one side.

"Is that you, Bear?"

"It is me. But not in the shape you're used to."

She was silent a moment, remembering the sound of feet, his voice. "You are a man now?"

"I am."

She lowered the ax slightly, then gripped it again as she felt the sudden rush of cool air on her face as the curtains were pulled aside.

"Don't come any closer." She could not see anything. Even the ax which she'd brought up in front of her face was just another piece of darkness.

"I want only to lie with you, make you truly mine as you agreed."

"I did not agree to be yours. I agreed to go with you." Astrid shuffled back on her knees, shaking, the ax still raised high.

"Yes, but you knew I wanted you as my woman. That coming with me would mean being my wife in all but name. Why, even your parents asked me about marriage. You could not have misunderstood." He spoke softly, calmly.

She wanted to say she had misunderstood, but he was right. "I thought, with you being a bear . . ."

"You hoped my enchantment would save you from my bed?"

"Yes." She whispered the admission.

"It would have anywhere else. But in terms of the agreement with my enchanter, I am able to return to my human form in my own castle from sunset to sunrise."

"Why won't you give me a light in this room? I can't see you."

"Exactly." The satisfaction in his voice sent a shiver down her spine.

"What is this enchantment all about?" She had to know, she couldn't remain caught up in this without knowing the stakes.

"I cannot tell you."

She shook her head at that, although she knew he could not see her. What did he fear she would do if she knew the truth? Was it that terrible?

She drew a deep breath. Perhaps it was.

"What is your name, then?"

He laughed, short and sharp. "What else but Bjorn? My enchanter did not choose my form at random. It amused her to turn me into my namesake."

She felt the mattress give way at the foot.

"I still have the ax ready," she warned.

"Then set it down, Astrid." He spoke as a mother speaks to a recalcitrant child, or a man speaks to his dog, making her want to draw blood.

"No. I have some oaths I would have you swear first."

Bjorn chuckled, a deep sound from his throat. "You are very good at making me swear oaths, my beautiful one. What would you have of me this time?"

"A promise that you will not take me until I say I am ready. I will not give myself to a stranger. I wish to know you first."

There was silence from the end of the bed.

Ha, he was speechless for once. She smiled in triumph.

"I will admit I do not want to swear an oath like that." His voice was dangerously low and her smile faded.

"I am not yours and you do need to swear that oath if you have no wish to be felled by an ax." She spoke sharp as the edge of the blade in her hands. "But even if I could not protect myself, would you not rather I went gladly to your arms? I agreed to come with you but had no idea what awaited me, and I have known you only three days." She paused, swallowed. "I am afraid."

Again there was silence, and then a sigh.

"I cannot find fault in what you say." He paused. "It is only that I have been waiting for this moment a long time. I have been alone so long . . ."

Stricken by the pain in his voice, Astrid lowered the ax, set it down on the floor to lean against the bed.

"Come then." She was used to sleeping in the same bed as Bets and Freja. It would be the same as that. "Lie with me as we did in the forest on our way here."

The cool draft cut off abruptly as the drape was dropped back into place, and she felt him crawl across the bed toward her.

Fingers reached out, touched her face, and then lifted back the blankets for them both.

Astrid began to lower herself down, and an arm snaked under her and pulled her close. His hard body was warm and naked. Tense. His skin smelled clean, with a hint of forest pine, and she breathed his scent in with delight.

Their movements caused the ax to slip down and clatter to the floor and Bjorn stilled beside her.

"What was that?"

"My ax."

"You really had one?" He sounded astounded.

"Of course. I asked the room for one when I heard you bump into the table."

Bjorn's laugh rumbled loud in her ear. "Remind me never to underestimate you."

"I will." She held herself back from him, unsure once again, like the first night with him in the forest.

"Come closer." He spoke mildly, but she could hear the strain beneath and at last, once again like before, she lay her head on his shoulder, giving up the attempt to see his face.

MICHELLE DIENER

And as she drifted off to sleep, she realized this was nothing like sharing with Bets and Freja.

56

Chapter Nine

He could stay no longer.

He breathed in the sweet smell of roses and crisp cotton that clung to Astrid and willed himself to get up.

Dawn was coming, and no matter how good it felt to lie beside her, curved warmly against him in deep, trusting sleep, the time to change was almost upon him.

He had to be far from her when it came.

The thought of the return of the pain he'd experienced last night filled him with dread. If it was to be a twice-daily ordeal, he would need to be stronger than he'd ever been before.

Astrid sighed quietly in her sleep, and the sound centered him. There were benefits to taking his human form. Going through the fires of hell to enjoy them every day would only make them sweeter.

He slipped from the bed, let the curtain fall back behind him and opened one of the four shutters, so Astrid would have light when she woke.

As he closed the door behind him, and heard the lock click into place, he was already making plans for his day. Astrid was all that stood between Norga and her goal, and she would never be safe until this year was over. From the moment he'd placed his paw on the mountain's stone door and declared his quest part-way fulfilled, Norga would have known he'd found his lady.

Which was why Astrid could not set one foot out of this mountain.

He, though, would be out today and every day for the next year, keeping the mountain free of Norga and her minions, whatever it took.

The tired, beaten down bear Norga had taunted in the mountains was gone.

In his place was a killer.

She woke soon after dawn. A chink in the drapes of her bed let a beam of light straight onto her face, and she squinted and looked to her side.

Bjorn was gone, and she thought of him with a strange flutter in her stomach.

She'd managed to calm the beast but she did not fool herself that it would last long. She shivered. Remembered the feel and smell of him. The way he held her close and still kept his word.

So different from the smelly, lusty-eyed boys of the market who leered at her and her sisters and called out to them.

Freja had someone who courted her when she

came to market, but neither of them had a chance of marrying unless they found a way to build a house of their own. Both their family homes were filled to bursting and they would have no life with either of their parents.

Well, perhaps that had changed. Two bags of gold were now at Freja's disposal.

For the first time, Astrid saw the reason for some of Freja's desperation. She put her complicated thoughts of her family aside and slipped out of bed, opening all the shutters and letting in the light.

Who was Bjorn to live in such a place, and have such powerful enemies? He seemed so powerful himself, she hardly dared think who or what had bested him, enchanted him and restricted him.

If he would not tell her, she would find out.

Decided on her goal, she wished up hot water, clothes and breakfast.

As she pulled the soft blue wool dress over her head she caught sight of her ax, and nudged it under the bed with her foot. It wouldn't hurt to have it handy for the future. For who knew what that future would bring?

When she was ready, in a dress and boots fit for a queen, she tried the door, and to her relief it swung open. She was free for the day.

She reached the top of the stairs and could see the main hall was deserted. There was an emptiness to the place that made her sure Bjorn was not here.

Her chance to explore. Get to know these rooms.

And find a way out.

⎯⎯⎯◄⟡►⎯⎯⎯

He'd wanted to be back inside long before dusk. But the sun had already begun to dip below the horizon and he was only now reaching the stone cliff.

Meeting up with old friends and allies had taken longer than he'd thought. He'd had to tread warily. Any one of them could now be in league with Norga, some a more obvious choice for her than others.

All paid him homage, had given thanks for his sacrifices, but it was impossible as yet to tell who meant it and who said it for a chance to get to Astrid.

They were wasting their time, though. He would trust no one with Astrid.

At least meeting up with some of the old guard had reminded him what this was all for. Why he'd never given up.

As he called the mountain door to open, he wondered uneasily where Astrid was within. He had been beyond foolish to risk returning so late.

As soon as the stone rolled closed behind him he ran up the stairs and toward her bedroom, slowing with relief as he heard the splashes of water from within.

He imagined her in her bath, soapy and naked, and his dread of the transformation to come eased. Until this was over, his man's body could never see her in her bath, but he could touch her skin, learn her inch by inch in the dark.

He reached her door the moment the sun set and rose up on his hind legs to take the pain he knew was coming, to face it head on.

It hit him like the vicious swipe of a bear's claw, felling him with a single blow. He'd thought knowing what was to come would make it easier, but it did not. He curled up tight. He would surely, surely die this time —

"Bear . . . Bjorn? Are you out there? Are you all right?" Astrid's fingers scrabbled on the wooden door, and it creaked as she leant against it.

As suddenly as it had come, once again the pain lifted, leaving him shuddering in shock.

He lay still a moment, listening to Astrid's bath water drip off her onto the golden stone floor.

"Bear," she whispered, and he could tell she'd knelt down and pressed her cheek to the ground, trying to see below the door.

"Go back to your bath," he managed to croak. "I . . . there is nothing to fear. I will come to you soon."

She did not reply, didn't move either, the only sound the drip, drip, drip of scented water.

Eventually, he heard her get to her feet and walk back to her bath. Heard the soft splash as she sank down into it. He straightened slowly, like an old man, his body still reeling from the memory of pain.

A small trickle of water had leaked from under her door into the passage. Bending, Bjorn trailed his fingers in it and lifted them to his nose.

Roses.

He breathed deeply.

He needed a hot bath of his own, to ease his muscles, help them forget. He needed to eat after the long, physically punishing day.

And he needed to go to Astrid.

Tonight his seduction would begin.

Astrid stood on a warm rug in her bare feet and nightgown, and looked straight up through the skylights at the night sky.

She needed to find a way out. The clues to Bjorn's enchantment lay outside this mountain's walls, not within them.

There was nothing in this place but beautiful furniture and empty rooms, their golden floors and silver walls oppressive in the flickering torch light. Silent and dark as a tomb.

She needed to breathe the fresh air, and the wind . . . she needed the wind on her face, whispering in her ear. She would die in this luxurious cave.

Just thinking of the wind brought tears, and as they stung her eyes she remembered all the times its fingers caressed her like a mother quietening her child, murmured sweet nothings after a hiding from Father, or a meal missed for punishment.

"Oh, wind," she whispered, and lifted her hands up as if to catch a star.

The wind whispered back. It blew down the narrow skylight tunnels, and swirled around her, lifting her long nightgown up around her knees as it danced and leapt and played with her hair.

A sense of joy filled her. She had called and it had come. She wondered now how often she'd done this without realizing it back home. Began to wonder about herself. About why Bjorn had chosen her.

"I wish I could be free as you," she told it, reaching out to touch the tight band of rushing air, as solid as stroking a cat.

It began to twist faster and faster around her, pulling and tugging her, lifting her skirts to her waist.

Astrid felt herself lift a fraction off the ground, then drop down.

It wished her free, too.

"Now," she called, and leapt, and the swirling air took her and held her, propelled her upwards for a short way. Dropped her again.

"I'm too heavy." It broke her heart to say it, and the wind calmed down, gently lifting her hair and the hem of her gown, tired out.

Astrid looked up at the sky light again. "If I had a

ladder . . ." A ladder! "I want a . . ." she stopped, her whole body trembling. Bjorn could be here any moment. And she wasn't running away from him, she just wanted the freedom to go outside when she chose. The freedom to discover his secrets if she could. She could ask the room for the ladder tomorrow.

The click of the lock made her spin round, her eyes straining in the dark to see the door. She felt the wind twist up her one last time, and rush out of the skylight into the night.

The door swung part way open and Bjorn stood just behind it.

"Get into bed, Astrid, and close the drapes."

"What if I don't?" She wished the wind was still with her, it would make her feel braver.

There was a moment of silence. "Then I freeze you in place again, and close your eyes, so I can come into the room and put you into bed myself."

There was a vein of steel in his voice, a hardness that she sometimes heard there. He would do it.

She would rather get into bed herself than have him make her.

"Very well." She made no effort to hide the anger in her voice. "I am slowly getting to know you, as I wanted."

He sighed. "I don't want to play the villain, but you leave me no choice. You cannot see me."

"Why not? Just tell me why and I will stop trying."

She climbed onto the bed as she spoke, pulling down the drapes.

"I have already explained. I cannot tell you. I made a bargain with my enchanter, and not telling you the details of my enchantment was part of it."

"Then be warned, I will not stop trying, for I made no such bargain."

He made a sound of frustration, entering the room and closing the door over-hard behind him.

"Do not try, Astrid. For both our sakes."

She did not answer him. She could not sit, quiet and obedient. She could not follow blindly with no information. It would break her.

They would not agree on this, and now she had a possible way out, she would go her own way, as she always did.

As for Bjorn, he was stubborn as she was, she could tell. The difference being she never took getting her way for granted, whereas he could hardly believe it when he didn't.

That was her advantage over him.

She heard him close the skylight shutters and move toward the bed, and an icy fist closed over her stomach. There wasn't enough air in this velvet tent to sustain her. She tried to fill her lungs.

"What is it?" The concern in his voice helped to steady her.

"Nothing." She drew in a deep breath.

"You are afraid?"

He slid down next to her, cocooning them in the soft down bedding, and the scent of him hit her. The forest after rain.

"You smell like roses," he whispered, and ran a light finger down her cotton-clad arm.

Mention of her bath scent reminded her of what happened earlier outside her bedroom. "What happened? You were in pain."

His finger stopped. "I don't want to talk of it now. The change from bear to man is . . . hard. There is nothing either of us can do."

"I'm sorry." She lifted a hand and touched his face, the first time she'd ever reached out to him. The first time she'd felt the lines and curves of his human face.

"One day, I will overcome it. It won't be forever." His finger began moving again, down her arm to the dip of her waist.

"How can I help you?"

"Do as I ask you, and you will be helping me very much." He opened his hand and slid his palm over her hip, held it there, warm and shockingly familiar in the dark.

Poor Bear. He had taken the wrong girl if he thought she would accept that.

Whatever happened between them in this bed would not weaken her will. Just as she knew no matter what comfort he took from her here, he would not bend

to her need to be outside.
So she would find her own way.

Chapter Ten

He needed to keep the oath he'd sworn clear in his mind. Remind himself he would not have her tonight. Nor even perhaps the night after this.

But through her nightclothes her skin was warm and firm, and he wanted no barriers between them. Knowing it would make his oath harder, Bjorn slipped a hand beneath her hem and ran it up her leg.

She stilled. "Please stop."

Bjorn sighed, and pulled his hand back. Leant forward in the dark and kissed her, his hands gripping her waist, his thumbs just below her breasts.

She trembled as his lips touched hers, but she did not pull back.

"Don't be afraid. Just lie here and let me show you what it could be like," he whispered to her.

She lay still a moment, and he heard her take a deeper breath, sensed a calming.

"Show me, then."

This would be a sweet torture, Bjorn realized as he lifted up on an elbow, heart thrumming in anticipation. He cupped a breast he longed to see in his hand, and bent to kiss her again.

His sweet Astrid, laid out for him, willing, to a point, and the only picture of it he could have was in his mind.

So be it. It was up to him to make their eyes unnecessary. To create a picture of taste, touch and sound. And by the gods, to remember his oath.

-------◄◢◢►-------

The dark lulled her and confounded her. Bjorn's mouth left a trail of fire down her body as he kissed and nuzzled. She was burning up for a man she had never seen.

Did it matter?

As she trembled beneath him, pulled between an urge to arch up against him or run, she couldn't think clearly enough to come up with an answer.

But why will he not let you see him? What is he afraid of?

At breaking point, unable to explain the tension growing within her, she cried out and rolled away, coming up on her knees on the far side of the bed.

"Hush, hush," he whispered, and only then did she realize she was all but sobbing.

"I don't know . . . what is happening to me," she gasped out.

"I know. I move too quickly for you, but not as

quickly as I would like. Come here and I will hold you a while. Start again more slowly."

She didn't want to. And she wanted to too much.

"I am constantly pulled in two with you," she told him, hesitating. If only she could see!

"I have stirred your body awake, and it wants me, but your brain is warning you that you don't know me well enough to accept me yet." He spoke quietly.

When had she ever accepted anything she hadn't wanted to? Even when it was the easiest course, the least trouble.

She had always taken the hard road.

She sighed, lay down and let him gather her close. This waiting game was at her discretion, and he'd proven himself to her by agreeing to it at all.

He had kept to his oath, and given the control in this bed to her.

He stroked her hair, his hands gentle, even though she could feel his hardness pressing against her.

She wanted to pull him even closer, taste him, ease the ache that he had coaxed to life in her body.

She fisted her hands. Did she commit to this like the north wind blowing a gale, or the east wind, barely stirring the warm air about? Full tilt or gently does it?

She heard the steady rhythm of his heart, felt the smoothness of his chest against her cheek, smelt his essence. She stuck out her tongue, touched the tip to his skin to taste him, and he jerked.

"Take me," she whispered.

North wind it was.

He reared up, making her heart pound with nerves.

"Now?"

"Unless you'd rather wait——" She didn't know if that was disappointment or relief she was feeling.

"No." He cut her off. "I would not rather wait." He felt for her hand, pulled it down to his erect penis and closed her fingers around his length. "I have been like this since I started down the passageway to this chamber. Be sure, Astrid."

She drew in a shaky breath. "I am sure." But she trembled.

He was quiet, and then he pulled away, lay back down on the bed beside her. She could feel his body, stiff and tense.

"The truth is, we have plenty of time. It is good, lying together like we did last night. We don't have to rush this. I have no right to ask you to go faster than you find comfortable." She heard the regret in his voice.

She felt her cheeks heat. "Yes. It is good." She reached out to him again, running a fingertip along his jaw, tracing the arch of his eyebrow. She levered herself over him, and bent to kiss him, becoming bolder as he groaned in encouragement.

And she found she did not want to wait. She wanted to leap into this, for once unfettered by rules or disapproval, and follow her instincts. She was safe with him.

He wanted her so much, she could feel him shaking beneath her, and yet he had exerted control. Respected her.

She lifted her lips from his. "Show me how it could be between us—"

He cut her off with a kiss of his own, his hand trailing between her breasts, over her stomach and down between her legs.

She gasped in shock as his fingers found the secret core of her, as her body responded to his touch. It may be the north wind, she thought as she arched into his hand, but for once, it was blowing hot.

⊷⊰⊷

She was free.

Astrid perched on the ledge below her skylights and felt the wind in her face. She lifted her arms out to her sides and closed her eyes, felt the warmth of the sun's rays on her eyelids, the chill bite of the snow-caps in the breeze lifting her hair.

It was a new day in every sense. From the ache between her legs, to standing in the sun at last. She was ready for anything.

Ready to find out what mysterious world she'd chosen for herself. What secrets there were to find.

Life with her father had schooled her well for this strange battle of wills Bjorn seemed determined to wage with her. Her Bear's disadvantage was he had no idea how deep her well of determination ran. The speed with which her father handed her over should have warned him.

She smiled, but she recognized the weight in her chest for what it was. Sadness.

Something had happened. Long ago, when she was too young to remember. Something about her frightened her father and he could not look at her without also feeling the fear. She had understood that slowly, hurtfully, as she'd grown older. Despite the shield of Mother and Tomas.

And since last night, she was sure it had to do with the wind.

"Come then," she whispered to the breeze. She scrambled down the rocks, making sure she could return the same way. It wouldn't do to have to ask Bjorn to let her in at the secret rock entrance.

Astrid didn't intend to lose this freedom to roam.

Chapter Eleven

She was changeable as the wind. The thought made Bjorn uneasy, even though he was more than pleased with the result. Leaving her chamber had been a physical wrench. He'd stood over her for long minutes, dangerously close to dawn, just to hear her breathing, hear each small movement she made.

The first human closeness he'd had in too long.

The chill of an autumn breeze cut through his thick fur as he stood waiting in the forest clearing. Since he'd found Astrid, the wind never left him alone. Blasting him with cold air, blinding him with sand and leaves.

He'd suspect Norga, but even she did not have mastery over the wind. Though he had no doubt she'd kill to get it.

Just then the wind died away, as suddenly as it sprung up, and for a moment Bjorn enjoyed the warmth of the sun fingering through the trees, and the peace of the forest.

"You are weary."

He jerked at the words, realized he'd closed his

eyes and had no idea whether minutes or seconds had passed.

Jorgen stood amongst the trees, so still he was almost invisible, and Bjorn understood if his old ally had taken Norga's side, he'd be dead.

The chill at his lapse stole the sun's heat from his skin.

"Where are the others?" He could show no chink in his armor, no matter whether Jorgen was true or not. He was their leader, and while it was not through choice, he had accepted his role.

"They are coming. But there is something in the woods today. Can you feel it?"

Bjorn shook his head, and Jorgen stepped into the clearing, his bearing alert.

He was clad in the brown and green of the vedfe, the fine cloth stretching across his broad shoulders and muscled arms, his skin dark as pine bark. Even in the open clearing, Bjorn knew if Jorgen stood still enough, most would pass him by without a second look, so well did he blend into his surroundings.

Unlike me, Bjorn thought, looking down at the white of his fur. Although, given the chill, in a month or less, he'd be the invisible one. Indistinguishable from the snow.

The branches stirred around them, and Jorgen cocked his head to listen. "There is a troll. Perhaps the others aren't coming after all."

Bjorn listened too. Not to the whispers of the trees, he could not understand their language, but for the troll. For once he was grateful for his bear body, with its sharp hearing and finely tuned nose. "Ask the trees where the troll is."

"They are not able to answer me that specifically," Jorgen smiled. "They are not talking to me at all. And it isn't the trees I'm listening to, anyway. It is a harmony of the wind and the trees together. I overhear some of it, and understand only a fraction."

Bjorn grunted. Pity. He'd like to narrow down where Norga's minion was, but if he had to do it the hard way, so be it. He was lucky to be forewarned as it was.

Jorgen folded his arms in front of his chest, the light hazel of his eyes startling in his dark face. "The forest has not ceased its whisperings since you returned with your lady."

Bjorn swung his full attention to his friend. "What does it say?"

Jorgen shrugged. "I haven't understood any of it. Just that there is much excitement. Your lady isn't the Wind Hag, is she?"

Bjorn thought of his ethereal blonde beauty and smiled. Shook his head. "She is not."

Jorgen smiled too. "You would know if she was. The Wind Hag's face is upside down."

Would he know? Bjorn felt his amusement drop away. Hadn't his father done just that? Taken a beauty, who turned out to be the opposite of what she seemed?

Jorgen seemed to sense the blunder. "I will go, then, if there is a troll. Be sure we will watch out for you and yours, my friend." He bowed, as if they were once more back in the palace hall, and Bjorn was the liege lord over the natural order.

"No need for that, Jorgen. That time has come and gone."

"It will come again." Jorgen hesitated on the edge of the clearing.

"Perhaps. But with changes. My father showed us what mischief could be wrought the old way. I won't let this costly lesson go to waste."

"And you have paid more than most," the vedfe acknowledged. "Stay away from the troll, Bjorn. You do no one any good if you die."

"I plan to protect my mountain," Bjorn said to the empty clearing, because he knew Jorgen was still there. "And if anyone dies today, it won't be me."

Chapter Twelve

The sound of vicious fighting made her freeze. It was coming through the trees to her left, and she hesitated. Was it Bjorn?

She needed to avoid him, but could she walk away from this? Leave him to fight whatever it was he fought and not help?

A snarl, low and rumbling, sent a prickle of fear up her arms. That was Bjorn as she had never heard him. Dangerous . . . deadly. She shivered.

What was it he fought?

Grateful for the dark brown of her cloak, and the soft soles of her leather boots, Astrid crept forward, staying close to the trees.

"Bearman," she heard a strange, grating voice say, and she crouched down, working her way slowly around a large tree to finally see the arena.

Out of the corner of her eye, a branch moved to her right, and her heart stopped with fear. She turned slowly to look, but it was nothing but a strangely shaped trunk, the height of a man.

She turned her attention back to the clearing.

Bjorn faced off against a strange creature. A hulking thing almost twice Bjorn's height; its eyes black beads, tiny in the massive head, with a long, misshapen nose below. Its body looked like a rock stained with moss and lichen, covered with layers of gray-green rags. But it moved too lithely, was too quick to really be rock and she saw the slash of a bear claw on its side. It bled red, just like every other living animal.

A troll?

"Norga has lost, either go back to her and stay there, or die." The growl rumbled in Bjorn's chest.

"I die if I go back without completing my task, Bearman," the troll said in its strange voice. "Or I die if you beat Norga."

"Is that what she's told you? If I win, you die?" Bjorn and the troll began to circle each other, their focus on the other complete.

"It isn't so?"

"No. If I win, the balance returns. Nothing more, nothing less." Bjorn stopped. Eyed his opponent.

Astrid leaned forward in anticipation. The key to his secrets was almost in her hand.

"It is Norga who seeks more than her share. It is she who will kill us all if she wins."

"I still die if I go back without killing the girl."

"Don't go back then." But Bjorn's easy shrug belied his posture. Tense. Ready. He didn't mean to let this creature walk away.

And the girl? Did that mean *her*?

She must have made a movement in shock, because the troll's eyes locked with hers as she stood loose-armed beside the tree.

"Help me," it cried to her, and suddenly it went from looming over Bjorn to being a small, wizened man, cowering back from the massive bear, paw raised to strike.

"What——?" Bjorn turned to look, and even on his bear face she registered his horror at the sight of her.

The little dwarf became the monstrous thing again in a heartbeat, its huge arm swinging, the blow lifting Bjorn into the air.

He fell with a thud that made the ground beneath her thin-soled boots shudder, and Astrid cried out, took a step to him.

"Run!" His roar made her jerk, and she saw the massive troll strike out at him with its foot before it turned back to her.

Bjorn lay still. She looked wildly from his strangely huddled body to the sharp black eyes of the monster. She spun on her heel, and ran.

It was too big to outrun, so she would have to outwit it.

"Can you slow it down?" she whispered to the

wind, wondering if it would answer. Wondering if she commanded it or whether it obliged her of its own accord.

Behind her she heard a rush of leaves, the whistle of a strong wind, and turned to look.

Around the troll was a whirlwind of sand, pine needles and twigs, and it was waving its hands in front of its eyes, stumbling as it was blinded.

Astrid turned her eyes back to the path, racing up through the trees toward the mountain.

She could hear the troll's steps, much slowed but still coming.

"Aaaargh." The monster screamed in frustration and pain, blundering into trees, swiping at the air.

If it caught her, there would be no mercy.

There would have been no mercy anyway, she told herself. Bjorn knew it, that's why he'd lied as he prepared to kill the thing.

The thought of Bjorn spurred her faster. She had to reach the palace, wish up a weapon and kill the troll so she could return to help him.

Behind her, the troll shrieked again, and Astrid reached the rocks. She began to scramble up, but her hands were slick with fear, her body heaving with exhaustion. She slipped down and sobbed as she tried again, finding the strength she needed when she felt the first sting of the whirlwind on her back. She managed to get up a little way, then ran out of handholds.

"Help me up," she begged the air, and at once there was support to her back, a boost just like Tomas used to give her, climbing trees. It was all she needed. Using her fingernails and her feet, she scrambled up to her ledge and swung her legs down the skylight, dropping through as the troll's hands gripped the rocks just below.

She slid down the ladder, not using any of the steps, her feet slamming into the ground. She stumbled forward to close the shutters, but just as her hand grasped the rod, a little dwarf fell through the ceiling and landed on her bedroom floor.

"Help me, help me," it laughed, then, with a look of surprise, turned back into a monster.

"I want an ax," she screamed to the room, but nothing appeared. "A sword." She looked at her empty hands in disbelief. "A knife."

Still nothing.

There was no magic in the room.

She made a run for the door, but the troll beat her to it, blocking the way.

"Are you a troll?" She started shuffling backwards to the bed.

"Yes," it answered. "Who are you?"

"No one." Astrid felt the bed against the back of her knees. She started edging right, to the side she slept on.

"Bearman's lady," it said, with a twisted smile.

"And Windlady." It breathed out the last word almost reverently, and Astrid held its gaze.

"The wind will hound you forever if you harm me. You will never be free of it." Around her, the air stirred, fluttering her cloak, and she felt a lift of hope. It was here, awaiting her command.

Bjorn's magic may have deserted her, but her own strange brand of magic had not.

The troll shrugged, not disbelieving her, she thought, but resigned to whatever consequences it would suffer.

Then it leapt.

"Blow the drapes," Astrid cried out, and the waiting air did her bidding, flicking the velvet into the troll's face. It came on, shouting as it ripped the fabric away. A few steps and it would reach her.

Astrid threw herself down and grabbed the hidden ax under her bed, then scrambled to her feet, swinging in an arc as she rose.

The troll shrieked as the wide blade buried itself deep in its chest, over its heart. It took a surprised step back.

"My heart," it keened, and fell over. Stone dead.

Her breath shuddered out her body, and Astrid sank down on the bed, legs wobbly as a fawn.

"Astrid!"

Full of rage and pain, Bjorn's shout echoed through the passageways, and she turned her head as he burst through the door, the streaks of blood from his wounds shocking against his white fur.

He reeled back at the sight of the troll, lying face up on her floor. The wind was still flapping the velvet drapes, obscuring her view of him.

"Astrid?" There was so much in the question. Relief, disbelief, and still a trace of rage.

Astrid bent her head into her hands and wept.

Chapter Thirteen

He came into the room cautiously, skirting the troll, his eyes on the ax, buried to the hilt in its heart. Stopping a troll's heart was the only way to kill it, and his innocent Astrid had felled this one with a single blow.

The strange wind swirling around the chamber had died, and the only sound was Astrid crying.

He took in the ladder up to the skylight. It was a far more mundane way to escape than he'd thought she'd found. Clever, but hardly mysterious. He hadn't known what to think since the troll gave chase to her.

He sat down on the floor, his body still clenching with pain where the troll's blows had landed.

"You are hurt," she said softly, swallowing her sobs as she lifted her head from her hands and stood. She took a step toward him.

"No thanks to you," he snarled back, suddenly furious with her, with what her disobedience could have cost him. She could have been killed.

"This is not my fault, it is yours," she cried—looking just as furious as he felt. "I told you already, if you won't tell me the truth, I will discover it for myself."

"What are you?" If the woman who could save him was not the sweet woodcutter's daughter he'd at first thought, he'd like to know who she was.

She looked at him in disbelief. "What am *I*? What are *you*?" She clenched her fists and lifted her head high. "Who is Norga? Why was a troll trying to kill me?"

He refused to answer, thinking of the small whirlwind of debris around the troll as he'd chased her up the hill. Thought of the constant bombardment the wind had given him since he'd taken her from her parents. Thought of an ax wielded with deadly accuracy. "Are you the Wind Hag?"

He saw her mouth fall open, her eyes widen. "The Wind Hag?" she whispered. "Who is the Wind Hag?"

"The mistress of the wind," he answered, even more unsure of her than ever. If she was not the Wind Hag—

"Mistress of the wind." She said it with satisfaction, a smile curving her lips. "I like that. I like Wind Hag, too. It sounds . . . powerful."

"If you don't know who the Wind Hag is, then you aren't her," Bjorn said harshly. "Why is the wind helping you?"

"Because I ask it to very nicely."

Her sarcasm made him want to smile for the first time since he'd seen her standing by the trees, watching him fight.

She studied the troll again, and crossed her arms

in front of her chest. "Why did the magic in the room stop? If I hadn't saved the ax from the other night, I'd be dead."

"I have safeguards in my palace. When the troll entered, his powers were stripped from him, but so was the magic of the room. He couldn't enchant you, or use the magic of the palace against you, but neither could you."

"He didn't need magic, he's twice my size."

"I never thought you'd leave the palace. I never thought anything could get in." *I was a fool.*

She stepped closer, as if drawn by the bleakness in his voice. "I thought you were dead, or seriously hurt," she said quietly.

"I had . . . help. From a friend. He has some healing powers. Enough to get me on my feet."

She bent forward, touched his fur. "I want warm water, please," she said to the room. "And cloths."

"Astrid—"

"Hush." Her words were an echo of his own last night. "Let's clean you up before you have to disappear. Will these wounds be on your real body, too?" She dipped a cloth into the basin of warm water which had appeared beside him, and squeezed it over a deep cut.

"They are troll-made, I won't be able to heal myself as easily as usual." He hesitated. "I don't know."

There was so much he didn't know, but for now, feeling her hands gently stroking him was all he needed.

"Well then, if they do, tonight, I will kiss them better," she whispered.

Bjorn closed his eyes, let his whole body relax. *Please*, he prayed to the deities. *Let her truly be mine. Let me not be my father all over again.*

———◄❧►———

"I think we should visit my parents." Astrid rose up on an elbow, gently tracing the lines of Bjorn's chest in the darkness.

"You want to go home?" He spoke warily. "You can't even step into the forest at the bottom of this mountain without being attacked."

"Exactly." She'd spent the last five days since the troll attack thinking of nothing else. Of how she was unable to walk free, imprisoned here forever. "I do not want to spend the rest of my days trapped within."

"It . . . won't be forever." He hesitated as he spoke.

"Well, how long then?" Could it really make such a difference if she knew how long? Did he trust her so little?

"A year."

Her heart sank. Even a year trapped within the gloomy confines of a mountain seemed like a death sentence.

"And this Norga? Will she stop trying to kill me now her troll is dead? Or will she try again?"

"Oh, she'll try again. She has everything to lose."

His voice was grim. In the dark, she imagined what his face must look like; serious, a frown creasing his brow.

"Then let's go. My mother knows something that can help us, I'm sure of it."

"What would your mother know of this?" Despite his words, he sounded relieved, and she realized he'd thought she meant to leave him, not seek out answers. And it struck her that leaving him had never entered her mind. All her thoughts, plans and ideas involved them both.

"The night you first came knocking on the window, she told me she'd once seen a troll. It had killed a hag, and there was a small boy there, too."

His big hands shot out, gripped her shoulders, moving so fast he frightened her. At her cry of surprise, he let her go and fell back.

"Tell me all she said." There was an intensity to his voice, a wildness.

"Nothing else. Except I was with her that day, but I was too young to remember it. My father made her stop the tale."

"Why? Why would he do that?"

"He didn't want her talking about it. It seemed to disturb him."

"If we go, we take the risk Norga will try to kill you on the way." His words came slowly. Considering.

"Whoever she is, will she not try to kill us both?" Why was he not worried for his own life?

"Never mind that. Is the risk worth it?"

"It is to me."

She had won him over. She could hear he was seriously considering the journey. But a new question niggled at her.

If Norga did not want to kill him, then it was because she needed him or was bound by some oath not to. And once again he'd avoided her questions.

His oath to his enchanter frustrated her beyond measure, but no matter what else lay between them, they opened up completely to each other in this bed. Skin to skin.

And there was an honesty to that she would never have believed.

Whoever she was, whoever he was, when they lay entwined like this, blind in the dark, they were at peace. And that was enough.

For now.

Chapter Fourteen

"You look much better." Jorgen seemed to step out of a tree trunk in the clearing, and Bjorn blinked in surprise.

"You become more invisible with each meeting." He gathered his wits. "I owe my wellbeing to you, my friend. I know it cost you to give me so much strength. I hope you have recovered."

Jorgen smiled, and gave a shrug. "I assume you were able to reach your lady before the troll?"

"No. I was not." Something huge and terrible squeezed his chest every time he thought about it.

Jorgen looked at him sharply. "She is not . . . "

"No." He wondered how much he could trust Jorgen, then decided it was worth the risk to hear his thoughts. "When I got to her, the troll lay dead. Felled in a single blow to the heart."

"Felled with what?" Jorgen's eyes strayed up the foothill, to the mountain.

"An ax."

"Your lady keeps an ax in her chamber?"

Bjorn grunted. He was not going to explain the ax

to Jorgen. He'd rather face the troll again.

"Well, I suppose she *is* a woodcutter's daughter."

"Is she?" Bjorn let his gaze follow Jorgen's up the hill. "Then why does the wind do her bidding?"

"What does she say?"

"That she asks it very nicely."

Jorgen shouted out a surprised laugh. "Why will she not explain?"

Bjorn sighed. "Because I cannot explain to her. She is stubborn, willful, and . . ." Mine.

"Beautiful," Jorgen said, surprising him. Disturbing him.

"You saw her?"

"We both watched you fighting that troll. I knew you wouldn't heed my advice to leave it be." He assumed a pose, still as deadwood. "She thought I was a tree trunk."

"And she is not the Wind Hag." It wasn't a question.

"Not the one I remember. Hideous creature. Eyes, ears, nose and mouth upside down. Topsy turvy, like the wind itself. But powerful."

"She has given the wind leave to obey Astrid, then. And we may discover why from Astrid's mother."

"That would be ill-considered, with Norga watching you. Your lady spells the death knell to her plans. Rather keep her within for a year, safe."

"I cannot keep her in the mountain that long."

Bjorn knew the admission weakened him, but it was the truth. "She will not accept it, and I cannot watch both her and Norga. She will find a way out again."

Jorgen said nothing for a moment. "You cannot order her to obey?"

"Can you order the wind to stop blowing?" Even to his own ears, Bjorn heard the thread of ruefulness, and strangely, pride, in his voice.

Jorgen smiled, and Bjorn thought his friend was enjoying the merry dance Bjorn was being led, even if the consequences could affect him just as much.

"If her mother can explain why the wind does her bidding, what will it help? The bargain with Norga remains."

"Norga has something to do with it, of that, I'm sure. And the better I understand Norga, the better I can defeat her." He didn't say it, but he knew the bargain's end left Norga with truly nothing to lose if he should win. What would stop her trying to kill them both, then, bargain or no? Astrid was right. Rather seek out answers, try to end it now, than wait.

"You are decided."

"I am. We will go in a week's time." He wanted more time to bind Astrid to him, to strengthen the connection between them that was growing beyond his wildest imaginings before he put her in proximity to her family again.

"Then good luck."

Bjorn acknowledged the farewell with a bow. Both he and Jorgen knew they would need all the luck they could get.

Chapter Fifteen

They left just after dawn.

Bjorn ran as if a troll were at their heels. And perhaps one soon would be. Clinging to his neck, Astrid looked back, and saw nothing but trees, their thick foliage already blocking the mountain from view, forcing the sun to poke through the leaves with pale fingers to find the ground.

She clutched her bundle of things tighter, remembering the small handkerchief of rags she'd brought with her just under a month ago.

How different things were now.

There was a flash of movement to the right. Something running from tree to tree, but before Astrid could tell Bjorn, he swerved left. He'd seen it, too.

"Be prepared to slide off, I will have to fight," he said to her, and Astrid felt a chill of fear grip her heart.

"Can you not freeze it, like you did me?"

"I could, but it would not help for long. That was Sigurd, and he has many tricks of his own. Strong magic that shields him against mine."

"You *know* him?" The cold morning air stole her

MICHELLE DIENER

breath as Bjorn ran toward a clearing a short way ahead.
No place for the creature to hide there.

"I know all in these woods," he said, reaching the
clearing and stopping dead center. "They used to answer
to me. Now some answer to Norga instead. Sigurd has
shown his hand, after kneeling to me and pledging his
allegiance only a few days ago."

Of course. The palace should have prepared her.
Of course he was the lord of this place. "Could he be
aiding us, rather than chasing us?"

"No."

He was so sure, Astrid did not doubt him.

"Get down, but stay close as you can. Within
grasp. Sigurd may not be alone, and I dare not let you
hide where I cannot see you. The trees are not safe."

Astrid slid down his back and stood facing the
opposite way to Bjorn, watching the far side of the
clearing.

From the way Bjorn stood ready, muscles
bunched, Sigurd was someone, *something*, to be feared.
She wanted to ask him what he was, or looked like, but
was terrified of making a sound.

Above the swish and sigh of the trees, the rustle of
leaves, something ran from one of the trees at the edge of
the clearing to another. So fast, once again Astrid could
not see them.

Bjorn turned toward the sound, forcing her to turn
too, to stay to his back. A low growl rumbled from his

throat, making the hairs on the back of Astrid's neck stand up. She shivered.

Another sharp burst of sound made her jump, and a sliver of tree trunk, twice Bjorn's height, levered out from the pines and reached across the clearing for her. A giant stick insect man with a thin face and cunning eyes, its weathered silver hands sharp and pointed, like dead wood.

She cried out as Sigurd lunged at her like a stork strikes forward to catch its frog, and Bjorn spun, his roar echoing through the trees as he swiped at Astrid, knocking her out of Sigurd's hands.

She landed hard and rolled to her feet, grateful the ground was thick with pine needles and spongy with autumn rains.

Bjorn had not spoken a word to his old subject, his teeth were bared and savage as he advanced.

She saw Sigurd freeze, his backward movement stopped, and knew Bjorn had enchanted him.

But with a cry he broke free of the spell and leapt, soaring up like a javelin over Bjorn's head. A massive branch snapped from a nearby tree and was hurled by an invisible hand into the clearing, catching Bjorn a glancing blow to his hind legs.

Sigurd most definitely had tricks of his own.

And so do I.

"Come, wind, to me," she whispered, and felt the first flutter of breeze against her face as Bjorn launched himself at Sigurd just as Sigurd leapt at him. They smashed into each other and Bjorn cried out as Sigurd raked him with sharp hands, then struck back with his own claws.

Sigurd's shout of pain was the strange creak of a tree falling. He flung himself up, flipping in the air and arrowing down straight for Bjorn, hands out in claws.

"Stop him," Astrid cried out, and the wind howled around the clearing, blowing Sigurd off course. Slamming him down into the ground.

Bjorn hurled himself onto Sigurd and stood over him, the pitch of his growl so low, so menacing, Astrid felt her arms pucker to gooseflesh.

A small ball of fire suddenly hovered in the air between them, and for the first time, Astrid saw Sigurd look afraid.

"Tell me why you do the troll's bidding, even while you swear loyalty to me, traitor."

Sigurd said nothing, his eyes on the flames that licked and leapt in the air.

Bjorn grunted. "It matters not. I could never trust you again, anyway."

With that, Bjorn stepped back and the fire ball dropped onto Sigurd's chest. It seemed to Astrid, unbidden by her, as if in revenge for Sigurd's attack, the wind fanned the flame.

Sigurd shrieked, was engulfed, and the there came an answering cry from deep within the trees. Sigurd struggled to his knees, twisting in the heat and then fell, blackened and still.

Bjorn turned his attention to the direction of the other call. "Leap on, that was another yggren, and I cannot trust they are not in league with Sigurd. Even if they are not, I have killed one of their own, and they will not be happy with that."

He crouched down for her, and she clambered on.

"What *is* an yggren?"

"They say they are the dead wood that dropped from the great tree itself."

"Yggdrasil?" Astrid gasped. She was over her head in these circumstances. She wondered again what Bjorn was, the most powerful of these powerful, magical beings, and then wondered if she truly wanted to know.

"You were not harmed by me?" he asked her as he began to speed through the woods again.

"No." She'd known why he'd knocked her out of Sigurd's hands. If the yggren had started running with her, Bjorn would never have caught him.

"I see the wind still does your bidding."

"Yes." And it still surprised her. Somehow, there seemed no limit to how much aid the wind would give her.

"Why do you?" she whispered as the air swelled around them, seeming to speed them along. She looked back and saw a wall of dead pine needles, cones and leaves rise up like a wall between them and the clearing, blocking them from view.

"Why do you?"

Chapter Sixteen

The tall trees loomed over them and the late afternoon light filtered through, green and gloomy this deep in the forest. They were less than a day from Astrid's home.

Even though she had never mentioned leaving him, Bjorn could not stop the dread that weighed him down. What did he have to offer her but the loneliness of an empty palace when before she'd had the constant company of her family?

She had not been his long enough for him to be sure of her. He had not bound her close enough.

And she was no meek miss.

She questioned everything and would not accept that he could not tell her, could not give her answers.

He found a clearing, protected by a thick stand of trees, and stopped early for the night, wanting to draw out their time together. Even though he knew it was dangerous to tarry.

"I would not like to bring my family into danger," Astrid said, leaning back against him, sheltering in his bear's bulk against the damp autumn chill that seemed to seep bone-deep. "Let us ask our questions and leave as soon as possible."

"I agree." Bjorn huffed out a contented sigh. She did not intend to stay behind, then.

"I suppose they have started spending your gold already," she mused. "Freja would have asked for money for a house, so she and Jonas can marry. Tomas will also want his own house."

He needed to be wary of Tomas. Of all of them, he held the most sway over Astrid, loved her the most. If he knew the truth, that Astrid was the touchstone in a power struggle, Bjorn's only point of weakness and Norga's only obstacle, he would beg her not to return.

"Please, promise me some things," he said.

"My turn to swear some oaths?" He could hear a smile in her voice.

"Yes. Do not mention what has happened on the mountain to your family. I would have them know nothing of Norga and her plans."

"I will swear to that. They would only worry if they knew the truth."

"Is your mother afraid of me?" Bjorn remembered the way the woodcutter's wife had looked at him, full of fear and anxiety, and already knew the answer.

"She is. She begged my father not to let me go. She said you could be anything."

"Do not let her turn you against me." He felt helpless at the thought of it. How could he compete with her mother's influence?

"No one could turn me against you, Bear," Astrid whispered to him. "I know your body better than I know my own. I know you keep your promises. I know you have a generous and kind spirit. I know you are courageous and brave." She tangled her fingers in his fur. "And I keep my promises, too. I said I would go with you, and I will not go back on my word, no matter what my family asks of me."

His heart soared, light as air. Free. Even becoming a man again had not felt as wonderful as Astrid's respect and regard.

But still, Bjorn wondered if she knew how hard it would be to deny her family's wishes, wondered how they would be received tomorrow.

Initially with dismay, he guessed. Her father and Eric would assume Bjorn had come to return her, and ask for his gold back.

If they hurt her feelings, if they made her unhappy, they would be very, very sorry.

She knew Bjorn was nervous. Whether because he feared she would want to stay, or because they were so exposed to the mysterious and powerful Norga, she could not say. Perhaps both.

She was nervous herself. She was not the same

Astrid she had once been, and her family would not be the same, either.

They had gold, but the price had been her. For some, that was a guilt-free exchange, for others, a burden.

"I want to get down and walk beside you, Bjorn," she called as they neared the forest's edge. She needed control, the ability to slow her steps, if this sudden fear within her became too much.

Less than four weeks ago this place had been her home. Now, as she slid down her lover's back her hand trembled, and her knees felt like buckling.

"I can hear an ax," Bjorn murmured, and Astrid stopped to listen.

At last, she heard it too. The rhythmic thud of metal on wood.

"I'd have thought they had no more need for wood chopping, with the gold you gave them."

"Shall we see?" Bjorn asked her, and she nodded, relieved to delay approaching the house for a while longer.

It was Tomas, his hair a halo of gold in the sunlight as he swung his ax, shirtless even though the air was cool, the sweat glistening on his back. He worked with total focus, hypnotized by the rhythm of his actions.

Astrid's heart lurched at the sight of him. Her handsome, strong brother, who had been her champion since the day she was born.

"Tomas."

His eyes flicked to hers and he froze, ax over shoulder. With a cry, he buried the ax-head deep into the tree and ran to her, sweeping her up and holding her close.

"You are safe."

She threw back her head and laughed in delight. "I am safe." Her gaze went to Bjorn, and Tomas lowered her, reaching for his shirt hanging on a branch and slipping it over his head before he turned to bow.

"You have brought her back, Bear?" There was an edge to his tone, and Astrid realized he thought Bjorn was unhappy with her, returning her like used baggage.

"Only for one day. She missed you, and wished to see you again. We leave this evening."

"Ah." Tomas' face was unreadable.

"We were on the way to the cottage, and heard you chopping. Do you still need the money, after the gold?"

Tomas looked in the direction of the house. "I chop because I cannot bear to sit around doing nothing." He looked deeply unhappy. "I chop because every bite I eat tastes like sawdust, my new feather mattress feels as though it is made of nails and my new clothes are like sackcloth."

"Because the price was me?" Astrid threw her arms around him. "Oh, Tomas. I am happy. Do not worry about that. It makes me sad to think you do not benefit from the gold, while Father and Eric do. Please, take some and build a house of your own. Get away from them."

"*Are* you happy?" Tomas held her gaze, and despite herself, Astrid blushed. Nodded.

"I am. I live in a magical palace, where my every wish is granted."

"And for company?" Again, she could not read his eyes.

"I have company."

"But you are not gone four weeks and you seek ours again?" Tomas looked at Bear, and Astrid thought she saw an accusation in his eyes.

"Your sister is better treated with me than she ever was here," Bjorn said, his voice quiet, the rumble of it sinister in the deep woods. "During the day, she is well cared for, and in the night—"

"What happens in the night?" Tomas cried out, looking between them.

"In the night, I am well cared for as well." Astrid spoke without flinching.

"What have we done?" Tomas whispered to himself, rubbing a hand over his face, but Astrid would have none of it.

"At night, my Bear becomes a man, and comes to me as a husband. And I say again, I am happy."

They fell into silence, and a robin started trilling its song again in the quiet.

"Come, the day is wasting." Bjorn started forward,

and Astrid could see from the way he looked from side to side he was nervous of their standing too long in the woods.

"Why do you not stay the night?" Tomas asked Astrid, and she shook her head.

"We must get back."

Tomas hesitated, as if to ask her why, then casting a glance at Bjorn, he pulled his ax out of the tree and picked up a small bundle besides the trunk. She had a feeling he would try to ask her later, out of Bjorn's hearing.

He waited for Astrid to walk ahead of him down the narrow path.

"I have to warn you. Things are much changed."

Things were much changed.

The fields lay in untended disrepair, and a lean-to had been added to the house. Parked beneath it was a carriage, and a horse stood grazing on the carrots she had once been in such trouble for neglecting.

"The house looks the same," Astrid said, surprised, her fingers clenching in Bjorn's fur. She walked with her hand on his neck, a nervous gesture she could not help.

Tomas snorted. "They are building a big house in town. Work started on it last week already, and Father spends his days there, ordering the workmen about."

"So Father will not be here?" Astrid was ashamed at the relief she felt. He could do nothing to her anymore. She did not have to endure his fists and his cruel words. She belonged elsewhere, now.

"I'm sure he isn't. The other wagon is gone. He and Eric both wanted one, so they got two."

"And Freja?"

"She is getting married. They announced the news two days after you left."

She didn't waste a moment, Astrid thought bitterly, then felt ashamed. How long had Freja waited already? And what would delaying the inevitable have helped?

"I am glad for her. I thought she might use her share that way."

They were almost at the house, and Bjorn stopped. "Can I trust my lady's safety to you?" he asked Tomas.

Tomas looked as if he'd been slapped. "You can." His cheeks burned red.

"Then I will wait outside, let Astrid go in with you alone."

"What will you do?" Astrid whispered to him, knowing he wished to give her time alone with Mother.

"Patrol around the house, and the woods. Make sure Norga did not work out where we went to." He spoke in a low rumble, and she hoped Tomas had not heard.

"I will see you later, then." She put her arms

around his neck and laid her cheek against him, then stepped back. Drew back her shoulders.

As she turned, the door opened and her mother stepped out of the house onto the porch. She cried out, her hand flying up to cover her mouth. "Astrid."

Astrid walked forward with Tomas at her side, and felt rather than saw Bjorn lope off again into the woods.

"Mother." Happiness kicked up within her at the sight of her mother in a pretty gown, her hair up and a less desperate look about her. But when she got nearer, she saw her mother's eyes were as pain-filled as ever.

"You . . . are back?" Her mother's gaze fell behind Astrid's shoulder, and she knew she was looking at Bjorn as he disappeared into the trees.

"Just for the day." She drew her mother close. "We must go back tonight. My Bear has many duties, and was generous to bring me such a long way for a visit as it is." She looked sideways at Tomas, and he looked straight back, unimpressed. He would probe further, she knew, if she let him. He would want to know what duties Bjorn had that were so pressing.

"Come in, and let me get you something to eat." Her mother looked flustered as she drew Astrid into the house, as if embarrassed at the bounty piled on the old table.

Another who looks at all the gold has bought and cannot accept the price paid for it.

"I have said this to Tomas, and I say this to you, Mother. I am happy. I want you to enjoy what Bear's gold can buy you. I want you free of worry, or I can never be."

"But he is a *bear*, Astrid. A bear."

"Not all the time," Astrid answered. "And bear or not, I love him already."

"When you say not all the time . . .?" Her mother looked desperately at Tomas.

"She means at night he comes to her as a man. As a husband." Tomas did not look away from her when he spoke, and the look on his face made her temper flare hot as a forge fire.

"Those were the conditions of my acceptance," she cried. "I was to be wife to him in all but name, and I have honored that. And found contentment in it." She paused, and looked him straight in the eye. "Joy, even."

She watched his cheeks flush again.

"Do not look at me with your accusing eyes, Tomas, as if I have somehow betrayed *you*." She clasped her hands before her, trying to still them in her agitation. "I did not see you following me to make sure of my safety. I did not hear either of you stand up to Father."

Her mother began to sob, and Tomas put a hand on her shoulder. Shook his head.

"You are right." His throat worked. "And I swear, there is not a day goes by that I do not regret that."

"Cast your regret aside," Astrid told him,

sweeping her fine fur-lined cloak from her shoulders and setting it over the back of a chair. "I have none of my own."

Chapter Seventeen

"Astrid, you must leave him. Come back to us." Her mother laid down a plate of cheese and meat, bread and apples.

Astrid looked out the window at Tomas saddling the horse to ride to town and fetch the others back to see her, and took a bite of apple before she answered.

"It is too late, Mother. I am his. You know that. And I do not wish to leave him."

"And some of the gold has already been spent." Her mother plucked at her new dress. "Is he handsome, your Bear? When he comes to you at night?"

Astrid took another bite of apple. She did not want to tell her mother the details, but she found she could not lie. "I do not know."

Her mother stopped fussing over the food and grabbed the back of a chair. "How can you not know?"

"He will not let me see him. He douses every light, and comes to me in the darkness." Frustration rose in her again, just saying it.

"Oh." Her mother's hands covered the lower part of her face, her eyes wide with horror. "Then it is true. He *is* a troll."

"He is not a troll, Mother. I have seen one, and the man I feel against me in the night is *not* a troll." She thought of the broad chest, the muscled arms her fingers traced. The straight, fine nose, and high cheekbones.

"Then why will he not let you see him?"

"He says he cannot tell me. It is part of his enchantment."

Her mother turned, opened a drawer and pulled out a small tallow candle. "Take this, and while he sleeps, light it and see what he really is."

"He has asked me not to do that." But she had not agreed to obey him.

Her mother tossed her head. "What he wants is of no concern to me. I only worry about you. See what he is, and if he is a monster, run back to us. Gold or no gold." She thrust the candle at Astrid.

Astrid took it, turned it in her hand, still undecided. "I will need a tinderbox, to light it."

"Here." Her mother found one and pressed it into her palm.

Astrid stood a moment, eyes closed, as she battled herself, then dropped the candle into the bundle she'd brought with her. She hated the gnawing sense of unease she felt. It bordered on guilt.

She'd told Bear she would not stop trying until she could see him. His deal with his enchanter was between them, and had nothing to do with her. But the guilty feeling did not subside.

"That troll. The one you saw long ago. Tell me the story." Astrid watched her mother's gaze flick to the window, to check they were still alone, then she slipped into a chair.

"You were no more than three, and I had lost Tomas in the forest. He was with us one moment, while we picked berries, then gone the next. I wasn't worried, he knew his way, but then I heard a cry, the sound of a small boy." She leaned back, and Astrid could see the fear she'd felt. "I picked you up and ran in the direction of the noise, burst into a clearing without even looking what was there first. I thought only of getting to Tomas."

Her mother clasped her hands on the table, and her fingers wove through each other, over and over.

"The clearing was wonderfully light. It was near the end of summer, and muggy. There were gnats buzzing, and birds singing, as if this was an ordinary, warm summer day. But there was also a strange breeze." She lifted a hand, and wiped across her forehead, as if there was sweat there. As if she were back in that hot, bright clearing.

"Strange how?" Astrid asked, her voice hushed.

"It was contained in the clearing, blowing nowhere else. There was not even the smallest breath of wind before I got there, and this breeze seemed to touch me. Touch you. Like it had fingers."

Astrid's heart beat faster, she struggled to keep

calm. Her gaze never left her mother's face.

"I hardly noticed the breeze at the time, I only thought about it later. What held my attention was the dead body on the ground. An old hag. Ugly beyond description, and towering over her, without a doubt the killer, was a troll. A female troll."

"What did she look like?" Astrid whispered.

"Like a gnarled old tree, but massive, much taller than Tomas is now, at least half a length taller than him. She was looking at the dead hag with fury. She lifted her foot and kicked the lifeless body."

Her mother paused, and looked out the window again.

"Go on, Mother. Please."

"When she kicked the body, I heard the child cry again, and I finally saw a small boy. Not Tomas, a bit older than him. He stood a little way from the troll, out of the sunlight. He was dressed in very fine clothes and . . . well, he was the most beautiful child I had ever seen. Like the child of Frey himself."

"'You will not tell your father this,'" the troll snarled at him, his cry reminding her he was there, it seemed to me.

'You killed her, and you are not beautiful,' the boy said, in that clear way children have. 'I *will* tell Father.' And when he said that, the troll grabbed him up by the throat. She meant to kill him too, I could see that. And I couldn't let it happen.

"I stepped forward and the troll saw me and lowered the boy.

'Be gone,' she shouted, but I did not go. I stepped closer to her, so the body of the hag was all that lay between us.

'Don't kill the child,' I said to her.

'You cannot stop me,' she replied, and she was right. I'd endangered us both by trying to save him, and I could see how strong and cruel she was. I had no hope of stopping her."

Astrid could see it all clear in her mind, and she wondered if it was her mother's evocative storytelling, or an actual memory that made her feel as if she were reliving the scene.

"You suddenly drew in your breath, Astrid, like a gasp, and for a moment I thought you were having some kind of fit. But then you struggled out of my arms, your eyes on the boy, and I couldn't blame you. He was mesmerizing. I couldn't allow him to be harmed. I think you spoke with him, holding out your hand for him to take, but I was too busy with the troll. Begging her to have mercy on an innocent child. And she looked down at the hag and nodded.

'You're right. He's more valuable alive. This Jotun wanted him, after all. That has to mean something.'"

Her mother looked at Astrid, her eyes grave. "I had no idea what she meant, but I murmured my agreement.

'Your father will not believe you, anyway,' she said to the boy, and frowned because you and he were caught up in each other, sitting talking quietly as if you were playing without a care. As if there wasn't a dead body and a murderous troll right next to you."

"I had done what I could, and from the way she looked at you, with such a scowl, I suddenly realized the danger I had put you in. So I scooped you up, and began backing away. The boy cried out as I pulled you apart, and I could hear his sobs for you even when we were halfway home. You were crying to, but worse, that strange wind seemed to follow us, a small whirlwind with us in its eye. I was calling frantically for Tomas, and when we got home, of course, there he was, playing outside the house and asking us where we'd been."

She leaned forward on her elbows. "The wind did not leave you for a day or two. Even in the house there was a little breeze that surrounded you. But it went away eventually."

"And that's why Father treats me as he does?" She spoke slowly, trying to work it out.

"Because when you were old enough to talk properly, you kept saying the wind was your friend, that it spoke to you. And the weather was colder. From that moment in the forest onward, we have not managed with the crops, the summers are too short."

"He blames me for the weather?" Outrage filled her.

"I think he does. He said that whenever he gave you a hiding, deserved or not, the wind would blow pine needles and sharp sticks in his eyes. That when he shouted at you outdoors, as soon as your back was turned he would get a mouthful of sand."

Astrid frowned. "And he never told me?"

"He thought you knew. He thought you arranged it."

She shook her head. "Although if I thought it possible to command the wind, I may have." It was true. She'd wished worse than a mouthful of sand on her father in the past. But a mouthful of sand was certainly better than nothing.

No wonder the animosity between them had been never-ending.

"Well, perhaps you can set matters straight with him. You never know when the Bear will allow you back here again. Do not leave feeling as you do toward your father, Astrid, you'll regret it."

"I don't think I will," Astrid said, and looked out the window again. She rose as she saw Bets riding with Tomas, and just behind them, the horse and cart carrying Freja, Eric and Father.

At the look on her father's face, a shiver of fear ran through her, despite herself.

He was beside himself with rage.

"Bets, I have missed you." Astrid breathed in the smell of new wool and lavender on her sister and held her close.

"Be careful. They are afraid you have been found wanting. That your bride price is expected returned," Bets murmured in her ear. "I would rather starve with you than feast without you, Astrid. I hope you *are* returned."

"I am not," Astrid stepped back, and nervously tucked a strand of hair behind her ear. She had killed a troll, helped defeat an yggren, but she was afraid of her father still. Too long under his power and too many times the loser in their battle of wills made it an automatic reaction.

"Astrid." Her father jumped from the cart, and Astrid saw Freja bite her lip. Conflicted between her own comfort and the brutality that was exercised in getting it.

Choose a side, Freja, Astrid thought. *You are less a person for wringing your hands while you watch me beaten down.*

For some reason, the thought steadied her. Bear was here somewhere, Tomas had promised to keep her safe, and she commanded the wind. She was not an easy target any more.

"Father." She bowed slightly. Formally. A princess greeting her subject, she suddenly thought, and had to fight the smile that tried to claim her lips.

"Why are you back?" He took a step toward her,

and everything about him was threatening.

"Did Tomas not tell you?" She saw Tomas had come to a stop halfway between Father and Eric and herself. Freja still sat in the cart, distanced from the action. Refusing to greet her, refusing to stand with Father and Eric.

"He said you would explain."

Astrid shot Tomas a sharp look, and he had the grace to look uncomfortable. His pique at her happiness with Bear was unworthy of him. Did he *want* her to be miserable?

"Why do you think I am back, Father?"

Her father hesitated, and she saw his eyes take in her proud appearance; the fine green wool of her dress, the beadwork at the neck like rays of light, glistening gold in the autumn sun.

She tossed her hair over her shoulder impatiently, and saw his eyes narrow. The movement was too confident, too defiant, for him to resist falling back into his old ways.

"You were always too contrary, Astrid. He's thrown you out. Well, I will not take you back. I have already spent some of the gold, and I'm not giving back any of it."

"You would throw her out? Alone and defenseless, with winter coming?" Tomas's voice was hard. She had never heard him use that tone with Father before.

"I'm sure her enchanted bear has taught her a few tricks that should help her find a bed, at the very least." Eric's words were crude and hurtful, and Astrid gaped at him. Saw Freja's hand go to cover her mouth in shock.

Bets made a sound behind her, and even Father turned to look at Eric. When he turned back to face her, she saw the shame in his eyes. But his greed overcame it.

"As Eric says. She will find someone willing to take her in."

"Isn't it lucky I don't need to?" Astrid spoke with a roaring in her ears, her vision narrowing to just Father and Eric. "Finding a place to sleep by working on my back won't be necessary."

That they would disown her had never occurred to her. That they could all but sell her and then refuse her welcome, was beyond what she had imagined them capable.

"Even if you did need to," Tomas said, "my share of the gold is yours."

They exchanged a look, and Astrid knew Tomas had broken with them. That he would do as she suggested and build a house of his own. Bets would perhaps go to live with him, and he would never sleep under the same roof as Father and Eric again.

"Do you mean he has not thrown you out?" Father spoke hesitantly.

"My Bear has kindly allowed me to visit with my family, thinking I may miss them. We were to leave this evening, but I will not set foot in your house again, Father." Her mother made a choking sound behind her, and she turned. "If I return, you can visit me at Tomas's, Mother." Her gaze shifted to the house. "I need to fetch my cloak."

"I'll get it," Bets said softly, and ran in.

When she returned, she held the soft, warm cloak to her cheek.

"Can I walk with you a little way?" she asked, and Astrid nodded. Swung the cloak around her shoulders.

"Astrid." Her mother stepped close and Astrid lay her head on her shoulder.

"I love you. Good bye." With a last squeeze, she drew back, and saw the tears pouring down her mother's cheeks. "Take your share of the gold and go, Mother. You and Bets and Tomas. You do not need to stay. The gold is for you all, equally. You have no need to be unhappy here."

Her father started at her words, as if the truth of them had just occurred to him. His fists clenched at his side.

"Take your poisonous tongue and go."

"She will go at her own pace, when she is ready," Tomas told him, and held out one arm for her, and one for Bets.

"She will go now," her father roared, then cut off abruptly.

Astrid turned, and saw Bjorn crossing the fields.

Her heart leapt, and she realized how much she'd missed him. How close her declarations of love for him were to the truth.

She could not hold back her smile of welcome when he joined her, breaking free of Tomas and walking to him.

"There is trouble?" he asked her, ignoring everyone else.

"Not anymore." She lifted a hand to his face, and he rubbed his cheek against it.

"Bets and Tomas will walk with us a little way. We can go now."

"You are not staying until this evening?"

He must know she was not, must have heard some of what was said, and he wanted a fight, she could see it in his eyes, in the way his muscles bunched under his fur. Perhaps he was not even aware of it, but he was growling, soft and menacing.

"I am not." She held his gaze and sent him the message there would be no confrontation. Not in front of her mother. She was terrified enough of him as it was.

He took a step toward her father and Eric, and the growl became a rumble. Something in the way he stood, as if prepared to leap, and to rend and tear, caused a deep, watchful silence to descend.

"Then let us go," he said, cold, hungry eyes on Father and Eric. They were pale-faced, and closer to the cart than they had been.

As they walked to the woods, Astrid did not look back, but she whispered one thing to the breeze that flowed across her face.

"A mouth full of sand for both of them."

Chapter Eighteen

"Did your mother tell you what happened with the troll?" Bjorn barely waited until Tomas and Bets were behind them to ask it. He even let up his pace so he could hear her reply properly.

"She told me everything, but it means almost nothing to me." He could hear the strain in her voice. It had been a hard day for her, and he wished he'd ignored her and killed her father. He'd dearly wanted to. Eric, too.

"Tell me what she said, it may make sense to me."

She was quiet for so long he almost halted.

"What will you tell me, in return?" she asked.

He stumbled on the path.

"Why did we make this journey, if not to find out what your mother knows?"

"You want me to tell you everything, while you tell me nothing."

He could imagine her face, a frown on her brow and her jaw set.

"You know why I cannot."

He felt her fists tighten on his fur.

"Explain the conditions of this bargain to me."

He had thought, from the way she looked at him when he'd come to fetch her from her father, that she was beginning to love him. Her smile had been bright as the sun off snow. She had been happy to see him, the warmth in her eyes stabbing at the remaining ice around his heart.

"Why are you asking this now, Astrid? I thought you trusted me, were happy with me."

She made a frustrated sound. "I do. I am. But you involve me, and then you do not give me the information I need to make sense of it all. You ask everything of me, but you do not give me your trust."

She was right. He had involved her, risked her life, without ever telling her the stakes. He had made so many mistakes.

"You know it's not a matter of trust, it's a matter of my bargain."

"Norga has broken her side of it by sending the troll to kill me. Why can you not break yours?"

Bjorn stopped, he needed to be face to face with her for this. Astrid slipped down from his shoulders and stood before him.

"I am afraid she never agreed not to try to kill you, Astrid. She broke no oath sending that troll after you. I was afraid she would think better of the deal we struck, and I agreed to her terms. I thought you would be safe in the mountain, and I did not think through the consequences of keeping the details of my enchantment from you."

Her eyes narrowed and Bjorn saw the outrage in them.

"You thought I'd accept everything you said, didn't you? You thought you would give me orders and I would happily obey."

She had him.

"I may have had that notion. I am aware of my error now, though." And he bitterly regretted his lack of foresight.

"Why me, Bjorn? When you saw what I am, why did you not look for some more biddable creature as your companion?"

Did she not understand she was the only one? That there could be no replacement?

He could not tell her that, though. He'd thought she would instinctively realize there was no other, but to explain he'd had to find her and her alone would break the bargain with Norga. She had been so long in his thoughts, yet she knew nothing of him. It was hard to remember that.

"It would be far easier for me if you were more biddable." He knew they'd stayed too long in one place, but he wanted this clear between them. "But I would never seek to replace you. Never."

Her eyes softened, and she reached out a hand to him. Sighed.

"You make it hard for me to deny you anything. I will tell you what my mother said."

He did not let the flare of gratitude show. She had enough hold over him as it was.

"Tell me as we go." He crouched for her to climb on, and felt her arms go around his neck for a hug as she settled on his back.

It cracked the final wall of ice inside him, and he nearly howled with pain.

Nearly cried with joy.

But instead of doing either, he began to run again, just like old times.

Yggren surrounded the mountain, standing like sentries at its foot, impossible to slip past.

Bjorn moved quietly through the trees, trying to find any weak point. He growled with frustration, and Astrid felt the tension in the muscles of his back. There was no weak point.

"It doesn't matter that we cannot broach them," he whispered to her. "I must make peace with them. I could enchant those near the entrance, and that would give us enough time to get within, but then we'd be trapped."

"Are they all in league with Norga?" Astrid asked, wondering what manner of enchantress could command the frightening, powerful yggren.

"No. Impossible." Bjorn turned deeper into the

woods, and Astrid had the feeling he was searching for something, or someone. "They have always been in favor of the balance. I cannot believe Norga could have won them all over."

"She hasn't."

Astrid gasped as the tree directly in front of them spoke. Then watched in shock as a man seemed to appear from the bark and leaves.

"Jorgen." Bjorn sounded relieved, and Astrid realized he had been looking for this strange man.

She looked at him curiously. He was tall, tall as Tomas, tall as she imagined Bjorn, when he lay beside her in the dark. He wore clothes of brown and sage green, cleverly layered to make them appear like bark and leaves. His skin was a dark brown and though he was broad-chested and muscular, he was hard to see even when you knew where he stood. Astrid rubbed her eyes.

"Good day to you, I am Astrid." She slipped off Bjorn's back and gave a pretty curtsey, speaking softly even though they were well away from the yggren.

"I am Jorgen, my lady." Jorgen bowed, speaking softly himself, quiet as the rustle of leaves.

"Why are the yggren standing against me, Jorgen? What do you know of this?" Bjorn cut across the pleasantries with impatience.

"I know only that since Sigurd's death they have been waiting for your return."

"Then I will speak with them. Can you act as my

messenger?"

Astrid watched Jorgen nod slowly.

"I will approach Reidar. He stands near your entrance. What would you have me say?"

"That I consider the yggren honorable. That I wish to speak with Reidar leader to leader, and discover what has turned them against me."

It seemed to Astrid no sooner had Jorgen nodded his agreement than he disappeared. She blinked.

"How does he do that?"

"It is not only his coloring. Jorgen is powerful in his own right. He healed me after the troll attack."

"And this Reidar. He will not harm Jorgen?" She noticed Jorgen had not hesitated to take on the task of mediator for Bjorn.

"Jorgen is a vedfe, a forest sprite. Reidar would be foolish to harm him. Their people have been allies always, their lives tied up in the forests. If their argument is with me, and me alone, he is safe."

"And if they are on Norga's side. And wish to harm all loyal to you?"

"Jorgen will not be easy to kill."

"Are there others like him?" Astrid looked through the trees and realized there could be a hundred vedfe right in front of her and she wouldn't know it. She wondered with a shiver how often she had passed one in her own forest.

"There are others. Jorgen is their leader."

"All men?" This place was full of men. Bjorn, Jorgen, Sigurd. Where were all the women?

"No. There are women vedfe."

Well, she was glad of that, even though she couldn't see them.

"Are the yggren all men?"

Bjorn shook his head. "I don't know. They are a mysterious, ancient race. There aren't many of them left."

Jorgen seemed to step out of thin air into the clearing. "There lies their grudge. Sigurd's death has shocked them. They would have you account for it."

Bjorn nodded. "So I thought. Will you take care of my lady while I'm gone?"

"Of course."

She saw a look pass between them, and she knew at once Bjorn meant he might be gone for good. That he was handing over permanent responsibility, should the yggren get the better of him.

She was not chattel. And she was not powerless. And she would most certainly not sit in the wood while he went off to battle, especially with the power of the wind at her disposal.

"Thank you, Jorgen, that won't be necessary." She kept her voice light and pleasant, and for a moment they did not catch her meaning.

"Astrid." Bjorn's voice held a warning.

"I will go with you, and help you if you need it," she answered, and began walking back toward the mountain, leaving them slack-jawed in the clearing.

"I see why you say you will never hold her within the palace," she heard Jorgen murmur.

"Quite right," Bjorn answered. "Either Norga will kill her, or I will."

Astrid smiled, and turned to him. "Come now, they are waiting, surely?"

"I could freeze you in place."

"So you could." She stared him down, and with a huff of breath he surrendered. Caught up with her.

"Stay hidden in the trees. I will not have you taken and used as a hostage."

She nodded. "Unless you need me."

He stopped.

"Bjorn, I will stay hidden. If your life is threatened, though, you can be sure I will step out from the forest and call on the wind to aid you."

He started walking again, slowly, because they were near the forest's edge, but she could see he had grave doubts.

"You are not alone anymore, Bear," she said softly.

He twisted his head round, and his eyes pierced her with their intensity. She would have stumbled had Jorgen not suddenly been at her side, steadying her.

"Keep her safe," Bjorn growled to his friend, and then he disappeared out onto the mountain side.

———⟨✦⟩———

Reidar was waiting for him, and though Bjorn thought it unlikely every yggren was in Norga's power, he felt a lurch of fear at the sight of so many of the powerful beings lined up around his mountain.

"Greetings," he called, stepping out from the trees.

Every sentinel turned his way, although none left their posts.

"You have done us a grievous injury, Bjorn of the Mountain. What have you to say?" Reidar's silver-grey limbs reflected the sun, and Bjorn could see he held a great anger in check. The yggren quivered with it, like an arrow shot badly from a bow. His tall, stick-like body hummed with tension.

Bjorn met his gaze, the silver eyes set in a head not much wider than his slender limbs, a man heated and stretched like glass, then turned to deadwood.

"Sigurd betrayed me and attacked me. He would have taken and killed my lady had I not stopped him." Bjorn watched Reidar's face carefully. There were murmurs from the other yggren up and down the line.

"Why would Sigurd betray you?" Reidar stilled for the first time since Bjorn had stepped from the wood.

"I hoped you could explain that."

"I cannot." Reidar frowned. "He was always in favor of the balance. Out of respect for the great tree. To side with Norga is a betrayal of everything we stand for. I do not believe it."

"Why would I lie?" Bjorn spoke quickly as Reidar

tensed for the attack. "I have no wish to anger the yggren. I have sacrificed for them, as much as for anyone. Ask yourselves, why was Sigurd fighting me?"

His words fell on deaf ears. The yggren began moving forward, their long legs eating up the ground.

"Stop."

Astrid's cry echoed off the cliffs and halted the yggren in their tracks.

"He tells the truth."

Reidar cocked his head, looked at her with interest. Bjorn turned to look at her himself, saw her standing fearless in her dark brown cloak, her golden hair spilling over her shoulders, bright as the sun overhead.

"You are his lady. You would say anything to protect him."

She acknowledged his point with a nod. "Yes, but would you trust the word of the wind?"

Reidar's silver eyes widened. "I would."

Bjorn remembered Jorgen telling him of the song of the trees and the wind. And what were the yggren but the magical deadwood of the greatest tree of all?

"Tell the yggren what happened in the clearing," Astrid called out, and Bjorn felt a breeze spring up, making the autumn leaves dance in the air. It seemed to spin and twirl around each yggren in turn, whispering in each ear.

When it at last died out, Bjorn could feel a change

in atmosphere. The yggren had gone from angry to shocked.

Reidar fell to his knees. "You have chosen your lady well." His voice was hoarse, choked. "I do not know why Sigurd would bring such shame to the yggren, but I swear an oath I will find out."

"I do not take the actions of one to be the actions of all, Reidar, but I would be grateful to hear if you do learn what hold Norga had over Sigurd." Bjorn watched as the yggren got back to his feet.

"My lady." Reidar bowed to Astrid, deeper than any bow he'd ever given Bjorn, and with a cry, the yggren raced down the slope and vanished into the trees.

"Thank you," Astrid murmured, and Bjorn realized she was thanking the breeze that surrounded her, dancing leaves at her feet and playing with her hair.

It seemed he'd taken the mistress of the wind for his own, after all.

Chapter Nineteen

The candle lay in her little bundle under the bed like a stone in her shoe. A bur in her clothing. Demanding attention, no matter how she tried to ignore it.

It seemed the only thing she'd gotten from her trip home was heartache and worry.

Her father had finally severed the cord, and her mother had given her the means to . . .

To what?

Betray Bjorn? Was looking on him a betrayal? She had made no oath to Norga. She did not even know who Norga was.

He had asked her not to look at him. And she had told him she did not accept that.

The arguments rapped like a woodpecker at her brain.

And still, night after night, she chose to honor his request. The candle remained untouched.

Bjorn had yet to explain what her mother's story meant. He'd listened, and told her he would think on it, but when she brought it up with him, he avoided a straight answer. And he had not let her out of the palace

back tonight."

He sounded as if he were talking of mundane subjects like the weather, or meeting with Jorgen in the clearing.

"Where are you going?" She forced the anger out of her words, pretended to be calmer.

"I have stayed too close to the mountain these last weeks. I need to patrol the far edges of my domain. Norga could cause mischief there and I would not know it."

"Will you take Jorgen?" She hoped beyond anything he'd say no. Jorgen knew something. He was Bjorn's closest friend.

"No. I have no need of him." Bjorn kissed her forehead in goodbye, his arms coming around her in a final squeeze before he slipped from the curtained bed.

"Be careful," she called after him, but she knew he would be. And now she had a full day on her own to find the invisible woodman.

As she heard Bjorn close the door behind him, she stretched out and smiled.

Today she would breathe the open air.

———⦅✿⦆———

They hadn't spoken of it since she last used the ladder, and Astrid realized she was trembling as she stood under the skylights. She drew the thick winter cloak she'd wished for around her, scuffed the fur-lined boots on the stone floor, waiting to find her nerve, steel herself for the possibility of disappointment. Would the ladder appear at her command, or had Bjorn banned it along with lights in this room?

"I want a ladder," she called softly, and there before her, a ladder stretched up to the roof.

He'd either forgotten or thought she would not do it again.

It didn't matter. It had appeared.

She climbed swiftly despite her bulky clothing, suddenly afraid, against all logic, Bjorn would return. But she reached the top and scrambled out onto the rock ledge unhindered, gasping at the cold.

The sky was only now brightening, and the horizon was thick with clouds. A storm was brewing.

She couldn't risk going for long. Despite her defiance, she was aware of the danger. Norga's spies could be watching her now. She pulled her cloak tighter.

"We must be on our guard," she murmured to the air.

We?

She'd begun to see the wind as a constant ally. Almost an integral part of herself. But the depth of the feeling, the instinctive nature of it, had only just occurred to her.

She tilted her face so her hood fell back and the icy lips of the wind brushed her cheeks. A bracing morning kiss.

"Let's go," she whispered to it, and an eddy of air swirled around her, floating her cloak around her ankles and nudging her elbow. "Call to Jorgen through the trees for me. I can meet him in the clearing."

She almost saw the air take shape, a lithe air nymph, and dive down the mountain to the forest to whisper the message to the trees.

It shocked her how instantly the air obeyed. It must be a mistake, this blind servitude, and she couldn't help be afraid there would be a later accounting for her use of it. What weighed more heavily was who she would have to account to, and what the payment would be.

She hoped Jorgen could shed more light. She'd defy Bjorn a hundred times over to learn what bound the wind and her together.

When she got to the clearing, her stomach churned with anticipation, and she looked hard at every tree. How did you find someone who could make himself invisible?

"Jorgen?" She called softly, afraid, even with the wind at her back, that she would alert Bjorn's enemies.

"My lady."

His voice came from behind her and she whipped round, the wind blowing her cloak up like a swan beats it wings. An attempt at intimidation. Had she done that somehow, or was the wind using its own initiative?

Jorgen held himself tense, his brow furrowed.

"Bjorn will be . . ." He trailed off, unable to put into words the extent of Bjorn's anger if he knew she was in the forest.

She nodded. "I know."

"Why then?" He held out his hands in disbelief.

"I am not his prisoner." *Liar. He is a loving warden, but he has put you in a prison all the same.* "I have questions he refuses to answer, and I think you can help me."

"Why would I tell you things my lord will not?"

"He cannot tell me because of his oath to Norga. You have no such promise binding you." She hoped. Norga could not have extracted oaths of silence from everyone.

"That is true." His eyes never rested as they looked through the trees. As if he expected an attack at any time. It set her even more on edge. "If I answer your questions as well as I'm able, will you return to the palace?"

"I promise." Relief and excitement made her breathless. She stepped closer to him, lowered her voice. "Who is Norga?"

He opened his mouth to answer, then closed it again. Shook his head. "I am uneasy about this. I don't know the consequences of answering you. Bjorn should tell you that. It is not my place."

Astrid glared at him. "Then at least tell me what this is all about. Why did she enchant him? What are the conditions of his pact with her?"

Again, Jorgen shook his head. "I cannot answer that without telling you who Norga is. I am sorry."

"Can you at least tell me why the wind obeys me?" She was desperate to learn at least that much.

"Because you ask it very nicely?" Jorgen answered with a wry grin, and Astrid blushed, remembering her flippant remark to Bjorn. It seemed he'd shared it with Jorgen.

"So I do." She stared him down, and at last Jorgen shook his head.

"That is the biggest mystery of all. I don't know why you have the loyalty of the wind."

Astrid tossed her head in disgust. "You have given me nothing."

"I am sorry—"

"*Danger.*" The wind whispered in her ear. The first time it had spoken to her so clearly.

"Where?" she breathed, saw Jorgen was listening to the noise in the trees. No doubt giving him the same message.

"*Not here. The bear is in danger.*"

"Where is he?" she choked out.

"*Come.*"

"Jorgen, Bjorn is in trouble. The wind will lead us."

Jorgen looked at her agape. "You are not going. I'll go. There are others in this forest I can call on, too."

The wind tugged at her cloak and Astrid let it

draw her out the clearing, ignoring Jorgen. "As fast as I can run," she told it, beginning to do just that.

"My lady, please." His call was desperate and she felt sorry for him, but didn't even turn round. Bjorn needed help.

The wind seemed to push her, support her, make her faster, and testing a theory, she jumped, holding her cloak wide and felt the wind lift her. Her feet touched the forest floor lightly, and she leapt again.

"My lady, wait."

Jorgen's voice was faint, and Astrid risked a backwards glance. Realized she had left the vedfe so far behind she could no longer see him through the trees.

She was almost flying through the forest. Flying to her lover's aid.

Chapter Twenty

B jorn looked down, stunned, at the body of Raidar, tumbled like a bundle of sticks over the rocks below.

He'd been right to patrol as far as he could go in one day and still be back by nightfall.

With this death, the mystery of the yggren deepened. For one of his own to take Raidar's life was a sacrilege of the highest order. So taboo, the murderer must surely contemplate suicide. Who else but another yggren could take on Raidar and win?

He had managed it with Sigurd, but he was the son of a disgraced Vanir, a demi-god. Bjorn knew few in the human realm could match his magic, or his strength.

Raidar must have gone up against Norga herself if another yggren had not done this. And he had lost.

He wondered how long Raidar had lain there. His fellow yggren could not know, they would have taken the body if they had.

He considered moving Raidar himself, and thought better of it. The yggren were likely to take offense at his interference. He would get word to them, and let them care for their own.

Norga was desperate if she was responsible. While the yggren had supported the balance, they had not actively opposed or hated Norga. That would change now.

Bjorn turned away from the tragic sight of a powerful force turned to matchwood, and started down the narrow path. He would skirt around the foot of the mountain where Raidar met his end and head back home through the forest.

He had hardly taken two steps from the edge when something landed on his back. Cruel, tight arms came around his neck and tried to lever him up by the throat, strangling him.

Gasping in shock, Bjorn twisted his head sideways and caught a glimpse of a silver-grey yggren. It took the strain, straddling him as it tried to hang Bjorn by lifting him in a chokehold.

Fool twice over.

He'd dismissed the possibility of another yggren killing Raidar, and he'd assumed the killer was long gone. But Sigurd had broken taboos himself, by siding with Norga. There was a rot within the ranks of the yggren, and he had looked at only one of the bad apples, assuming the rest were still untouched.

He threw a freezing spell upwards, his eyes blinded by spots of bright light as he struggled to suck in air. It worked for a few precious seconds, enough for him to slip from the chokehold and turn, snarling, on the traitor.

As with Sigurd, the yggren shrugged the spell off in a moment, screaming at him, its eyes protruding from its face in rage and grief.

"You killed your own." Bjorn's voice was rough and scratched, barely audible after the crushing hold.

He could not run. An yggren was faster than he'd ever be. And this one had an edge. It did not care for its own life. He felt its elemental magic resisting his own, a stalemate that left physical strength and intelligence the only decider.

The yggren leapt at him, and Bjorn charged, skidding underneath it, so they were both forced to turn again on the narrow mountain ledge. A cliff to one side, a solid wall of stone to the other.

It surely did not attack him on Norga's orders. Her plan was nothing if he should die. She needed him to fail, but most of all, she needed him alive.

"You killed Raidar, and now you want someone to kill you?" Bjorn called to it. "I will do it gladly. Just tell me why."

With another shriek, the yggren whipped out a long arm, clawed at him with lethal fingers, and Bjorn could see all reason had gone. It was maddened beyond thought, beyond any sensible reply.

Bjorn threw up a wall of fire between them, stretching across the whole of the path. He felt the immediate push of magic as the yggren countered him.

Searching for a way through the flames.

There was no way through, but he wondered how long he could hold the barrier against the battering of its power.

Then, without warning, the yggren launched off the mountain.

"Shhhreeeee."

Its scream echoed off the cliffs as it fell, but Bjorn had seen its eyes, its bloodlust, and was not fooled. He collapsed his fire wall and braced, ready for the yggren to return from some ledge or foothold below, but even though he'd expected it, he flinched as it shot up like an arrow, its trajectory slamming it into Bjorn, pinning him to the rocks.

He roared, fighting its thin, wiry strength with his weight and bulk. Desperation allowed him to punch through its magical buffer, flick a tiny flame onto its leg.

"Shhhreeee." Its cry deafened him. The pain of fire making it wilder, fiercer. Undeterred.

It leant in, its arms crossed against Bjorn's throat, its feet digging in to the hard rock of the path. Bjorn felt the first flick of panic. Felt the first tongue of fire singe his coat as it crawled up the yggren's leg.

If the yggren would not yield, would not give in to the flames, they would both burn.

Astrid rode the wind, and as she rode, an army gathered behind her.

A horn had called from behind, faint through the whistling in her ears. Since then, each place she passed, each time her feet touched the forest floor, a sprite or vedfe seemed to step out of a tree, a rock, or the streams that tumbled through the forest, to run alongside her.

At first she'd thought Jorgen had called them to stop her, but as she looked, startled, into the eyes of a rock nymph, he'd sketched a salute, and begun running at her side.

Every time she leapt, arms holding her cloak out like a pair of wings, she left them behind, but a quick glance over her shoulder showed her they still followed, a forest-hued retinue in grays, browns and greens, silent and strangely intimidating. Their beautiful faces were serious and their feet swift.

Jorgen said he had others he could call on, and he had not lied.

She saw the wind carried her toward a mountain on the far east end of the forest, its steep cliffs and jagged ridges just discernible in the distance. It seemed impossibly far away.

"Hurry," she pleaded. The wind had not spoken again since it whispered to her in the clearing, and she sensed it was expending great energy in lifting her as she ran. It need only have enough strength to get her to Bjorn, and once there, aid her in saving him. She didn't care how long the walk back was.

They must just get there in time.

———◄✐►———

Bjorn fought for his life, desperate as the heat singed him. He clawed at the yggren, trying to push it away as the flames took hold of it, licked their way higher up its body.

It could not end this way.

He'd tried already to douse the flames, but he could no longer get through the shield of ancient magic the yggren threw over them both. It wanted to die. And for some reason, it wanted Bjorn to go with it.

It would not succeed.

With a roar that echoed off the cliffs, he twisted in the yggren's hold, every muscle, every sinew in his body straining to throw off the living torch hanging on with steel-like fingers.

He could not shake it and the pain of the fire made him half-mad with panic.

A wind sprang up, he could feel it against his fur, and then a gale was blowing, coming out of nowhere.

"Fire to the head," he heard a voice—*Astrid*—call out, and before his eyes he saw a flame scooped off the yggren's burning body by the hand of the wind, and thrown into its face.

With a scream, it finally let go, unable to endure

the pain. As it stepped back, the wind, as with Sigurd, breathed on the fire and in a moment, the yggren was a pyre of flame.

Bjorn fell, his sides heaving as he fought for air, fought the pain and fought the fear. Astrid was out of the palace, exposed to danger again.

"Bear."

He felt her alight next to him as if she were a bird, landing from the air, and she knelt beside him, smoothing his fur, her eyes wide with horror.

"Can you help him?" she cried to someone behind her, and he lifted his head a little way, and saw a stone sprite running up the path, the pale gray of her skin, the silver of her hair, making her swim in and out of focus against the rocks.

"Only Jorgen has enough power for that," she said, her voice the soft clink of pebbles against each other.

"Then we carry him down to Jorgen. We mustn't waste a moment."

Bjorn wanted to ask Astrid how she thought she could carry him two steps, let alone down the mountain to Jorgen, but she scrambled to her feet, and he was shivering too much to get the words out.

"If we help, can you try to lift him?" she whispered, and he knew from her tone she was talking to the wind.

The air strengthened around him, its cold fingers forcing under him, and he lifted a little.

"Please help me," Astrid called to the stone sprite, and he felt her hands coming under him. They were going to carry him with the wind. He would laugh at the idea, if he could just stop shaking, could open his eyes. They seemed weighed down with rocks.

But then another set of hands took the strain, and another, lifting him to shoulder height, and they began moving down the path, the wind a tight whirlwind beneath him, keeping him stable.

How many sprites and vedfe had Astrid managed to rope into this crazy scheme?

He at last forced his eyes open a crack, and the sight that met him snapped them open wider. He was surrounded by a throng of vedfe, two hundred at least, taking turns to carry his weight, as they moved off the mountain and back into the forest.

Astrid alone would not be replaced, holding him up near his shoulder. Her cheek was smudged with blood, and he realized with shock it was his own.

"Set him down." The bellow from the path before them could only belong to Jorgen.

"By the gods, Bjorn. Do you want to kill yourself and do us all in? Do you want to break the balance?"

He was lowered slowly to the ground, laid to rest on the forest path as light as an autumn leaf.

"What happened?"

Bjorn wanted to answer, but Jorgen was not looking at him, but Astrid.

"Another yggren. Bjorn set it alight, and it clamped itself to him, trying to burn them both. It was trying to strangle him while they burned."

"What madness is going on with the yggren?" Jorgen knelt beside him and placed his hands on either side of Bjorn's neck wound.

"My friend, you test my powers to the limits."

"Will try to help," Bjorn gasped out, but he knew in his weakened state, he would be of little use.

"Form a chain," Jorgen called out, and Bjorn saw the vedfe line up, each one touching the shoulder of the other, the first in line touching Jorgen.

They were sharing what power they had with their leader, and he was giving it all to Bjorn. Bjorn felt it flare within, felt the soothing touch of energy as the pain in his burnt legs and chest receded, as his neck slowly healed.

It stopped long before it needed to, but it was enough. Enough to get him on his feet and back to the palace. Enough to give him time to heal himself.

"I am deeply in your debt." Bjorn struggled shakily to his feet.

"As we are in yours, my lord," one of the vedfe answered, and suddenly every one but Jorgen and Astrid was gone.

"Can you walk?" The flecks of blood on Astrid's cheeks were in stark contrast to her white face. Her voice shook. "Shouldn't we carry him back?"

It annoyed him that she turned to the vedfe, even though Jorgen could barely stand himself since pouring his power into Bjorn's healing.

They were so exposed. Neither he nor Jorgen could protect her should Norga choose this moment to strike. If her spies were watching, they'd be foolish not to take this opportunity.

Come to that, what was Astrid doing out of the palace? His lady had a death wish.

Jorgen must have seen his eyes, because he swallowed nervously.

"Can you walk back?" he asked.

"I can." Bjorn struggled for control. There would be time for arguments later. Besides, his throat hurt too much to speak. He had to whisper. "Astrid get back to the palace. We'll follow as quickly as possible."

She looked at him with astonishment. "I am not going back alone. I just raced across the length of the forest to save you."

"I can't protect you." He swayed on his feet, his teeth clenched.

"No. But I can protect you," she replied, her eyes snapping as angrily as his own.

"Please." Fighting her, forcing her, was not the point. He was too weak to do it anyway, and it seemed she had Jorgen well and truly under her thumb. "Please."

"But you are hurt . . ."

"Astrid. Please. I need fear nothing from Norga,

whereas you . . ."

She spun in a circle, her fists clenched, her robe swirling around her. "We go together. I've just spent the last hour worried you were dead, and now you send me off? No."

She was so angry she vibrated like a bowstring after the shot. His blood marked her brow and she flung back her head—a warrior princess.

"Keep close, then." His words were resigned. "We are all vulnerable."

"The wind is tired," she agreed, and lifted out an arm, moving her fingers as if she ran them through water. He saw her start at the blood on her hand, and her whole body shuddered. With a cry, she flung herself to her knees next to him, burying her face in his fur.

"I didn't know what was happening. I was so worried." She drew back her head and he saw tears streaming down her face. "If I'd been a moment later. . ."

He'd have been dead.

"Come," he said quietly, nuzzling her, even though for the first time in a long time he wanted to roar until his throat bled that he was trapped in this bear body. He wanted to scoop her up, hold her close.

Carry her home in his arms.

Chapter Twenty-one

It hurt to see Bjorn walking as if on thorns. His every step was tortured as they neared the palace. Jorgen mumbled a farewell as they reached the treeline, startling Astrid.

She kept forgetting he was there.

She wondered, in one of the strange meanders her mind kept taking on this interminable journey, if Jorgen could set foot out of the forest.

She called out a goodbye, unsure if he'd gone or was still standing there.

Bjorn stumbled ahead of her, his eyes on the ground in front of him, just getting one foot in front of the other.

The sun edged toward the horizon, lighting the dark gray storm clouds to the west with dramatic oranges and reds, and the long shadows made the last part of her journey up the rocky path treacherous.

Bjorn was already at the palace entrance, raising a weary paw to the stone.

When had she fallen so far behind?

The sound of stone grinding on itself galvanized

her. The mountain was opening.

She tripped, scraped her hands, and was on her feet and running again before her tired muscles could protest.

Bjorn, leaning against the rock face, collapsed through the entrance as the door slid past him.

Her heart felt lodged in her throat by the time she reached the opening. She couldn't get enough of the thin, cold air into her lungs.

Blood smeared the floor where Bjorn had fallen, half in and half out of the mountain, and she leapt over his legs. She needed to pull him in.

The door began to rumble shut, the grinding of rock on rock ominous. Astrid grabbed hold of Bjorn's fur, bending her knees and tugging with all the strength fear gave her.

He slid a fraction and stopped, and gritting her teeth, she hauled at him again. He seemed stuck to the floor.

The stone door hit him mid-back and began pushing him before it.

With a cry of pure panic, Astrid grabbed a back paw in each hand, using Bjorn's forward momentum to swing him around. If she didn't get him in before the door closed, his legs would be crushed.

Slowly but surely his body slid inward, and with an echoing thunk, the entrance closed.

Her knees gave way, slamming onto the granite

floor, and she shuddered, the pain out of all proportion to the injury.

They were in complete darkness.

Bjorn cried out, making her jump. A hoarse, agonized cry that made every hair on her body rise. A strange rush of air—not her kind—swirled where he lay.

Dark magic.

The sun must have set.

She knelt next to him, fear-stricken, imagining him change from bear to man. She heard his nails scrabble on the stone floor, his body twist in pain, and shoved her knuckles in her mouth. Bit down.

What could she do?

Again she felt the brush of ice-cold evil on her face and then sensed it dissipate into the air.

The groan Bjorn let out this time was a very human one.

"Turn on the lights," she whispered in the echoing hall, and nothing happen. *"Turn on the lights,"* she screamed, leaping to her feet with her hands clenched to fists at her side.

Her panic echoed back at her eerily.

Bjorn must have made sure she had no power to command the magic outside of her room after sundown. She knelt again, despairing.

She was tired. Tired of not understanding. Tired of being locked in at night. Tired of being in darkness.

She felt him move, shiver from lying on the cold

stone, and he groaned again. She reached out to touch him and found he was freezing. He needed blankets and clothes.

Standing unsteadily, Astrid lifted her hands in front of her and headed in the direction of the stairs. It seemed to take forever, but at last her fingers touched the wall, and she edged left until the wall ran out. Bending, she felt for the first stair, and stifled a sob when she found it.

If she cried now, she would not stop.

She crawled up the stairway and then leant against the passage wall at the top, walking with her body touching the smooth stone until she came to her door.

She knew it would not open from the inside, but surely it would open from the outside?

Steeling herself for disappointment, she found the handle and pulled down. The door swung open, and her chamber lay before her, as dark as everywhere else.

She held the door and stepped in. "I want a doorstop," she called out, not willing to chance being shut in. It appeared in her hands, and she jammed it firmly in place.

She wished up blankets and cushions, and after some thought, a shirt and loose cotton pants for Bjorn, water and food. She lay it all on a blanket she could pull along behind her.

Then she found the bed and crawled to her side of

it, feeling beneath the mattress for her bundle. She felt within for the tallow candle and the tinderbox, stroked them with her fingers.

If there was ever a time to use them, it was now.

He was beautiful.

Handsome in the way gods are handsome—blindingly. She could not look away.

His hair was white blond, his skin golden. The proportions of his face were an artist's dream.

She crouched beside him, lifting the candle closer to his face, and saw his neck was bruised and black.

The body her fingers knew so well lay naked before her. He was big, his frame as broad and muscular as she imagined it. The burns on his legs wept and the slashes on his chest bled. She could not waste time drinking him in.

She arranged the cushions and blankets, and as gently as she could, tugged him onto them. The hot water she'd brought was now warm, and she dipped a cloth into it, moving quickly to clean him.

Even as she wiped away the blood, she saw in the weak candle light his wounds were healing, the skin knitting together and smoothing over.

He shivered as the water cooled on his skin.

With infinite care, she lifted the soft white cotton

shirt she'd wished for over his head, slid his arms into the long sleeves, and then struggled with the pants. His leg wounds were well enough healed by now that the soft fabric would not stick to them, and he desperately needed the warmth.

She was breathing hard by the time she'd finished dressing him, and she knelt back, candle raised, to look at him again.

He moaned in his sleep and she smoothed back his hair and kissed him gently on the forehead.

Bjorn jerked awake with a cry, startling her, and three drops of tallow fell, hot and black, onto the white of his shirt.

"Astrid?" His voice was hoarse from the yggren's strangling hands, and befuddled. He struggled up to his elbows.

She could say nothing. She could only look at him, wide eyed, suddenly shy; overcome with emotion and a sense of strangeness to truly see him at last. See his eyes when he spoke.

"Astrid." He looked at the candle, nothing more than a stub in her hand, and then back to her. "What have you done?"

<hr />

They were doomed.

Every sacrifice he'd made, every check and balance he'd put into place was for nought.

And it was his fault. He could have left her alone.
Let her be, instead of making her his lover, drawing her
deep into his world, but he had taken the chance.

And he had failed.

Astrid's eyes were wide in the waning candle
light, and he saw hot tallow drop on her hand, unheeded.

"What *have* I done?" she asked, and her voice
trembled.

"You have lost me," he replied, the words
scraping over his throat and tongue like sandpaper. "I
have lost you."

A roaring, desperate anger built in him and he felt
the tendons in his neck stand out, the muscles in his arms
bunch. "We are lost to each other." He could barely
speak, the roaring filled his ears and thundered in his
heart, and he pushed up from his elbows, and stood.
Looked up to the ceiling in the dark hall, his hands
clenched.

"You win, your majesty!"

His shout bounded and echoed in the chamber
and Astrid jumped, dropping the pitiful piece of wax that
had brought them so low, extinguishing the struggling
flame.

They were engulfed in darkness.

"Because I saw you as a man? I have lost you
because of that?"

"Why do you think I went to such lengths to
ensure you never saw me? Why do you think I begged

you, *begged you*, Astrid, to never try?" He spun in her direction, snarling as if he were still a bear.

"I didn't know why!" Her cry was anguished and angry, all at once. "And I've abided by your request. I've had the means to see you for weeks and I haven't done it. But tonight you needed help."

"It wasn't a request, it was an *order*." His roar echoed all around him, and he sensed Astrid stand up.

"You do not order me, Bjorn, and you never have. You have put me in the middle of this, without ever telling me all the stakes."

He closed his eyes and breathed deep. "You are right." He could not help the desolation in his voice. He was blind with regret, consumed by the enormity of his loss. "How did you come to have that candle? Did you want to make sure you slept with a man, not some dark creature from your mother's nightmares?"

She gasped, the sound clear in the darkness. "And if I did? You have seen me for all I am, but I haven't seen you. Tonight, tending your wounds was the reason for bringing out the candle my mother gave me, but I admit, beholding you was an added benefit."

"I had no choice," he shouted, then clenched his fists, bowed his head, and fought for control. Her pain, the agony that ran through her voice, calmed him. "I had no choice."

"What happens now?" She tried to match his calm.

"As I haven't already disappeared, I think Norga

will take me at dawn, when I become a bear."

"Take you?"

"To her palace." He moved forward and found her in the dark, pulled her to him. She came easily into his embrace, her arms tight around him.

Why were they stumbling around in the dark? There was no more need. "Lights!"

He blinked as the sconces lit, flooding the hall with a warm glow. He saw the little nest she'd made on the floor for him. It made a lonely island in the vast space, and he realized she had managed it all in complete darkness.

"Let's go to your room."

She nodded. Allowed him to lead them up the stairs.

"What will happen to you? Why does Norga want you?"

"It's a long story." By the top of the stairs, he was breathing hard and his legs felt like giving way. He lent against her.

"We have until dawn." Her voice was strong—defiant, almost—but he could hear the thread of fear. The note of panic.

He opened the door to her chamber and felt like an old man. Every movement hurt.

He used some of his strength to create sconces and light her room. Astrid followed him in and sat on her bed, her eyes bright on him, missing nothing.

"Use all your power to heal yourself," she said as he limped toward her. "We have no need of light."

He looked at her a long moment. Sighed. "No. We don't." As he reached the bed, he plunged the room into darkness.

--------◄⟨⟨⟩⟩►--------

"Norga enchanted me while I sat beside my father on his deathbed. When I was at my lowest, and so that he would see, the moment before he died, how she had tricked him. What plans she had for me."

Astrid made an inarticulate sound at the back of her throat.

Bjorn eased himself onto the bed, and pulled her close.

"She laid out my future. She had plans to take control of the realm, but she was not interested in keeping the balance. She wanted to rule as a tyrant, not as an arbitrator like my father, where everything is in harmony. Because of that, most of my father's subjects would not accept her. She could only count on support from some of the darker corners of the realm."

Astrid said nothing, feeling Bjorn's arms tense, the muscles rippling under her hands.

"She has a daughter, hidden in her palace. And her plan was for me to marry this troll daughter, and command the vedfe and the others to accept us as the new lord and lady."

"Why would you do that?"

"If I did not agree, she swore we would go to war. Her and those loyal to her, against me and those loyal to me. It would be carnage. And an end to the balance, no matter what the outcome."

"But that would have cost her, too."

"Which is why she agreed to the bargain. She knew a war could destroy that which she sought to control."

Astrid sat up, her mind racing. "She thought the bargain gave her a better chance of winning."

Bjorn sighed. "I had to walk a knife's edge with that bargain. Making it seem likely she would win, but giving myself a chance of winning, too."

"What was the bargain?" This is what she'd longed to know since she'd met him.

"I had a dream. One that came to me every night, sometimes. Of a clearing, and a girl, and a dead hag, and Norga and another woman talking about me. I told Norga I wished to marry none but the girl, and I wanted a chance to find her. That if, after a year, I could not, I would marry Norga's daughter."

"The boy in the clearing was you."

"While we sat together, you whispered something to me, something that stayed with me from that day until this one."

"What did I say?" Astrid turned her face toward him. How could she not remember?

"You said: I will love you forever."

Chapter Twenty-two

"I *will* love you forever." With the words came determination.

Bjorn pulled her back down, into his arms, and she forced herself to lie calmly beside him when she wanted instead to pace and plot. To think up a way around their predicament. She wanted action to overcome her fear.

His voice was strong. Back to normal. "I have loved you since that day in the clearing. You gave me an escape from Norga's spite and my father's spell-blinded eyes."

"How long did it take you to find me?"

He shivered beside her. "Almost my full year."

"But you *did* find me. You beat her." Astrid felt the first surge of hope.

"Norga agreed to my bargain on a condition. That I take you to my palace, and keep you for a year. She would allow me to take my human form at night, but you could not see me as a man for that whole year. If you did, the bargain was broken and I had to marry her daughter."

"She thought to torture you by having me under your roof and not be able to come to me as a man."

"I was so pleased to know I would have time as a man again, I agreed readily. I thought I could live with you without touching you for a year, and then, I came up with the plan of visiting to you in darkness. That way, I kept to the letter of the bargain, but not in a way Norga intended."

"Until I came with my tallow candle." Astrid's voice cracked. She should have listened to the niggle of doubt she'd had since her mother first pressed the candle into her hand.

"Shhh. No tears or blame." He brushed her hair back. "I should never have come to you at all."

"Can you not reverse this? Enchant Norga somehow?" She tried to grab any idea, however unformed, that swirled through her mind.

"No." He held her even closer. "I am not as powerful as my father. I'm half-human. In a physical fight, I might be her match, but she has older magic than me."

"Where does Norga take you, then? Perhaps I could rescue you, somehow."

He shook his head. "That is impossible. Norga's palace can only be found east of the sun, and west of the moon."

"But that's . . ." She lifted a startled face to his.

"Yes. That's no place at all."

"I do not care. I will find a way."

"Astrid." His voice was dead, despairing. "I gave my oath, and must fulfill this bargain."

"You gave your oath, but I did not give mine."

His fingers tightened, clamped her waist. "Norga becomes even more powerful the moment I marry her daughter. Do not endanger yourself."

She did not reply, and eventually his hold on her relaxed.

"Let us not waste our last hours on this." Bjorn brushed his lips to her cheek, and light, soft and mellow, bloomed like a flower, filling the room.

He looked almost completely healed, and she stared at him, filling her eyes so she would never forget.

"I want to see you, to not waste a minute more. So I have this memory whatever may happen." He reached behind her and tugged at the ties on her dress, his fingers clumsy with haste. When he raised his eyes to hers, they were molten. Sea green mixed with fire.

Her heart lurched as it caught his urgency. She pushed her dress off her shoulders and began wriggling out of it.

He raised his white shirt off his head, and then looked at it, perplexed. "Where did this come from?"

"I wished for it. You were so cold." Astrid fingered the soft cotton, marred only by the drops of tallow over the left breast.

"Something truly from you. From your heart." He

looked thoughtful. "I shall wear it when Norga takes me."

He laid it carefully aside, and the light gleamed off his skin and hair as he turned to her. Framed her face with his hands.

Astrid traced a finger over his lips as their bodies slid together, familiar and yet unfamiliar.

"If there is a way to find you, then I will." She found a center of calm in her words. A new resolve. When dawn came, she would not lie, crying and wishing for him back. She would push away the anguish and she would *get* him back.

Astrid woke to the pale, cold touch of early morning. She stretched out and then froze. With a cry, she twisted up and onto her knees, her heart thundering. Her gaze went to the empty place beside her in the bed.

How could she have slept through? How could he have gone without waking her?

The empty bed was proof she had and he did, but how could it be?

They had lain together, soft and sated, and she had closed her eyes to savor the moment. The smell of his skin, the feel of it against hers. How could she have slept?

Unless . . . she looked again at the dented pillow, the ruffled sheets on Bjorn's side, and wondered if he had made the choice for her?

"As least now, I know nothing is unsaid between us."

He had whispered that to her only a few hours ago.

Could he really have enchanted her one last time? Thinking to save her from the trauma and heartbreak of his leaving. Thinking to force her to be angry with him, move on and find a new life.

"No!" She pounded the bed with her fist and leapt up. "You do not get rid of me that easily."

"Hot water," she called. Nothing happened. "Breakfast?" Again, nothing. The magic in her room was gone.

So was everything else, she realized, except the furniture that had been in the room the evening she arrived. The bed and a chair and table were all she could see. The ladder was gone. The dress she wore yesterday, her bath—all gone.

Naked, panicked, Astrid fell to her knees and began scrabbling under her bed. As her hand touched her old rag bundle, tears of relief stung her eyes.

She dug in the cloth sack and lifted out her old dress. The one she'd worn from her home the night Bjorn came for her. It had once been cornflower blue, now faded to match the winter sky; thin, scratchy, and over-patched. Before her, Freja and Bets had both worn it.

It had served her well enough before. And it would do so now.

She pulled it over her head. Threw the sack over her shoulder, and winced as something within it struck her back in the pendulum swing of the bag. She dug her hand inside, and came out with the gift Eric had given her before she'd left home the first time.

The tiny carving of a bear.

He'd sanded and oiled it, and it was smooth in her hands. Why had he given it to her? Guilt, perhaps. Some strange idea of a parting gift.

Whatever the reason, it comforted her. Increased her determination. She slipped it back in the sack and walked to the door, her hand resting a moment on the handle. Would it open for her?

As she pushed the handle down, something dropped from the skylight, and Astrid looked over her shoulder to see what it was.

A little dwarf. And then another. And then another. Red capped, blue shirted, with little leather boots.

The first one looked at her and let out a laugh at the surprise and horror on her face, and she did not wait a second longer.

Trusting the castle was free of all magic, she flung the door back and ran for her life.

The first mistake they made was turning back to trolls in her chamber. As they struggled out of the door on knuckles and knees, she gained a small lead.

She could only see them because the light from her

skylights spilled into the passageway, but the sconces were no longer lit. It may be daylight, but within the palace it was black as a tomb and she flew down the steps in pure darkness, the thud of massive footsteps behind her.

A troll cried out as it fell down the stairs, and the others slowed their chase.

Hands outstretched, she raced across the massive hall to the door, running too fast to stop herself slamming into the stone.

"Open," she whispered. "Please open."

The rock did not budge.

Then she would *force* it open.

Air in the palace, to me. She commanded the wind with her thoughts, desperate not to make another sound. The first brush of air on her face made her lean weakly back against the rock.

It had worked.

The trolls could be anywhere. Right on top of her, for all she knew. And she needed time.

With regretful, shaking fingers, she pulled her carved bear out of her sack and pitched it as hard as she could at the far wall. It skittered on the smooth granite and made a satisfying thunk as it hit its target.

She heard a grunt, and the sound of footsteps in that direction, but not three sets. At least one still stood, listening.

She could feel the pressure building as the air

flowed toward her. *As much strength as you have to offer. I must open this entrance.*

As soon as she'd thought it, the pressure increased, the air whistling as it moved to her. Filling the hall with an eerie sound.

Her hair whipped her face, the wool of her dress flattened against her body, and she took the strain herself, gripping what handholds she could find in the stone and pushing with all her might.

The trolls were muttering, uneasy. And the one who'd been listening took a step toward her, his footfall a clear slap of sound on the polished floor.

The air was now like the blast of wind through a narrow gorge, concentrated, terrifying, its fingers digging into the fine crack that separated the stone door from the wall of mountain. The pitch of its whistle grew higher and higher as it cried out in exertion.

Astrid's ears ached.

She felt the door move. A miniscule jerk. She strained against the rock, grazing her hands, pushing harder. The shriek and whistle of the wind was deafening.

Hurry.

If the trolls were coming closer, she could no longer hear them. But she could smell them. The air blasted their scent at her. The smell of rock, lichen and moss.

The door inched wider, vibrating with the strain,

and a tiny crack of light penetrated the hall.

They would see her. Panic gripped her as she pressed back against the rock.

She knew the moment they had. One gave a cry of triumph loud enough to be heard over the pounding noise of air, and the thin line of light from outside illuminated it, a strange stripe of brightness, as it leapt at her.

Astrid was forming her scream when the troll was batted back, the wind turning its full force toward it for a moment. The troll stumbled and fell, and the air went back to work, howling in the confined space.

In the growing light, she saw the trolls look at one another. Nervous and confused. Their hesitation gave her the time she needed, and with a final shove, the door moved just enough to let her through.

She dived through the narrow gap, grazing her shoulders, and the moment she was through the air ceased pushing. The gate snapped back with a grinding screech that set her teeth on edge.

She lay on the ground for only a moment. How long would it take the trolls to get out the palace?

Astrid didn't wait to find out.

Chapter Twenty-three

She was gathering the wind to her, running full tilt at the trees to make her first leap when an yggren stepped into her path.

She was going too fast on the slithering stones, and she willed the wind, like a limb, like a part of herself, to lift her up, and she jumped.

As she sailed high above the yggren's head, she looked down, giddy with delight and fear, and saw it had craned back its neck to look at her. Its bark-brown gaze alien and unreadable.

"Do not run," it called in the strange, high call she'd heard before. "I am not your enemy."

Astrid landed hard enough to jolt her legs, stumbled and raced on, readying herself for another leap.

"Stop."

Jorgen stepped from the cool shadows of the trees, blocking her way. He was too close to jump over, too close for anything but collision.

She slammed into him and he went over like a felled oak, taking the brunt of impact on the cold, hard forest floor.

Astrid rolled off him, but before she could find her feet he had a lock on her legs.

"Wait, my lady. This yggren can be trusted."

"It isn't with the trolls?" she gasped out, and saw the flash of surprise in his eyes.

"Trolls?"

"In the palace." She sucked in air. "Tried to kill me."

"Where is Bjorn?"

There was no mistaking the panic, the fear for Bjorn in his voice, and Astrid let herself flop gratefully back to the ground, her eyes closed. He had not betrayed her.

"Norga took Bjorn at dawn." Her throat was suddenly bone dry, every word painful to speak.

The yggren gave a cry, and Astrid sat up again, looking at it warily.

"The bargain is lost?"

Jorgen's face, the sorrow, the despair, mirrored Astrid's own.

"Oh, Jorgen. I am sorry. It was my fault. I had a candle and I lit it last night to care for his wounds. I saw him as a man."

"After everything . . ."

Jorgen sat back down, pale under his dark skin.

The sound of stone crunching beneath running feet filtered through the trees.

"The trolls." Astrid leapt up, grabbing Jorgen

under his arms and hauling him with all her might.

"Leave the trolls to us," the yggren said, its voice like the shriek of two branches rubbing together in the wind. It let out a cry, strange and terrible, and suddenly there were yggren all around.

Before she could even count how many, they were gone in their disturbing way; faster than a blink, the crackle of leaves and the swish of disturbed branches the only sound of their leaving.

Astrid shivered. "Jorgen, quickly. I must know. Have you heard of the place that is east of the sun and west of the moon?"

Jorgen blinked, his old self again. He shook his head. "That's where Bjorn is?"

"Yes and I am going to find him."

From behind them, between the trees, they both heard the queer, high-pitched scream of a creature in pain. It cut off abruptly.

Astrid glanced back uneasily. "I need to know the best way to start."

"You are going on a journey?" The yggren was back, no mark on it. It might never have been away.

Astrid could not look it in the eye after it had just shed blood for her. "Why are you helping me?"

The yggren bent down on one knee. "I gave Bjorn my loyalty. So did the others. It is a mystery to us why two of our own broke their word, but we have not. Will not."

The declaration touched her, and she nodded. "I seek the place east of the sun, west of the moon. Do you know it?"

"I have heard of it, but do not know where to find it." The yggren cocked its head like a bird. "Why do you not ask your loyal subjects, Wind Hag? Does the wind not go everywhere?"

Wind Hag. Was she?

Of course she was. Since the moment Bjorn asked her, she'd known it, deep within.

She bent her head. "I'm a poor mistress of the wind. I can command it, but cannot talk with it."

The yggren shrugged. "These local air sprites do you good service, my lady, but they are not the same as the great winds." He gestured east. "Perhaps the East Wind will know, if this place is east?"

The East Wind. Power seemed to lift up from her feet, to flow through every part of her. "I am in your debt, yggren."

"We will watch for your safety where we can." It stood, and then, in a blink it was gone.

"If I could be of help, I would go with you." Jorgen watched her, his face unreadable. "My power is tied to this place, and I am more useful here."

Astrid went down on her knees before him, and bowed her head. "Thank you for everything, my friend. More than anyone else, Bjorn and I are in your debt."

He was before her in an instant, hauling her to her

feet.

"You do not bow to me, my lady."

"I am only your lady if I can recover your lord." She smiled at the surprise on his face. "But I plan to." She leaned forward and kissed him on each cheek. "I will get him back."

⋯⋯⋘⫘⋙⋯⋯

Astrid was freezing. She clenched her jaw to stop her teeth from chattering.

A snow-topped mountain stood straight ahead, its slopes glowing red and gold in the setting sun. Giving a false impression of warmth.

The wind had carried her in great leaps east, but like her, it had begun to tire, the jumps becoming lower and shorter as the day wore on. And now dusk was seeping across the winter sky and she had no cloak.

She needed to find shelter.

She'd seen a light earlier, as she approached the end of the valley, winking through the trees at the foot of the mountain, and she jumped one last time to land just in front of the treeline.

She straightened her dress but her hair was beyond help. Whipped and twisted into knots, it stood out from her face like a writhing nest of snakes, and there was nothing she could do about it.

She made her way through the tall pines, wincing at every step. She could smell the wood smoke as she got closer to the light, the sweet smoky scent mingling with the aroma of a stew or broth.

Her stomach growled.

What if they turned her away?

She felt the light touch of the wind on her shoulder, felt the air sprites crowding behind her, and she took comfort.

If she was turned away, so be it. She would manage.

She pulled her spine straighter and followed a narrow path just visible in the gloom. It led her with a twist and a turn around massive pines, and there, nestled with its back against the mountainside, was a small cottage.

Light spilled from the edges of the shutters, and as she approached a horse whinnied from an outbuilding attached to the side of the little house.

She came to the rough wooden front door, and after a moment of hesitation, knocked three times.

There was a shuffle from within, and the door was opened by a tiny old woman, wizened as an end-of-winter apple, with cheeks just as rosy. She stood protectively in the narrow wedge of light, blocking any view of the interior.

"Yes?" Her eyes, beady and dark brown, missed nothing. They took in her worn and ragged dress, and lingered on her hair.

"I . . . I come to seek shelter for the night,

mistress." Astrid winced. Even through all the years of poverty with her father, she had never had to ask for the charity of another. Her father's pride would not allow it.

"Who are you?"

Astrid hesitated. Who was she? Just a short time ago, she would have had no trouble answering this question. "I am Astrid."

"And why are you traveling so late?" The old woman's eyes narrowed suspiciously.

"I am looking for the East Wind."

"Ah." The woman pursed her lips and looked over Astrid's shoulder, as if she could see the air sprites.

"Come in." She stepped back, opening the door wider, and the wafting smell of cooking, the gentle touch of warmth on her cold-stung face, enticed Astrid into the room.

The old woman closed the door, and Astrid stood numb within, the heat of the wood fire pricking her eyes to tears. Eyes watering, nose dripping, she took in the cosy little room, the far wall of which was the mountain's bare rock face.

She closed her eyes to blink away the tears, and when she opened them again, the room had fallen away.

Chapter Twenty-four

Shock and fear froze her to the spot.

Back in the dark.

In some kind of cave. She could sense the vastness of it, the terrifying breadth and height.

Astrid could smell the damp rock, the stale air. She drew in a deep breath of it, forcing down the panic. Bending on one knee, she felt the floor. It was clammy, slippery with moss and mold. Slime coated her fingers.

Trapped? Tricked? What was this?

Somewhere to her left a single drop of water hit stone, the sound echoing in the massive space.

How did she know it was so big?

The thought diverted her fear, and she latched onto it. How *did* she know? She could see nothing.

And yet she felt the air. Instinctively knew how much surrounded her. Knew she stood exactly in the middle of the space. And knew, she realized with a little leap of excitement within, that there was a passage out.

She felt the air flow down like a stream of water into a large reservoir far to the left.

She took a step in that direction, and as she did

someone—*something*—whispered near her ear, and she spun to face it.

"Hello?"

"We have a test for you." The voice was gritty, earthy; the smell of rich soil and the metallic tang of stone danced on the air to her.

"Who are you?" Astrid strained to see in the dark, holding her hands before her to at least have some forewarning if something got too close.

"We see you have discovered the door. You have to walk to it without bumping into any of us."

"What are you?"

"Not something you want to bump into." The speaker sniggered.

"But I can't see." Astrid's voice faltered.

There was no reply, and Astrid winced at the weakness she had shown.

She thought about it. The air could be her eyes.

It already told her where she stood, how large a place she stood in and the way out. Everything her eyes could have told her.

She needed to trust it now. To trust her mastery of it. She turned back to the opening and took a step, felt the air compress slightly.

There was something just in front of her, and she stepped to the right of it and around, moved forward again. As she made her halting way through the cave she learned the language of air pressure, of compression.

She wondered what strange dance she was performing, gliding, stopping, twirling around her unseen partners, silent and still, earthy and dark. She felt them loiter with an edge of cruel interest.

As she moved faster and faster, more and more sure-footed, she learned her connection to the air was far stronger than she'd ever realized or admitted to.

That it spoke to her on an instinctual level.

And as she took the last step to the passage entrance, she was so connected to the air, so close, she was certain she could fly up the narrow, twisting staircase she found.

Awe caught in her throat, and for the first time, she truly believed she had a chance of finding Bjorn. She was not just Astrid. She was something more.

She put her foot on the first stone step, and heard the shuffle of feet behind her.

"You take your leave of us, Wind Hag?"

As she spun, light suddenly seeped down the staircase, as if above her, someone had opened a door. Astrid's eyes widened at the sight of the creature before her. If her invisible companions were air sprites, this was surely an earth sprite.

Deep brown, orange and cream, as if cut from the stone stairwell above her, streaked with the sage of lichen, it hulked and shuffled in the weak light. Unused to eyes upon it.

Its face was knobbly as rock, but in the angle of its

chin, in the turn of its shoulders, she could see the majesty of a soaring rock outcrop, the jut of a cliff over the land.

She got down on one knee and bowed her head. "You have given me a precious gift. I give my thanks."

The earth sprite was silent, and Astrid looked up at it, saw approval in its eyes. She rose, and placed a hand on its face, kissed its cheek. Felt the smooth, cool grain of stone on her lips.

"Was a time, thanks was given with blood," it said gruffly.

"Do you wish it?"

"No." It smiled. "Dame Berge wanted only to make sure you were the Wind Hag. But you are very different from the last one."

Astrid found she liked that. Was freed by it.

"Go well, mistress." It stepped back from the passage, vanishing into the depths of the cavern, and Astrid lifted her head to look up the long flight of stairs before her.

Dame Berge waited above, no doubt, fire crackling, stew bubbling.

She wondered who the old woman really was.

———⟨✦⟩———

"So you are the one who should have married the Prince." Dame Berge pushed a bowl of stew across the table to Astrid, and Astrid forced herself to nod, to not grab up her spoon, as her hostess ladled a bowl for herself.

"Eat, eat. I can see you're hungry." The old lady began eating herself.

Refusing to let herself behave like a starving beggar, Astrid lifted her spoon to her mouth, savoring the flavors on her tongue.

The old woman nodded. "You carry yourself well."

At last, Astrid allowed herself to relax. Her legs felt leaden and the table looked as good as a feather pillow.

"How do you know the Prince is mine?" she asked.

"You seek him, don't you?" Again, Dame Berge spoke sharply.

Astrid nodded.

"Well then." She ate another spoon of stew, the matter obviously decided. "You may never find him, you know?"

The question revived her. "I will find him."

"Hmm." The old woman cackled. "I don't think Norga bargained on going up against the Wind Hag, eh?"

Astrid looked up briefly, saw the cool intelligence in the eyes upon her, and took another mouthful of stew. "I only discovered I was the Wind Hag this morning."

"Ho, ho! Even better!" Dame Berge grabbed up a loaf of bread and cut a slice with gusto. "Norga won't have even the smallest inkling then, will she?"

Astrid was not as certain. For all she knew, Norga knew exactly who she was.

"Can I ask you . . ." Astrid took the slice of bread offered to her, wiped her bowl clean. "Where is the old Wind Hag?"

Dame Berge rested her hands on the table. "The Wind Hag has been missing for a long time. The weather has been colder because of it. Without her to keep the four great winds in check, the strongest one, the North Wind, has prevailed over the others. But as you are sitting here, the new Wind Hag, it can only mean one thing."

There was a soft sigh of air in the room, and Astrid kept her gaze fixed on Dame Berge.

The old woman leant back in her chair and folded her arms. "The old Wind Hag is dead."

"The dead woman in the clearing." That meant somehow the Wind Hag had passed the mantle on to her at the age of three. It meant . . . "The Wind Hag used me to tell Bjorn she'd love him for ever."

Dame Berge rose to clear the table. "Always had an eye for beauty, did the Wind Hag, though as a Jotun, she had a face like a dog's behind."

"She saw Bjorn and wanted him. Even though he was only a child." Excitement drew Astrid to her feet.

The answers were slowly finding their way to the light.

"Oh, she mentioned him before to me. Could not get enough of his fair countenance. Hoped he would grow used to her ugliness and when he was a man, would consent to marry her."

"She stole him away, and Norga caught her and killed her."

"Without knowing who she'd killed, no doubt." The old woman went to a small cupboard near the fireplace. "If she'd realized it was the Wind Hag, she'd have tried to get the great winds on her side too."

Astrid watched curiously as the old woman opened a drawer, and then raised her hands to shield her eyes as Dame Berge pulled out a golden sphere. It caught the firelight and reflected it, its golden rays brightening the room.

"What is that?" She spoke as if in a holy place, and surely this was an object of the gods?

"This is the gift I give to you, a golden apple. To help you on your journey." Dame Berge offered the apple to her, and with trembling hands, Astrid took it, felt the smooth, cool metal of it beneath her fingertips.

This was a gift fit for a king or queen. "Thank you. For everything."

Dame Berge smiled, nodded her head as if well pleased. "Sleep well tonight, and tomorrow, I will lend you my horse. If you take him, you can cover enough distance to bring you to . . . a friend of mine by nightfall.

She will take you in. But I need Cirrus back. After his night's rest, tell him to go home, and he will return to me."

"Thank you for your offer, Dame Berge, but I am the mistress of the wind. I ride it in great leaps. Faster than a horse."

Dame Berge shook her head. "You do not understand. Cirrus is not an ordinary horse. He was a gift from the old Wind Hag. Cirrus rides the wind."

Astrid sat bareback on Cirrus and used the reins to guide him through the trees, down the path toward the open valley.

How did a horse ride the wind? She would just have to find out.

They broke out into the open, but the mountain was still in the way. Light seeped from either side of it, and Astrid realized it lay directly east, blocking the sun from view.

"We go over it, then." She urged Cirrus into a trot, then a canter, until finally they were galloping along the valley floor, straight at the craggy heights.

"Show me how you ride the wind," Astrid whispered, but Cirrus did nothing, and she imagined the wind around them, imagined it solid beneath Cirrus's flashing hooves.

She felt his angle change, clamped her knees tighter on his flanks as he rose up. Felt her heart soar as they climbed higher and higher, until the forest was below them and they flew up like eagles, rounding the side of the mountain.

Her hair, which she'd fought into submission and braided that morning, streamed out behind her, and the old, threadbare cloak Dame Berge had given her flapped like a brown wing. She pulled it closer around her, tucking her sack beneath it. Last night, when she'd placed the golden apple in her sack, she'd heard the clunk of two hard objects hitting each other. She'd tipped the sack up to see what the apple could have hit against and there, on the bed, lay the wooden bear Eric had given her.

But she had thrown it against the wall in the Mountain Palace.

She'd stood looking down at it, her exhausted mind churning over the possibilities, but she could think of only one that made sense. The air sprites had returned it to her. Unnoticed, while she pushed against the stone door, they had recovered her carving and slipped it back into her sack.

She had picked it up and climbed into bed with it clutched tight in her hand, and fought with her tears.

Astrid blinked. Just thinking of the returned talisman again, a single drop leaked from the corner of her eye, stinging her cold cheek with its warmth. She dipped her head and rubbed her face on her shoulder to dry it, leant into the shelter of Cirrus's neck, and held on for the wild ride.

Chapter Twenty-five

They alighted in a meadow cast deep into shadow by the hill above it. Snug up against the hillside was a cottage, and to the right of it, a waterfall fell from nearly half way up the hill into a large pool. In the pale pink light of dusk, Astrid saw the water churning and foaming, the ripples reflecting the pastel sky as they eddied to the banks.

Cirrus nickered as they approached the house and a horse answered from the stable. Astrid slid off his back with a groan, every muscle stiff and sore, and led him into the tiny courtyard, rubbing his nose.

"It has been a long time since Cirrus stood in this yard."

An old woman in a homespun dress as white as her short, wavy hair stood at the door.

"Good evening." Astrid curtsied low, and to her surprise, the wind sprites lifted her cloak behind her, as if it were a train. "Dame Berge lent me the use of Cirrus for today, and said I might find a welcome here from you."

"A curtsey from the Wind Hag. That's worth a good dinner to you alone." The old woman chuckled and stepped from her doorway into the little yard, and Astrid saw her face was pale and smooth despite her age; she had once been a great beauty. "I am Dame Elv. Go within and rest before the fire a while, or make use of the hot water to wash. I will get Cirrus comfortable."

"I will do it." Astrid lifted a hand to Cirrus's neck. "He has served me well today and I should be the one to brush him down and feed him."

The old woman looked at her with eyes that caught the last rays of sun. Pale green as the ice in a glacier. "Very well. We will do it together."

She took up the reins and led Cirrus into the stable. Within was a horse identical to him, and the two nuzzled each other ecstatically.

"Nimbus will be happy of the company tonight."

Astrid looked curiously at the small stream that ran through the stable, bubbling up on one end, running down a deep channel and disappearing back into the ground near the door.

"There is one in the house, too. Spring water." The old woman handed Astrid a brush and went to fetch a bucket of oats.

The rhythm of brushing Cirrus felt good; calming after the long day, and Astrid sniffed in the sweet smell of hay, the normal, comforting scents of the barn, and thought how not so long ago, there would have been nothing remarkable in this for her. She had wished for a new world, and she had been given one beyond her imagination. But the only thing of importance to her in it was Bjorn. And she would find him again.

When they were finished, Dame Elv dusted her hands with a quick slap, one against the other, and then rubbed them down the front skirt of her dress.

"Come, let's wash, eat and sleep. I will lend you Nimbus tomorrow. He won't want to miss an adventure of his own after a night hearing Cirrus recount his."

Inside the house, just as she'd said, a spring bubbled up into a basin on the floor, spilling over the sides and disappearing into the smooth stones set around it. The air seemed fresher because of it, and Astrid drew in a deep breath.

Dame Elv led her to a chair beside the fire, and Astrid had just lowered herself into it when her hostess produced a bowl of stew for her lap. Despite her hunger, Astrid struggled to keep her eyes open, lulled by the murmur of the fountain, the warmth radiating from the hearth, and the muted, steady hiss of the waterfall outside.

Her head dropped further and further forward, and she cried out as she suddenly fell head first—not into her bowl of stew, but into the churning foam of the waterfall's icy waters.

———⟨✦⟩———

Cold and shock slapped her awake, and panic had her heart racing.

Astrid tried to kick back up to the surface, but the water was so full of bubbles, there was nothing to kick against. She sunk straight to the bottom and was held there by the pounding water.

Think. Think!

There had to be a way. Lungs already burning, Astrid tried using the uneven, rocky floor of the pool to launch herself back up, but she got caught again in the swirl of air-laden water, pushed back down again.

"Stuck?"

Astrid caught the image of a naked woman in the water, gone before she could be sure.

A soft tinkle of laughter, cold and frothy, swirled around her.

She flayed in panic, dizzy with the need for a breath, her lungs on fire. She pictured the air above and within the water coming to her, spiraling down, and willed it to be so. Through the lights dancing in front of her eyes she looked up and saw a whirlpool coalesce above her, the air drilling down through the water. Fighting its way to her.

She glimpsed the curious, transparent face of a woman, peering through the swirling water, her features sharp, and with a final, panicked shove of her will, the air punched down to the bottom of the pool, shoving the water aside.

Astrid heaved in a shaking, gasping breath.

The water had flown from her to a spinning

vortex, narrow enough she could touch it if she lifted her arms out at her sides. She balanced on the slippery, weed-covered rocks at the bottom of the pool and looked up to see the star-filled night sky above her.

The pool was deep and the amount of water around her, stretching above her, sent a skitter of fear through her body.

"Very dramatic." The water sprite's voice was fuzzy through the spinning water. She pushed up against the inner edge of the whirlpool as if it were a glass window, then poked her head through into the air-filled eye of calm.

Rage swept through Astrid, the aftermath of a close encounter with death, and she clenched her fists. Her hair stuck to her cheeks and water dripped from her clothes. The chill winter air from above clamped a clammy hand over her.

"You . . ." She heard a roaring in her ears, and only the nervous flash in the water sprite's eyes made her fight for control. "You almost killed me . . ."

The water sprite stared back, her face neutral.

"What is this test about?" Astrid stood, shivering in the whirlpool's center, and crossed her arms over her chest.

"How are you going to get out of the pool?" the sprite asked.

Astrid had wondered that herself. Away from the pounding, churning water directly under the waterfall, she could simply do away with the whirlpool and swim up. Except that would leave her in the water with the water sprite, and she didn't trust it.

"I don't know."

The sprite nodded. "Those who do not appreciate the power they wield, do not deserve to have it."

With that, she seemed to kick off of something, shooting herself to the top of the whirlpool and water began pouring down on Astrid, spilling over the lip of the air cylinder she'd created, to rain down on her.

It pummeled her, bowing her under its weight.

She had held this all in check without a thought only moments ago, and she suddenly understood her lesson. Took a huge breath as the water closed over her head.

She was the mistress of the wind. She was powerful. She needed to respect her own strength.

She called the air back and it formed beneath her, a massive bubble, rising from the bottom with her standing upon it. She rose to the surface, the water streaming off her, and she stood on the water as if it were a solid thing. Willed the air beneath her to sweep her to the shore.

Dame Elv was waiting for her with a towel as she stepped from the lapping waves onto the rocky pool's edge, but before she took it, Astrid turned back, knelt and touched her lips to the water.

"Thank you."

"Nicely done," came the tinkling reply. "Nicely done, Wind Hag."

———◅✍▻———

Wrapped up in a soft blanket, her dress dripping by the fire, Astrid swallowed the last of her stew and shivered. Not from cold, but from the strangeness of everything.

Dame Elv regarded her steadily with her green eyes, and Astrid thought she saw a hint of iciness, the flash of cold interest she'd seen in the water sprite. But when the old woman took the soup bowl from her, there was nothing but friendliness and concern in her face. She smiled, and it transformed her back to a little old lady.

What she had been before the smile was more puzzling. Sharp-eyed, powerful. Magical.

When Dame Elv sat down again, her hand dug deep into the pocket of her dress.

"You may find this useful to you where you're going." She lifted out a comb; golden, lovely beyond anything. Even the apple in Astrid's sack could not compare to the delicate intricacies of the design along the top. The perfect marriage of art and function.

Astrid knew her eyes were wide, her mouth open, and she slid off her chair to her knees, blanket clutched in front of her, to take the gift from Dame Elv's offered palm.

"Thank you. I have never seen anything so

lovely."

"Haven't you?" Dame Elv asked, and Astrid jerked her gaze up.

"Nothing man-made," she conceded, thinking of a dew-covered spiderweb, the forest spread out before her yesterday on Cirrus. Bjorn's face.

A lightning jab of pain pierced her and she fought back the crippling sense of loss. She would find him.

"It is lovely, you're right." The old woman rubbed her eyes, and Astrid wondered if she regretted her gift, but she did not so much as give the comb another look as she rose.

"I'll show you to your bed."

Astrid got up from her knees and slipped the comb into the bag with her other things. How these gifts would be of use to her, she had no idea, other than their great value.

But she was sure Dame Berge and Dame Elv did not give their treasures lightly.

She hoped she could reward their sacrifice with success.

Chapter Twenty-six

Nimbus was as swift a wind steed as Cirrus. Astrid watched the landscape fall away, thickly forested hills that seemed diseased with their patchy snow, valleys muddy with early winter slush and swollen rivers spilling into narrow fjords so deep their waters were inky blue.

She knew her journey's end today was the home of another friend of the two old women, and felt the claw of panic, the gnawing fear that time was wasting. She still did not even know where Norga's palace was, and Bjorn could even now be swearing his marriage oaths to her troll daughter.

But panic would not serve her well. She could not travel faster than she was. With her breath snatched from her lips and the icy fingers of altitude prying through her clothes, she truly was swift as the wind.

Despite the feeling her hours were running out, that the ax of time was lowering on her neck, she welcomed the nightfall and the prospect of rest. Even with the borrowed cloak, her body was close to freezing, her face stiff with cold. When she could, she dipped her head and lifted the edge of her cloak, covering part of her face, even though it felt worse when her numb fingers fumbled and the fabric was ripped from them, her face blasted by the cold again.

When Nimbus touched down and staggered to a stop in front of a neat house, she slid off his back with relief.

Astrid saw the door of the cottage was open—strange on this cold night—and she took a longing step toward it, the flicker of candlelight promising comfort within.

Nimbus blew warm breath on her neck and she turned and pressed her cheek against his nose. "Come, let us find our hostess. She must be in the stable."

Astrid led Nimbus to the small barn just visible around the back of the house but there was no one there save another wind steed.

She brushed and fed Nimbus and trudged back to the front of the house. As she approached the door, the small ball of unease she had not realized she carried became heavier. Dropped deeper in her chest to her stomach.

What test this time?

She stepped across the threshold and peered in. Candles lay on every surface. Thick, scented, they were far above the miserable tallow stick that had been her downfall. She sniffed in pine, burnt orange and rose. Even less at her ease, she rolled her shoulders, wincing at the stiffness in them.

"Are you afraid?" a woman asked from behind her.

Astrid gasped and spun, her mouth already forming a 'Yes.' Her eyes widened at the beauty who stood just outside the door, her red hair glistening, the burnt umber of her eyes gleaming as they caught the light of the lamp she held in her hand. This woman could have been any age, although Astrid guessed her to be as old as her mother; with a vibrancy and glow her mother had long lost.

A woman in her prime.

Was she afraid?

"No."

"You should be." The woman swung back her arm and threw the lamp at Astrid's feet. The oil within spilled out and the fire ran after it, hungry.

Astrid stepped back, her eyes meeting the woman's in shock across the fence of flames. The woman's lips gave a slight twist, and she shrugged her shoulders as she turned to go.

As if this was their signal, the flames leapt higher, head height, and Astrid was surrounded by a ring of fire. She spun, desperate for even the smallest of gaps, but there were none. She was enclosed as neatly by flames as she'd been by water the night before.

They began edging closer to her, and the air shimmered in the heat, pulsed against her. Astrid ripped off her cloak and wrapped it like a massive scarf over her mouth. Her eyes stung and panic clawed like a leashed beast against her chest.

She blinked, forced moisture into her eyes, as she caught sight of sprites dancing in the fire, their heads thrown back in glee.

"Come join us," one called as it leapt and spun, dizzy with joy.

There was a wildness, an abandon to their dance, and Astrid found herself leaning forward, dangerously close to the heat. The smell of singed hair jerked her back.

The sprites laughed harder, twirling closer and closer as they gave themselves up to the crackle and hiss, to the heat.

"You can be wild as we are, our dearest one. Come join the dance."

Astrid had the clear image of Tomas blowing the bellows on the fire, the air feeding it, strengthening it.

Fire needed air. They didn't call her their dearest one for nothing.

But air did not need fire. She would not obey.

When do you ever? It was as if Bjorn had leaned over and whispered in her ear, and confidence surged through her. She smiled beneath the scarf her cloak made, at once sure of herself, and her strength.

Her instinct was to draw the air to her. To blow this fire out in a gale of wind. The rush of air tugged the curtains at the windows inward, but the sprites fell upon her gale like starving wolves on fresh meat, leaping higher still.

A sprite boldly fingered Astrid's dress with a flame-tipped hand, and she slapped at it with the edge of her cloak.

If air fed it, would no air kill it?

Through the wool of her cloak, Astrid took a deep breath and sent the air away, imagined it flying out, a whirlwind in reverse, with her at the epicenter.

There was sudden silence, as if a heavy door had slammed between her and a raucous party, and every flame was extinguished.

She waited one more beat of her heart in the pitch dark to make sure every spark was dead, and then willed the air back.

Expecting smoke, she took a breath through her cloak, but it was as if there had never been a fire. She could only smell the sweet oils in the candle wax.

She stood in the room, in the dark, and waited.

The candles suddenly relit, and the woman stepped into the cottage.

"Welcome." She looked Astrid straight in the eye, with no apology. "I am Dame Ild." The corners of her mouth turned up when she said the word 'Dame', as if it amused her.

"You wanted my power." Astrid felt slightly apart from herself. Detached.

"It was part of the test, but I'm sure Berge and Elv

had misgivings leaving this one to me." Dame Ild smiled suddenly, a genuine smile, and her face lit up, warm and inviting. "There is nothing more tempting on a freezing night than a fire, eh?" She laughed.

"I am one of you." Astrid spoke slowly, her whole body trembling at the revelation. "The four of us . . ." She looked absently for a chair and stumbled to one. Flopped down.

"Hmmm. We've been wondering where you've been. Must be seventeen years since we saw the old one, at least."

"I . . . didn't know."

"So we realized. Seems you've landed on your feet though. Caught the prince before he had a chance to work out what you were." There was a slender thread of heat in her words. Of spite.

Astrid shook off her daze. "Would that have made a difference? Why shouldn't he love the Wind Hag?"

"Do you see any of the three of us with a man in tow?" Dame Ild moved to her fireplace and Astrid saw for the first time a stew pot sat simmering there. "We're too powerful. The men don't like it."

"There aren't many like Bjorn." Astrid stood, and joined her hostess at the fire. They were sisters of sorts, and the youngest two of the four. She sensed they would have a long future together.

Dame Ild's face softened. "No. There are none like him. You found the only one strong enough to accept you as you are."

"And I lost him." Astrid was surprised how stark her voice sounded. Shocked when she felt tears on her cheeks. The second time she'd cried in as many days.

Dame Ild moved to the table near the fire and picked up a slim golden object lying there. "Here. This is all the help I can give you. That and the use of Stratus for your final day's journey to the East Wind."

Astrid took the delicate golden flute, struck by its elegant simplicity. "Thank you. I am in your debt."

"Ah. The Wind Hag owes me a favor." Dame Ild smiled. "Let us eat and drink to that."

"Dame Elv said something similar." Astrid frowned. "What does it mean?"

Ild shot her a wicked grin. "You'll work it out soon enough."

Astrid turned the flute in her hand, her fingers tracing the smooth gold lines. "You owed the favors, before."

Dame Ild did not answer as she laid the bowls upon the table. Her eyes glinted in the firelight. And for a moment, Astrid saw her as she truly was. More powerful, more magical, than she could ever imagine being herself.

And yet, Dame Ild once owed the Wind Hag so dearly, her delight at now having the balance in her favor made her smile like a child at a birthday celebration.

Which meant Astrid could be as powerful as her one day, if not more so.

And the question that kept bumping up against her mind, a small fishing boat against a storm-swept dock, was did she want that for herself?

Chapter Twenty-seven

Stratus sped on the back of the wind sprites, over rolling plains and low mountain ranges. As she clung to him, as the muscles in his legs and back bunched beneath her, Astrid felt a stab of nervousness at the thought of facing the East Wind. In theory, she was its mistress, yet who was she to command it?

Bjorn would say if she was the Wind Hag, she must act like the Wind Hag. Be bold. But he had a right to his power. Had sacrificed himself for the greater good and shown himself worthy.

What had she done?

Perhaps it was not what she had done but what she could do? Astrid's heart lurched as Stratus suddenly dived through the air, angling down toward the highest peak in the range before them.

The time for vacillating was over.

She was not capable of bluster and lies, of presenting herself as more than she was. Neither was she powerless—the dames had shown her that.

An 'oh' escaped her lips as she took in the significance of her thought. Perhaps the tests were to help her control her winds as much as anything. What good was a Wind Hag otherwise?

An eerie whistling rose and fell in the buffeting gale around the peak, low as a moan, high as a shriek.

Stratus alighted on a wide stone ledge near the top of the mountain and Astrid slid reluctantly off his trembling back. With a snort, he broke free of her hands and ran straight off the far side of the ledge, banking in the air, his eyes wild.

The sight of his terror chilled her. But fear and doubts had no place in her life. Time was wasting.

She imagined Bjorn treading toward his waiting troll-bride in time with the seconds beating past.

She set down her sack, smoothed her hair and straightened her back.

"East Wind," she called.

"You have come at last." The whisper was in her left ear, from behind, and every hair on her scalp and arms rose. Warm, humid air enveloped her, making her cold fingers and nose tingle.

"I came as soon as I realized."

"Realized what?" the voice breathed.

"Who I am."

An arm, solid, but solid as air becomes solid when channeled at speed, slid over her shoulder and came to rest just above her breast. Near her heart.

"Do you understand what your absence has meant?"

"Tell me." Astrid turned, forcing down her fear, keeping her voice steady and her face calm.

An image of a man stood before her, an outline of gray-blue cloud. A strong, handsome face framed by hair so long, it flirted with his thighs. Long robes swirled around his feet, and she saw his hands were strong, his wrists thick. There was challenge in his eyes.

"We have been left to fight among ourselves, to battle about who has reign over the lands. Without you to give orders, we have turned against each other."

"Did you not think to find me?" Astrid wondered now why they never had. She couldn't take her eyes off him, the way he shimmered insubstantial as a mirage, yet the force of his presence was unmistakable.

The East Wind lifted both his hands and shrugged. "We thought the Wind Hag had not passed her mantle on."

"But the air sprites knew where I was. They have been with me always."

The East Wind stilled, his hair and robes no longer moving in constant motion. "They would only have kept your location secret if . . ."

Astrid watched his face change, saw a flash of hurt.

"If what?" The answer came to her before he could reply. "If the Wind Hag bade them to do so?"

He nodded, and warm air rippled over her. "How old were you when the Wind Hag died?"

"Three years old."

"Too young to exert your will over us."

"And if one of you no longer wished to be commanded by your mistress . . ." There was a hitch in her throat, a tremble within for her younger, vulnerable self.

"Kill the new Wind Hag?" The East Wind's eyes seemed to blaze, even though they were made of nothing but smoky cloud, and heat radiated off him. "Never."

"Yet she thought there was a chance of it," Astrid said. "And why would she if she didn't already suspect one of you did want to be rid of her?"

She crossed her arms over her chest, her mind tracing all the threads.

"How did Norga find the Wind Hag? How did she come to kill her?" She'd thought, from Bjorn's story, that Norga had seen the Wind Hag take him and had followed her, but what if she'd been told by someone else? By one of the Winds.

"She was killed taking the boy, wasn't she?" The East Wind spoke bitterly. "She was obsessed with him."

"Did she really mean to keep him?" She couldn't imagine it.

"She thought he would consent to stay. To marry her, when he got older." He said the words like he was swearing.

"What would a husband have meant to you?" Astrid asked. Nothing good, by the sound of it.

The East Wind's hair flew out around his head, humid air radiating out with it. "A master as well as a mistress. As if we were not enough for her. She looked at the human world and longed for the love of man and wife. Longed for beauty."

Despite the heat, his words chilled Astrid. Was she no longer human? Had the Wind Hag's gift changed her that much? Then she thought of Ild's jealousy of her love for Bjorn, and saw in it a reflection of the Wind Hag's need.

"Who of you had most cause to feel aggrieved?" She needed to know if one of her Winds wished her ill.

The East Wind pondered the question, his hair lowering and swirling around his shoulders. "The North Wind. The Wind Hag liked to walk the earth looking for a husband, and she liked to do it in warm weather. Which meant either me, or South or West carried her. North rarely had a turn."

"Would he have tried to kill the Wind Hag?"

The East Wind shook his head. "I cannot believe any one of us would have." There was a thread of iron certainty in his voice.

Astrid grimaced. She had no time to uncover a possible plot against her. "This is something I will have to sort out later. I need to know if you can tell me where the place is that is east of the sun and west of the moon."

The East Wind shook his head. "I have never heard of such a place. Why do you need to know?"

Astrid swallowed down her panic. "The troll who killed the Wind Hag has taken my lover there. I would defeat her and get him back."

"Always this one troll, interfering with us." The East Wind's fists clenched. "And always the Wind Hag searches for a lover or a husband."

And in this one thing, she and the old Wind Hag shared the same object of affection. Astrid tossed her head, her hair flying back in the East Wind's angry blowing. She would not apologize for her love. And she would not give it up for her Winds.

"Would the West Wind know where this place is?" Her heart thundered in her chest. Desperate for any chance.

"West of the moon?" He nodded. "Perhaps."

"Would you carry me to the West Wind?"

"You do not command me to take you?" The East Wind held her gaze and they stood for a long moment saying nothing.

Should she command him? She was not used to this indecision. She was out of her depth.

"Until I have your respect, I have no right to command you," Astrid said at last.

"The West Wind and I have fought for dominance over each other for the last seventeen years. You ask me to carry you to my enemy."

Astrid knew the simple clarity of fear. She needed his help at any cost or her quest to save Bjorn was doomed. "I promise I will do everything in my power to reconcile you with your brother. Consider this a favor to me and the first step to regaining the balance."

"A favor? Beware, mistress, of putting yourself in my debt. Of being beholden to one of us, and not the others." He turned from her and looked west.

Astrid realized the mistake she could have made and shivered. All she wanted was to get to Bjorn, but she would not find him unless she set her house in order first. Only if the winds were hers to command could she receive the aid she needed.

She drew herself up. "Take me to the West Wind." She bent and took up her sack full of precious gifts, stepped to join the East Wind on the very edge of the ledge.

"You have decided to command me, after all?" He looked at her, a slanting, probing look. She held his gaze and nodded.

"Your wish, Mistress," he said solemnly, turning to bow low on one knee. "Let us fly."

He expanded, becoming three, four times larger than he had been. He reached out and scooped Astrid up in his hand, turned back to the ledge, and leapt off.

———⟨≪⟩———

If she thought the wind steeds were fast, the East Wind was lightning. The air fought them as they whipped through it, ripping at Astrid's clothes and forcing her to close her eyes, cover her head with her hands.

Like she was cowering.

When she realized what she was doing, when she remembered who she was, her cheeks burned. What kind of Wind Hag was she?

She fought the buffering, lifted her head and then, with eyes still closed, willed a shield of calm around her body. When she opened her eyes, all resistance had faded.

Now she could look ahead with the East Wind, his face determined and solemn, as he sped toward the brother who had become his enemy.

They flew high, far higher than the wind steeds, and the earth lay mapped out below her, a patchwork of valleys, mountains and twisting rivers gleaming in the late afternoon sun.

After many hours they came to a plateau, a long escarpment ending in a massive ridge of peaks. The East Wind gripped her a little tighter, and Astrid felt the familiar clutch of fear in her throat.

She saw a shimmer in the air far ahead, a moving mirage, and peered forward.

"What is it?"

"The fore-guard," the East Wind said, and brought his other hand across, to hold Astrid more securely.

"They're attacking us?" She leaned even further

forward.

Attacked? By her own subject? She didn't have *time* for this.

She saw them coming, fast as the East Wind, speeding toward a headlong collision.

"What will they try to do?"

"Force me back."

At last Astrid could see the shields in the approaching air sprites' hands. They were going to smack into the East Wind and drive him back.

"I could send out air sprites of my own?" The East Wind lifted an eyebrow, and Astrid shook her head.

"I will deal with this. We're wasting time." She imagined the air around her, completely under her control. The air sprites sped closer and closer, until they were only a field away.

With a firm nod of her head, a projection of will, she threw up a solid wall of air before them, and watched them slam against it.

"Fly over them," she called to the East Wind, and dropped the wall.

He lifted up over the sprites as he sped past, then began to dive, almost in freefall through the pale blue sky.

Astrid looked back, and saw the sprites trailing them, their shields no longer raised.

"Brother," the East Wind shouted over the shrieking gale as they came to the West Wind's mountain top. "I bring the Wind Hag—"

Before he'd finished his sentence, something smashed into them, knocking Astrid out of the East Wind's careful hands.

She fell downwards, tumbling, her scream echoing against the sheer cliffs of the mountains.

Sharp rocks and outcrops flew past, and below, growing larger and closer, a narrow river, edged with trees.

She needed to do something at once or she would die.

If she could create a vertical wall of air, she could create a horizontal one. Astrid focused on the air beneath her, created a cushion of it, and bounced to a stop just short of the tree tops. She lay, weak with relief, then dragged herself to standing, shaking with fear and rage.

"Up," she commanded her platform. She rose fast, giving it a spin so she spiraled up, looking on all sides so nothing could take her by surprise again.

The two winds twisted and fought each other over the edge of a sheer-faced cliff, the West Wind's smoky mirage clearly whiter against the East Wind's gray. Clouds boiled above them and the West Wind drew back a hammer's fist.

"You!" Fury burned in her, her dress and cloak billowing as the agitated air around her spun and twisted. She imagined the air as an extension of her own hand, grabbed the West Wind by his long hair and jerked him back. Smacked him into the ground.

He lay, stunned, for a moment. "Wind Hag?"

As he rose, his sharp etched face was comical in its surprise and disbelief, as if he'd had no idea it was his mistress he'd just thrown down the side of a mountain.

Of course, he could be lying. He could be the one the Wind Hag had been afraid would harm her. He'd certainly just had a good try.

Astrid willed her air platform over, and stepped onto the rocky ledge. Looked the West Wind straight in the eyes, feeling the sparks of anger flying from her own. "You do not attack each other again, or you deal with me."

The West Wind bowed. "I have no need to fight him if you are back."

Astrid gave him a cool look.

"I'm back."

Chapter Twenty-eight

"I have never heard of a place east of the sun and west of the moon." The West Wind shrugged.

"I had hoped you would know it." Fear closed up Astrid's throat, and she could barely speak. But she couldn't let the fear control her. Then she would never win. "We will have to ask one of the other winds. Between the four of you, there is surely no place on this earth you do not go."

"I'll take you," the West Wind said.

She flicked her eyes to his face, distrustful of his eagerness. The East Wind was tired, slower than the West Wind would be, but trustworthy and safe.

"Try the South Wind first." The East Wind looked north thoughtfully.

"You think the North Wind is the one?" Astrid turned north herself.

"What one?" West looked between them.

"The Wind Hag suspected her death was no accident." Heat radiated off East again, and Astrid saw how deeply hurt and insulted he was, still. "She thought one of us . . . " He could not even say it. "She set some air sprites to guard our new mistress and keep her hidden from us."

She saw West half disappear in shock, then he drew himself up to double his size, his dry air sucking up East's humidity. "That is . . . " He seemed speechless.

Her reservations toward him evaporated like the moisture from East's breath. She would accept his offer of a ride.

"To the South Wind then." She bowed to East, and he blew a kiss to her cheek. The West Wind extended his hand for her to climb upon and as soon as she knelt in his palm, he flew straight up in the air.

When they were so high Astrid felt she could reach out and touch the stars appearing in the deep-dusk blue of the sky, he turned south. Racing against time.

"Who is stronger? You or the South Wind?" Astrid's voice was thick with sleep. She'd closed her eyes shortly after the West Wind began the journey, and she was not sure how many hours had passed.

"The South." West's answer was short. "But you'll see that soon enough."

While she was sleeping he'd flown lower, and the full moon shone an eerie silver light over the red dunes of the desert below them.

"Waves of sand," she said, wonder-struck.

"We are close to where the South Wind lives." West dropped lower still, and like the East Wind had done, gripped her tighter. "Be ready."

"What do you expect?"

"Dust devils, for a start. Are you afraid?"

"No, I'm not."

Ahead, she saw a swirl of sand on the horizon, twisting in tiny whirlwinds that raced toward them.

"Dust devils?" she asked, and West nodded, his sharp face tense. He looked as if he were braced for impact, and Astrid focused ahead of her.

These air sprites were messier than West's fore-guard. Less controlled as they spun in their blasting sand spirals.

"Throw me into the middle of them," she said to West.

He jerked his head to look at her, his mouth open.

"I have a plan." She kept her tone mild.

The old Wind Hag would perhaps have spoken sharply, angrily, but Astrid was too new to her power to blame him for doubting her. "Get ready . . . now!"

"As you command." His voice was skeptical, dry as the air he blew across the earth. But he threw her. Perfectly into the middle of the advancing dust devils.

As she hoped, they were confused. Expecting only the West Wind, they did not know what to make of the woman hurtling through the air at them. She saw their slim, narrow faces and bodies where the sand blew against them, creating shifting glimpses, making their movements seem jerky.

She formed her platform just before she touched the sand, then spun it up like she'd done on the mountain, this time sucking all the air with her as she went. Creating her own whirlwind. Creating chaos within chaos.

The strength of her tornado far outweighed the power of the sprites, and they shrieked in rage as they were sucked into the vortex. She rose up through the eye, passed the screaming sprites caught in their whirling prison and found the West Wind waiting for her at the top.

He met her gaze with respect. "Let us find the South Wind."

She stepped from her platform back into his palm and they drifted slowly forward, toward a rocky outcrop standing alone in the vast desert, glimmering silver-gray and orange in the moonlight.

"I bring the Wind Hag," West called out, his shout a high whistle against the rocks.

"You lie." The answering cry engulfed them in hot, dry air that sucked the moisture from Astrid's lungs. And then it seemed the desert sands rose up around them, and every tiny grain bombarded them.

Shocked, Astrid widened the layer of air she'd had around herself since she'd traveled with East, bringing West under its protection, and looked in astonishment at the sand storm assaulting them.

Anger sparked within. She could lose Bjorn. This discord could cost her everything.

She sent the sand flying at them back with equal force.

She knew the South Wind started feeling the sting of his own attack when the bombardment slacked off. Then slowly came to a stop.

At last. Relief coursed through her.

"Wind Hag?"

"Enough proof for you?" Astrid unclenched her fists. Saw the hazy red cloud of the South Wind shimmer into view. Like his sprites, he was lean and sinewy, with high cheeks and a thin, patrician nose. He bowed.

"Mistress, I apologize, I thought . . ."

"I was gone forever?" Could he have been the one who set Norga on the Wind Hag?

"I thought our old Mistress had not passed her power on. I cannot believe . . . Where have you *been* all this time?"

There was a note of relief, of joy, even, in his tone.

"You are happy to see me?" Astrid watched him carefully.

He looked astounded at the question. His mouth worked as if as he were at a loss. "Yes."

She believed him.

"Can you tell me where the place is that is east of the sun, and west of the moon?"

South frowned. Shook his head. "I have never heard of it."

———◆———

The South Wind flew low, and Astrid, tucked safely in the crook of his arm, could see by the way he threw his head back, how he closed his eyes, that he loved twisting through the mountains and swooping over the plateaus.

But he was tense, his brows drawn together, and Astrid sensed his deep unease.

She shared it.

The North Wind was the most powerful of the four. And the only chance she had left to find Bjorn.

They were flying slower now over the quiet forests, the snow sliding off the trees they passed over, melted by the touch of South's hot air.

The ground no longer flashed beneath them as they made for the mountain tops in the distance, glistening white in the sun.

"We are long past the midway point where the North and I usually clash." South slowed even more. "I will be too tired to help you against him if I don't rest. The cold drains me."

"Just get me there as fast as you can. If I'm not strong enough to take him on alone, we are lost anyway."

South struggled up and over the high peaks, leaving a groove of melted snow behind him, and at last let the cold air drag him down the other side of the mountain range, unresisting.

They were both dumbstuck by the endless fields of ice stretching before them. Dunes of snow piled high on an open plain, the glare so bright, Astrid had to turn her head and look down in subjugation.

There was no cover, nothing to hold the cold back across the icy wasteland, and it battered against Astrid's protective layer of air as they sank down the mountain side, so insidious it seeped through. Its strength was a shock, and she flinched as its fingers reached out to claw at her face. South slid down the slope, coming to rest in a slushy puddle, his smoky red barely visible, even against the bright white of the snow.

"I need to rest." The heat of his voice was greedily absorbed by the cold.

"Get back your strength, I'll go on alone." Astrid jumped from his hand, the snow crunching under her old leather boots. The bite of cold was immediate, as if she'd dipped her feet into a frozen fjord. She created a platform of air at ground level, stepped onto it to keep her feet from freezing.

She placed her sack of treasures next to South. "Watch this for me."

The time had come to face her strongest enemy. And perhaps her strongest ally.

"Forward," she whispered, and her platform skated across the snow smooth as a skier down a mountain. She widened her bubble of air and the extra layer against the cold brought relief.

She looked back and saw South huddled a good distance away. He would hopefully go unnoticed where he lay. There was no more reason to delay calling her last hope.

She threw back her head. "North Wind."

The absorbent silence of the snow plains swallowed her shout, and it seemed to have been muffled and killed.

She tried again. "North Wind."

Behind her, a rumble began. The air trembled and she spun her air platform in the direction of the sound as a boom echoed against the steep cliffs. An avalanche of snow slid down the mountain, throwing up a plume before it like foam on a massive wave.

Her eyes wide, Astrid saw South lying directly in the path of the avalanche. Astrid shot her platform forward, swooping toward him and her precious sack, dived to grab them up just as the snow engulfed them all.

For a moment, the world was white and mad. She tumbled through the loose snow, and felt the touch of an icy hand on her arm.

Immediately, it was as if she were floating in calm shallows. She jerked her head and looked straight into the silver-blue eyes of a snow sprite as large as South.

"My mistress gives me leave to aid you." The sound of the sprite's voice was like the hiss of snow sliding over snow. And her hands were carrying Astrid safely through the maelstrom. "What would you have me do?"

Frozen water. Dame Elv to the rescue. Astrid felt her heart sing. This was no mere sprite. This must be Dame Elv's equivalent of one of Astrid's Winds. She owed the dame another favor, and she didn't care.

"Find the South Wind and my sack. Lift them out of the snow and keep them safe, please."

The Snow Sprite looked curious, as if she would like to ask a question, but she nodded and released Astrid, diving to the right, away through the fast-flowing snow.

The moment she let go, Astrid began to tumble again. She relaxed, stopped fighting it.

Somewhere above, North hovered, watching. Astrid could think here in this chaos of white, despite the cold and the somersaults.

Was this North's test of her strength or a show of deadly force?

Whatever his motivation, he would expect her to come straight up, she was sure. Expect her to fight her way to the surface, panicked.

Ah, the dames had taught her well.

She would not do the obvious. She looked sideways, to the edge of the avalanche. She could escape from the side, and fly upward, against the flow. Hopefully come up behind the North Wind. The last of her subjects to be chastened.

She created a tunnel of air through the snow, curving to the left, and shot along it fast as a bobsleigh. The avalanche spat her out into air even icier than it had been before and to keep low, she formed the platform beneath her stomach, sliding uphill through the air just as she'd once slid downhill on a plank as a child. She kept close to the roaring avalanche, tucked under its left shadow, out of sight, as she sped up the mountain.

When she reached the top, she stood, her eyes screwed against the glare, searching the slopes.

Where was he . . . there!

A shimmer of white, almost invisible, half way down the mountain.

He would respect and obey her only if she could outwit and outmaneuver him. Ruthless as he was himself.

Ruthless.

Astrid took a deep breath of thin, cold air, and dove down the mountain.

Chapter Twenty-nine

As the air whistled past her in her free fall, she snagged a ribbon of it in her mind, made a taut, strong rope of it, gave it a loop. Her hand opened and closed, as if to hold the invisible lasso, and it was there. Cold and strangely alive against her palm.

There he was, just a little way below her, looking for her, waiting to see if he'd buried her for good or whether she would try to fight her way out.

She drew back her arm and threw the rope. Willed it to catch him in its noose and then pulled it tight. Shot herself past him and swung up the other way, looping the air rope a second time around him.

She risked a look at his face and she was glad she hadn't seen it before.

Cold as frost, sharp as an edge of ice, dangerous as a snow storm. The look he sent her was fury and hatred combined.

Yet she had him tied.

Just as the thought formed, he spun upward, arms pinned to his side, but still free to fly.

She hung on to the rope. Was pulled up with him.

"Was it you who arranged for the old Wind Hag's death?" she called.

She felt a jerk on the rope as he stopped dead, mid-air.

"No." His shout was loud enough to cause another, smaller avalanche on the lower slopes.

"What then? Why did she try to hide me from you?"

He didn't answer, instead he spun, higher and higher. Astrid looked down and saw the earth falling away from her, the heavens coming closer, no longer blue, but black.

The time had come to end this. He was strong and rested, and he could drag her around for days. But up here, she had the bubble of air around her, and he had nothing. He was running out of raw material.

Astrid could feel from the way she moved through it that the air was thin here. Very thin.

Then North brought them up against the very edge of sky, and for the first time, Astrid felt a real, deep fear. North's flight hadn't been unthinking instinct. It had been ruthless calculation.

There would be no coming back if he pushed her out beyond the thin membrane that held back the universe.

If he used his body as a battering ram, if she wasn't quick enough in this slippery, thin air, it could happen.

"The others said you weren't capable of this." She allowed none of the fear to show in her face, or her voice. She was only too aware the air in her bubble would not last forever. "They said you were strong, you had reason to feel aggrieved, but you would never harm the Wind Hag."

Something flickered across his face. But so high up, in the strange light, she could not decipher it.

"What is the Mountain Prince to you?"

"Bjorn?" She frowned, confused. "My lover. My love."

"Again," he breathed, a sharp blast of icy air. "After all this time, he comes back again, and will not die."

"Die?" Her mouth snapped shut, and she stared at him, at his face, his eyes. "The yggren." Her voice seemed small and insignificant up here. Tinny.

It was as if one of the stars above focused its light on her, and she could see clearly at last. Wind and wood. Their ties were deep, their relationship forged at the beginning of time with the old tree itself. Far more powerful than Norga. Norga was insignificant against something this strong.

"The yggren were after Bjorn, not me. Trying to kill him. For you. At your request." Her voice caught on the last sentence, and she realized the air in her bubble was nearly gone. She glanced below, a quick flick of her eyes, and she saw the earth curve away to the right.

Her heart jerked.

She was bobbing like a fish just under the thin skin of ice on the water's surface, at the very, very top. She would be just as out of her element as a fish if she broke through to the unknown beyond.

The scale of it hit her, and she wanted to gasp in a huge breath, had to content herself with a quarter of that.

She needed to get down. But even more, she needed North to bow to her. She would never have his allegiance if she ran now.

Again, as she lifted her eyes back to his, she saw the flicker of something across his features, saw he was weakening. He'd taken her to his outer limit and he was feeling the effects.

"I am not the old Wind Hag."

He made a movement, a furious dismissal.

"No." Her voice could be as sharp as his. "Bjorn is my lover, not my everything. I love him, I don't worship him. And he has his own obligations, his own principality. You would not have two masters."

"Why always him?" The words were wrenched out, in pain.

"Because of *you*. He was in the forest near my house because of you."

She expected defiance, or anger, but instead she saw sadness and shame settle on his face.

"I told the troll the boy had been stolen, but I didn't think she would kill my mistress in the fight over him." He spoke so quietly, she barely heard him. "I didn't think anything could kill her. I just wanted the boy gone. Taken away so the Wind Hag would forget him."

"Make amends. Tell me where the place is that is east of the sun and west of the moon."

He drifted closer, and she did not flinch as he reached out an icy hand, sprinkled dancing stars of frost across her bubble.

"I know where it is only because I followed the troll there. It is like this place." He looked around them. "The outer reaches of everything. I only just had enough strength to get there the first time. But I know where it is."

"Then let me get my sack, and take me." She said the words calmly, on her last gulp of air.

He met her eyes, and nodded. Took her bubble like a fragile glass ball in his hands, and dived.

"You followed Norga after she killed the Wind Hag?"

Sack safely on her lap, Astrid knelt on North's palm as he blasted over the frozen plains.

"I could never trust her again. So I kept an eye on her, and the boy."

He rose, then dipped suddenly, as if to shake loose a difficult memory. "If only the Wind Hag had never seen him."

Astrid heard the bitterness in his voice, sensed his
deep bewilderment at the Wind Hag's fascination with
Bjorn. His old mistress had loved Bjorn for his looks, as a
young child. Astrid had fallen in love with the man,
without ever seeing his beauty. Had fallen in love with
who he was.

They came to the same man through opposite
paths.

North sighed, a sound as desolate and raw as the
landscape. "When I saw he was close to finding you, high
in the mountains above your valley, I found the troll and
told her where he was, and hoped she could persuade
him to give up."

"But he never did."

North glanced at her. "No, he never did."

Leaning forward, Astrid rested her cheek against
his palm for a moment, rose back up. "He honors me. He
believes in my strength. I will not give up what I am if we
find him, I give you my word."

North said nothing, but she thought perhaps there
was a lightening of the frown on his face. That his mouth
turned down less at the corners.

They reached the sea. North flew low and Astrid
glimpsed ivory-tipped waves of marbled green bowing
as they passed. Islands of ice floated in the distance, stark
white against a slate sky.

"What is Norga's land like?"

North huffed out a breath and churned up the sea. "A dark and terrible place. On the edge of a cliff where the sea is always cold and hungry, and the sky is always gray and listless. A place without hope."

Astrid clutched her sack tighter, dipped her hand within and felt the golden beauty, the soothing preciousness of the treasures within.

She didn't care if there was no hope in Norga's palace. She was bringing hope with her.

The piercing cries of gulls ripped Astrid out of a deep, dreamless sleep, and she sat up, heart fluttering, and looked over North's curled fingers.

Black cliffs loomed in the distance, the gulls flashes of white against the rock face as they dove from the ledges into the sea. A massive castle squatted on top, black as the rock it rose from. Astrid could not spy a single window in the wall facing the sea.

Exhaustion splintered the cold mask of North's face, and she glimpsed the strain. They flew so low it was as if they were skimming the surface like a skipping stone.

With a final effort, North landed them on a rocky beach which lurked beneath the cliffs like a surly, dirty tramp. It was littered with debris; old wood, rotting ropes of kelp, and the sand was covered with sharp, broken shells.

North collapsed just beyond the watermark. "I
had to rest here for two days last time I came." His voice
was barely audible.

Astrid leapt from his hand and as she did, he
shrunk down to the size of a man. She dissolved her air
bubble, and the decaying stink of the beach and the sharp
slap of cold air assaulted her.

"Thank you." Leaning forward, she smoothed his
hair. For the first time, it did not move constantly in the
eddies of air around him. There were none.

He found a large rock to lie on and closed his eyes,
the white vapor of him stark against its blackness.

This journey had cleaned the slate between them.
She was happy never to discuss his part in the old Wind
Hag's death, or her debt to him in finding this place
again. All tallies were cleared from the book.

"Will you tell the Mountain Prince I tried to kill
him? That I set those yggren on him?"

Ah. Not quite cleared.

"He deserves to know. The yggren are worried
that some of their number have turned to Norga. They
are deeply disturbed by it."

"I only spoke to two of the oldest ones. Ones who
remembered the time when it was just us and them. The
wind in the trees, with no other chatter around them."

"And both those two are dead, along with one
other."

North moved as if uncomfortable on the rock. "I am sorry for that. Sorry for all the deaths."

She rubbed her temple. "You are my responsibility now. We will find a way to appease the yggren."

North opened an eye. "The old Wind Hag told the air sprites to keep you hidden from my brothers and I, but I was watching that day in the forest with the troll, and I always knew where you were. I didn't think you'd be much of a Wind Hag, watching you grow up." He closed the eye again. "You seemed too slight. Too timid."

"And what do you think now?" Astrid felt a tiny stream of his cold air stir through her thin dress, and shivered.

"I have changed my views."

She smiled. "I'm going to spy out the land. Rest well."

Then she walked, ankles turning on the loose pebbles, toward the cliffs.

Toward her final obstacle to happiness.

Chapter Thirty

The cliff face was damp and her hands, slimy from clambering over rocks to reach it, could find nothing to hold. Her nose tingled in the cold, her cheeks flushed with the effort of getting even this short distance on the boulder-strewn beach. Her gaze traveled from the sack at her feet up the rock-face, disappearing beyond her sight.

"You could fly up." North's whisper was in her ear, although he still lay near the shoreline.

"I don't want Norga to learn I'm the Wind Hag," she whispered, putting her hands on the small of her back and blowing out a breath as she tilted her head up. There was no air here, that was the problem. Just as North said, it was the outer reaches of nowhere. Even the smallest action left her breathless.

"You won't have to convince her of anything if you're lying dead at the foot of these cliffs."

True enough.

She picked up the sack and thought of her air platform. Her feet did not so much as lift from the pebbles. "It isn't working."

"No wind sprites. No energy in the air." North

curled up on his rock. "It was worth a try."

Astrid stepped back to see more of the cliff, looking for a way up. She noticed for the first time the gulls were like none she'd seen before. Their wings were tiny, and they did not fly down to the sea, they dived. None were circling the air above her.

There were no air currents here for them to ride. Instead, they had to climb back up the cliff.

She watched one launch itself into the air and dive into the waves, then saw another shake itself out as it hopped through the foam of a retreating wave and made its way to the cliff. It began climbing up, jumping and scrabbling with beak, feet and wings.

If a little bird could do it, so could she. She bent to her sack and took out the golden apple. Put it in the deep pocket of her skirt. She was going into the unknown. Best to be prepared. North barely stirred as she trudged back to him and hid the sack beneath his rock.

She returned to the cliff, huffing for breath, and found the first hand and footholds. Hauled herself up. This lower part was relatively easy, she realized, when you found the right path, but from the level where the gulls nested, upwards, the cliff seemed an unbroken vertical slab of rock.

After a while, she stopped looking further than the next foothold or handhold. Taking every tiny advance as a success. She was gasping for breath, and felt she would never get enough air into her lungs.

When at last it seemed there was nowhere else to go, she started looking sideways, for a way to move across to a place where she could find another way up. She leaned against the freezing rock and tried to get her breathing under control.

Something ran across her hand, and she gave a low, breathless scream. A spider, black as the dripping, slick cliff face, furtive and hideous, scuttled off across the rock.

Another movement caught her eye, and then another. There were hundreds of them.

She shivered in revulsion at their protruding eyes and long, spiky legs. A few moved curiously toward her fingers, and suddenly the ledge she'd been eyeing didn't seem as impossible to reach as before. She leapt, gripping with the tips of her fingers, arching her back to push her body up against the rock.

When the pounding in her heart and head subsided, she saw there was a new way up and began moving again. As long as she was in motion, the spiders left her alone.

The castle wall was built from cliff stone. It grew seamlessly upward where the natural rock ended, and she saw as she climbed up each weathered and pitted stone slab there were no windows.

Their lack made her think of a fish she'd seen in the market once, churned up from the depths of the fjord by a storm; blind and disturbingly alien.

It gave her an uneasy sense of climbing over a living thing, sightless but sentient. Waiting for its moment to strike.

When she reached the top of the wall she clung just below the last layer of stone, her stomach clenched with nerves, her arms and legs quivering with exhaustion. She needed air. She tried to gulp it in as soundlessly as she could, afraid there would be a watcher or some guard above.

Inching up to peer over the top, she glimpsed a deep parapet, wide enough to hold twenty men abreast, and realized if she wanted to see into the castle beyond, she would need to risk crossing it. She looked carefully left and right, but there was no sign of anyone, and she struggled over the wall and forced her legs to move across the parapet as furtively as the cliff spiders below.

She knelt on the far side, legs trembling at the relief of being on a flat, solid surface, and peered over. The castle was built in a square, with the parapet running all around it. Below her was a massive courtyard and on the far side of it, opposite the wall she clutched with white-knuckled hands, were double doors leading out of the castle.

She'd expected to see trolls, but while there were a few standing or sitting around a huge wooden table in the center of the yard, there were more men and women. They did not walk about their business, they scuttled, crab-like, across the massive courtyard from one wing of the castle to the other, carrying food and linen.

They steered a wide path around the trolls and were dressed as poorly as she was herself.

Slaves?

Two of them, men in rough pants and stained tunics, were up on ladders, tying pine branches into an arch over the big doors.

A buzz started in Astrid's ears. Those pine branches were a gate of honor. Built over a bride's doorway in preparation for her wedding ceremony.

It seemed the world fell away for a moment before snapping her back to the present.

She had arrived just in time.

Astrid watched the men secure the final branch. Now she was here, the next step was to find Bjorn, and with the abundance of servants, slipping into the castle in her rags looked easier than she dared hope. But as she looked for a way down, a troll emerged from below and walked across the huge open space of the courtyard. Everyone she passed, the stable hands, a woman mopping the flagstones with an air of resignation, bowed low enough to touch their foreheads to their knees.

It could be Norga, but the troll looked young. Younger than the ones who'd attacked her after Bjorn had left. Young enough to be the bride-in-waiting.

Astrid watched her walk beneath the pine branch arch, nodding to the men as they scrambled down their ladders.

She was going for a walk. And she was the one person Astrid could be sure had contact with Bjorn.

She was the way in.

Crouching low, Astrid ran along the parapet, keeping close to the wall until it turned sharply inland, forming the right-hand wall of the courtyard. An open stairway angled down into the courtyard itself, but though it would be faster to take it and sneak out the front entrance, Astrid did not dare take the risk of being stopped.

Instead, she continued on until she was in line with the great entrance. She heaved herself over the wall, stopping for a moment to see which direction the troll was taking.

Norga's daughter, if it was her, crossed the open land beyond the castle entrance and disappeared over a low rise.

Astrid climbed recklessly down the wall, scraping her hands and knees against the rough stone in her haste. After her climb up the wet stones on the seaward side, it seemed much quicker and easier.

She turned again to spy her quarry, catching her breath at the same time, but the troll was nowhere in sight.

This side of the castle was built facing down the

peninsula, a gray-green moor that ended in a line of hills.
A river tumbled from their slopes and then twisted
sharply right, away from the castle, as if to avoid it. Near
the cliffs it cut a deep gorge into the rock and fell into the
sea, out of sight.

Panting, her palms stinging, her dress sticky
against her skin despite the chill air, Astrid leapt the final
distance to the ground. She landed hard, hobbling
forward until the pain in her shins subsided. Then she set
off swiftly through the low, scrubby bushes, in the same
direction at the troll princess.

The troll had a ten minute start but Astrid decided
that was to her advantage. She needed to be beyond
suspicion. She needed the troll to come to her. So she
would find a spot the troll had to pass on her way back to
the castle.

She came to a small meadow of grass and bush
beside the river, an open place where she was sure to be
seen, and sat down to wait.

What would draw the troll to her? After a
moment's hesitation, Astrid dipped her hand into her
pocket and brought out the golden apple. It almost
throbbed in her hand, and for a moment, her fingers
closed hard around it, and she struggled with the idea of
giving it up.

But she would. That was why she had it.

She began to toss it in the air like a ball, and
watched it gleam and shine in the sun, throwing wild

reflections into the water slipping past.

She did not know how many minutes had gone by before she felt the fine hairs on the back of her neck lift, felt the prickle of awareness of quarry under a hunter's gaze.

She looked up sharply, and saw the troll princess watching her from the path. As if the touch of Astrid's gaze broke some sort of spell, the princess strode toward her, and it took all the self-control Astrid possessed not to scramble to her feet as she loomed closer.

She hadn't expected the troll to be so big, although that seemed foolish now—she knew the size of them. The princess was more than head and shoulders above her. Her gray-green body was covered with a layered dress of the same colors, and she looked like a massive stone on the move.

There was also something in the set of her jaw, the gleam in her eye. She was intimidating. A power in her own right.

Not just a poor thing in the shadow of her mother.

"Good day," Astrid called, and her voice cracked.

The troll princess stopped just in front of her, and Astrid could see her nose grew almost to her lips, bent a little to the left. A pungent scent of hot rock wafted from her.

"What is that you have?" The beady eyes barely looked at Astrid's face, they were fixed on the golden apple, glowing softly in Astrid's cupped hands.

"A golden apple." Astrid struggled to stop the quiver of her voice.

The princess reached out a hand, her fingers bending into a claw, her fingernails black. She stopped a mere snatch away.

Astrid did not draw back, but her hands closed more tightly around the cool surface of the apple, and at last, the princess looked her in the eyes.

"I want it."

Astrid shook her head, unable to say a word under the force of that gaze. They both knew the only thing stopping the troll from taking it by force was the magic of the apple itself. Magical things could only be given freely, otherwise Astrid would not be in a position to bargain at all.

"I will give anything for it." There was a wistful, childlike quality to the troll's voice and Astrid saw her eyes were dreamy as she gazed at the gleaming treasure.

The troll's wistfulness gave her confidence and strength. "You cannot give me what I want for it."

"Name it." The troll knelt beside Astrid, still looming.

"I hear there is a prince locked in the castle over the hill." Astrid moved the apple onto her lap, covered it completely with her hands. She gripped it tightly, to stop them trembling.

The troll went still. "So there is."

"I hear he is handsome as a god. They say he is a

god. Or the son of one."

The troll snorted. "He'd like to think so."

"I'm getting married soon." Astrid managed to lower her eyes demurely. "They say if a woman spends the night with a god, they are blessed with fertility forever."

"Do they?" The troll princess barked out a laugh.

Astrid took a deep, stuttering breath. "I will give you my precious apple for a night with the prince."

The troll lifted a hand to her face, tapped her fingers against a cheek that looked fuzzy with mold. "For all the good it will do you, I agree to those terms."

Relief engulfed Astrid as if she'd been dunked in a bracing sea, but she kept her head down, her eyes on the sparse dry grass of the field. "How will you arrange it?"

"Give me the apple and I will tell you."

Astrid shook her head, and she didn't need to pretend the stubborn line of her mouth.

The troll looked regretfully at the treasure.

"Come tonight to the castle. I will meet you at the gate after the evening meal and take you to the prince's chamber. I'll come for you again in the morning at first light."

Astrid nodded. "You will get the apple when your end of this is complete."

A snarl escaped from the troll's mouth, and she drew herself up. "Do you know who you address, peasant?"

Astrid opened her eyes wide and shook her head.

"Princess Dekla. Show some respect."

Astrid nodded, but she did not apologize and she kept the apple tightly clasped.

"You're either simple or you're impertinent." Dekla jumped to her feet, amazingly quick, and for a moment, Astrid thought she'd strike out.

But her eye fell on the apple again, and she took a step back, as if to put the temptation of a sound beating out of reach.

"I will see you tonight." With a final, longing look at the apple, Dekla turned back to the castle.

Astrid watched her go, and wondered what Dekla would do if she realized the man Astrid intended to marry was the very one the troll princess was shutting her in a room with that night.

Astrid stood, small and insignificant, before the barred doors of Norga's castle. She fiddled with the apple deep in her skirt pocket, North's entreaties for her to reconsider echoing in her head, and the weight of Dame Elv's bread heavy in her churning stomach.

A scrape of wood on slate sounded to her right, and a sliver of light shone from a small door cut into one of the massive wooden gates.

"Come," Dekla whispered, and Astrid took a

tentative step forward.

Dekla shifted uneasily, glancing over her shoulder into the dark courtyard.

"The guards are inside, having their ale. Hurry."

Astrid gathered her courage and slipped over the threshold.

The moment she was through, Dekla closed the door and shot the bolt across, careful not to make a sound.

Without a word, she strode to the inner-castle entrance, and Astrid had to jog to keep up. When they reached it, the troll princess blocked the open door and peered inside before jerking her head for Astrid to follow her.

As she stepped into the castle, Astrid was hit by the smell of troll. Iron-scented rock and moss. She remembered leaning up against the mountain door, smelling that same smell as the wind bombarded her, as Norga's killing team closed in, and shivered.

Dekla led the way to an open staircase and Astrid stayed close to the wall as she pulled herself up the massive, uneven steps.

They reach a passageway, and Dekla stopped at the third door on the left. "I do not care how badly things go. I don't care what happens to you in there. You stay within, quiet, until I come for you at first light. I cannot risk standing here to listen for you."

Astrid nodded, keeping the smile from her face,

hoping her eyes wouldn't give her joy away.

She hid her impatience as Dekla unlocked the door and held it open for her. As she ducked under the troll's arm and glanced back, she saw the satisfied smirk on her rival's face as the door swung closed.

A cold fist closed around her stomach as she took in the room. A small candle gave off an unsteady light, revealing a prison cell.

A narrow bed lay against a wall, and a chair and small table stood in the center of the chamber. There were no windows, and Astrid realized they were in the sea-facing part of the castle, that the wall before her was the one she had scaled early that morning.

But all these realizations were just background to the focus of the room.

Bjorn lay on the bed, his eyes closed.

"My love," she whispered, kneeling beside him. "I have come for you."

He made no sound, and suddenly stricken, Astrid reached out a hand and touched his face. He was warm, alive. But she could hear now from his breathing he was in a deep, unnatural slumber.

The horror of that realization seemed to stop time.

"No." Her anguished cry was echoed back at her by the dark walls. This could not be. After everything, after managing to do the impossible, to be right here with him, for him to be enchanted . . .

She turned to look at the small table, at the

remains of food on the plate. Sniffed the air. The smell of the rich stew lingered, and was at odds with the starkness of the cell.

So, enchanted, or perhaps . . . drugged.

There would be no joyful reunion tonight.

Chapter Thirty-one

Bjorn lay as if dead. He wore the shirt she'd wished for him, but the three drops of tallow over his heart were no longer the only stains marring the snowy white linen. They were lost in the grime and grey now.

Still, not even the filth of Norga's castle could dim his beauty. Her breath caught as she watched him in the weak light of the candle.

Something moved, furtive and sly, and she jerked her eyes up. A cliff spider, as big as her hand, eyed her from the dripping cell wall above Bjorn. It did a little to-and-fro dance, as if undecided which way to leap.

Astrid watched it warily and shrieked as it dropped onto Bjorn's chest.

She flapped her hands ineffectually and it stared up at her with shiny black eyes, unconcerned. Dekla's little watchdog.

Astrid edged to the table, too afraid to take her eyes off it, even for a moment. She reached back, slid the plate off.

She lunged, flicked the repulsive thing off Bjorn and onto the floor, and jumped on it. Jumped until it was a squashed nothing beneath her worn-out shoes.

Then she lay her head on Bjorn's chest and wept until the weak dawn light edged beneath the door.

———⟨✦⟩———

She was standing, waiting, when Dekla opened the door, her face a careful blank.

"Cried all night, did you?" Dekla's eyes were full of hard amusement. "Why is that?"

Astrid said nothing and Dekla glanced into the room.

"He doesn't look like he's moved since when I first let you in."

Astrid clamped back the scream within her. She looked at Bjorn one last time.

He stirred, on the brink of waking, and Dekla moved as if stung. She grabbed Astrid by the shoulder and shoved her out the door, slamming it closed and turning the lock in one panicked movement.

"Time to go." She spoke as if short of breath and her hand trembled slightly as she held it out expectantly.

Astrid forced herself to plunge her own hand into her pocket and bring out the golden apple.

Moments before she dropped it into the troll's palm, the whisper of a footstep on stone sounded just behind them.

The shock, the abject fear in Dekla's eyes, made

Astrid clutch the apple to her chest, and drop it back in her pocket. She stepped back, crouching down, deep in the shadows, and Dekla turned toward the footsteps, blocking Astrid with her body.

"Mother?"

Astrid saw her palms slide up and down her sides, the jagged black nails of her fingers snagging and pulling the wool. When there was no answer, no further sound of footsteps, she bunched the fabric up in fists. Squeezed until her knuckles were white through the sage green of her skin.

"Mother?"

At last the footsteps moved again, and the shadows around Astrid deepened as something big blocked off even more of the dawn light coming from the thin slits of the windows facing the courtyard.

"Who were you talking to?"

"No one."

Dekla had been expecting the question, Astrid could tell by her smooth response. She'd recovered well from her shock at her mother's spying presence.

"You said something." The voice was menacing, and Astrid was suddenly aware of the strength of her opponent. This troll had captured Bjorn and enchanted him. She must never forget how powerful she was.

"Just talking to myself."

The smack of flesh against flesh, the crack of a hand across a cheek, made Astrid bite back a cry. She stuffed her fingers in her mouth and stared up from the dark corner where she crouched. She'd rather know if a blow was coming her way than be taken by surprise. She always had done. It had made her father hit her harder. To him, her looking him in the eyes was a challenge.

"That's for all the sulking you've been doing," Norga said, her voice icy. "Going out for long walks, skulking in passageways talking to yourself. I'm making you the Mountain Princess. I'm putting you over the yggren, over the sprites. And what thanks do I get for it?"

Dekla said nothing, as if she knew no response would be the right one. Any answer would earn her another blow.

Astrid watched Dekla's nervous fingers, and remembered her own twitches with her father.

This scene had been played out many times between mother and daughter.

Had Dekla been happy when her mother was with Bjorn's father, playing princess? She'd been abandoned for a more beautiful life, even though it was all a pretense.

Dekla was sobbing quietly, holding her cheek with both hands. She did not even glance Astrid's way.

"Stop sniveling. Not here."

Dekla moved a little, and at last, Astrid could see Norga. She looked an older version of her daughter, but her face was harder. Crueler. She was bigger by at least a head. Double Astrid's height.

She pointed at Bjorn's door and lowered her voice. "Get some backbone. You'll need it to control the golden boy." She half-raised her hand, as if to strike out again, but changed her mind, and instead lashed out with her foot at Astrid.

Her clog clipped Astrid's hip and pain exploded in her side. Astrid could not help the whimper that escaped her gritted teeth. When had Norga noticed her?

"Get to work." Norga carried on along the passage, and panting with nausea, Astrid heard her thunder down the stairs. She leant back against the wall, trying to banish the stars before her eyes.

The chill stone on her neck steadied her, but there was something wrong with the silence.

She looked up, and found Dekla staring down at her, her eyes gleaming at Astrid's pain. Her pride assuaged by her mother's kick.

The witness to her own humiliation, humiliated.

"Get up." Dekla did not offer a hand.

Slowly, using the wall to her back to help her, Astrid pushed herself to her feet.

Again, Dekla extended her hand, but this time, Astrid did not need to force herself to pull out the apple. She knew what she faced, now. What Bjorn faced.

She put the apple in Dekla's hand, and limped out into the world again.

Bjorn heard a door slam, voices, and he jerked up from bed.

Astrid?

His head was fuzzy, as if he were sickening, but he was sure he'd heard the impossible.

Blank walls stared back at him.

Perhaps he was going sick *and* mad. Perhaps Norga's spell to strip him of his power within her castle walls was having a deeper, more insidious effect than merely rendering him a watered-down version of his former self.

He swung his feet down and grimaced when he saw a pulpy mess of spider spread across the stone floor. One of his hideous visitors, squashed to a paste.

He frowned.

He'd hit more than one with his boot, and he knew from experience they were robust. This one looked as if it had been ground down.

And he hadn't done it.

Had Dekla come in while he slept?

The thought gave him an uncomfortable tingle down his spine. He wouldn't put it past her. But to take the time to kill a spider while she was here? That didn't ring true.

She barely noticed the things.

He frowned again. Toed the mess.

Was he so desperate, he was trying to find hope in a pulverized spider? Hope that Astrid had achieved the impossible and somehow found a way to this pit. Found a way past the guards and through the labyrinth of Norga's castle to his room.

And what? Sat beside him while he slept and did not wake him? Vanished before he did?

He laughed at himself, even as his heart ripped in two.

Could Norga have brought him any lower?

"So the daughter is as slippery as the mother." North spoke without looking at her, his eyes closed, stretched across his rock. Still barely there.

Astrid swallowed her self-pity—a bitter pill—and rubbed her hip. "She's not as violent, but she enjoys watching her mother hurt others." North half-opened an eye at that, and his lips thinned as she gave the swollen bruise one last rub. "I know where he is now. I know there is no window we can rescue him from. I know Dekla . . ." What did she know about Dekla? That the troll princess was possessive. That she longed to be admired as well as feared.

That when she looked at Astrid, her fingers twitched with their desire to claw her face, grind her head-first into the dirt.

She threw a stone into a sea as restless as herself. "He doesn't even know I was there."

North said nothing, and the gulls cried for her as they dived from the cliffs into the murky waves.

Astrid threw another stone, squinted at the horizon, trying to work out the time.

"It was around this time yesterday Dekla went for her walk."

"You will arrange another meeting?" North spoke as if he did not care, but it seemed to her his voice was sharper, the air slightly colder.

"Of course."

"What will you exchange this time?"

Astrid pulled the sack from its hiding place under North's rock and brought out the comb and the flute. Touched each lightly with a fingertip.

"The comb."

It was the one she least wanted to part with. The most beautiful.

Dekla would not be able to resist it.

"She'll trick you again." North's voice was barely a sigh in the still, bitter air.

"She'll think she is, anyway." She clenched her fist around the comb, winced when its teeth dug into her palm. "I'll take some charcoal I found on the beach and write Bjorn a message on his wall. And I will leave him something he knows could only come from me."

"What is that?" North lifted up from the rock for the first time in over a day, a cloudy eyebrow raised a notch.

Astrid dropped the comb into her pocket and took the carved bear from the sack. She lifted it up to show him, rubbed it against the bodice of her thread-bare blue dress to make it gleam.

North grunted, lay back down, and Astrid slid the sack with its one lonely treasure and what remained of the bread and cheese from Dame Elv under his rock. She slipped the bear and a crumbling piece of charcoal in to join the comb in her pocket.

"I think the wedding is on Friday. After the raising of the gate of honor, that's traditional. It's what makes sense."

"And today is Wednesday."

"Yes." The things that could go wrong, the danger she was in, went unspoken between them. She had two nights left to rescue Bjorn and she would do what she needed to do.

The time she had was more than she'd expected. She'd feared the worst, and she was grateful for every second she had.

"Wish me luck," she called to North, but he didn't answer as she set off along the cliff bottom, weighed down by the sky and her troubles.

When she reached the deep gorge where the river fell in a sheer curtain into the sea, she climbed up beside it and started inland, following the twisting ribbon of water to the meadow where she'd met with Dekla the day before.

Waiting had never agreed with her, and while she sat and pretended not to watch for the troll princess, she realized her edginess had everything to do with the stillness.

There was no wind stirring here.

There had never been a time when she had not had the wind dancing around her when she went outside.

It was the most evil thing about this place. The dark sky and darker sea, the way everything loomed, sharp and threatening, were nothing to the wind-forsaken atmosphere.

Astrid lifted her hands behind her head and worked the knot of the cord fastening her braid.

It came free and she burrowed her fingers deep, massaging her scalp. She shivered with the pleasure of unbound hair.

Then she took the comb and began to work it through her tangles, the only chance she'd have to use her gift. She bent her head forward and her hair fell in a curtain of gold silk, a few shades lighter than the comb itself.

A shadow fell over her, and Astrid forced herself not to check her movement. She looked up easily.

"Princess." She nodded as if they were casual acquaintances.

The princess's eyes were blank, but Astrid had seen the longing to rip Astrid's hair out with her black-nailed fingers before she'd mastered her jealousy.

"I want it." She breathed the words out on a possessive sigh.

It was on the tip of Astrid's tongue to tell her owning the comb would never make Dekla more like her. Never make Bjorn love her. But she held her tongue.

And most likely, Dekla did not want Bjorn's love, only his admiration and obedience. And she would never have that.

"I cannot trust you," she said instead. "The prince slept through my visit last time." She went back to brushing her hair.

Dekla hissed, and leant over her, her fingers twitching to yank her hair.

"It was nothing to do with me, that he slept." Her eyes gleamed, vicious in their lies.

Astrid kept her expression neutral. She needed to be a believable dupe. Not too stupid or Dekla may find her suspicious. But not too bright, either. She had to get into Bjorn's room tonight *and* tomorrow night to have any chance of saving him.

"Well?" A hint of fear spiked Dekla's tone.

"I don't know." Astrid tugged the comb through her hair one last time and laid it in her lap, then lifted her arms back to braid it, as if she had all the time in the world.

Dekla's gaze burned her thighs as she focused on the comb.

"Decide." The word was sharp with panic.

"It is a lot to risk for another night of him snoring through." Astrid widened her eyes as she looked up at Dekla. Uncertain naivety.

Dekla lifted a fist to her heart and knocked it once. "I will see he gets a hearty meal for lunch and dinner. He will be strong as an ox for you."

Warmth crept up Astrid's cheeks at the troll's words, offering her her lover like a whore. Dekla would think it maidenly blushes.

"What if he sleeps again?"

Dekla shrugged. "Wake him up."

"Same time as before?" Astrid's voice quavered. Only she knew it was anger and not a virgin's uncertainty.

"The same time."

Dekla almost gave herself away, the glee leaking from the corners of her mouth.

Astrid turned her head, fussed with the comb, so she could pretend she hadn't seen it.

"Until later." Dekla began walking away, but backwards, her eyes fixed on the comb. She unbalanced on the uneven ground of the field, and fell over with a shout.

That's right. Astrid stood herself, shaking with rage, and walked away. *This comb will trip you up.*

Chapter Thirty-two

D ekla shuffled, uneasy now they were at Bjorn's cell. Proof of her deceit lay just beyond the door, if Astrid was any judge.

She stood still and relaxed, watching the troll, her hand in her pocket. A reminder to Dekla of the precious thing within.

Dekla's eyes followed a cliff spider scuttling down the corridor. "Keep silent. If someone realizes you are in the castle, I cannot protect you."

Astrid lowered her gaze. "I'll keep silent. I only cried last time because I was so disappointed."

"I am sure you will not be disappointed this time."

Astrid did not answer, but raised her eyebrows as she looked at Dekla. Saw the slyness in the set of her jaw, the way her eyes shifted over Astrid's shoulder. She turned and slid the key into the lock.

"I'll see you at dawn." She edged the door open just enough for Astrid to slip through, then slammed it behind her.

Exactly as Astrid hoped she would.

She leant back against the rough wood a moment

but she could sense Dekla on the other side, ear pressed to the lock.

Astrid shivered and stepped away, the door tainted by Dekla's leaning presence. She took in the room in the fluttering candlelight; the glint of moisture off the walls, the gleam of black spider eyes in a corner.

Bjorn lying fast asleep.

She had known he would be. Had been certain of it. And yet, one tiny part of her must have hoped otherwise. Because suddenly she wept. Heart wrenching sobs that tore from her chest.

She walked to Bjorn's bed, clambered over him and lay squashed against him and the wall, holding on to him as if he were a life raft in the sea of her tears.

She heard the sharp, ringing steps of Dekla walking away, no doubt satisfied that the little village girl had been disappointed once again. The thought helped calm her.

She hadn't lost.

She and Dekla had tied this round, and she intended to win the last one.

She sat up, eased herself off the bed and took the piece of charcoal from her pocket. Lifted the candle, wobbly in its holder, and looked for a place to leave her message.

The walls all seemed too dark, too damp, but she tried a few strokes. Writing black on black was not going to work. She turned to the door, but the wood was blackened as well, and just as useless.

Her eye fell on the dull grey wood of the table, a surface both light enough and dry enough to leave her message. She kept it short and could only hope Dekla did not notice it.

Then she took the little wooden bear and placed it in Bjorn's hand. Closed his fingers around it.

There was nothing more she could do except wait until morning, so she wriggled back between him and the wall, watching over him until the candle burnt out. Then lay with her head on his heart until morning.

⋘━━━⟨✦⟩━━━⋙

He woke to the sight of Dekla's back as she closed his cell door, a dripping cloth in her hand. Astrid's scent seemed to cling to him, and though he hadn't cried since he was a child, tears pricked the back of his eyes as he breathed in her fading perfume, fresh as sunshine.

He noticed water dripping from his table to the floor, and remembered the wet rag in Dekla's hand. He frowned, struggled up, trying to make sense of the nonsensical. She wouldn't have been cleaning it, surely?

He took the single step necessary to reach the table, and saw that far from cleaning the table, Dekla seemed to have rubbed black soot into it.

He sat back down on the bed, holding his pounding head with both hands, wondering what was wrong with him, and felt something hard digging into his thigh.

He patted the bed and his hand closed over a small wooden bear. It stood with head held high, sniffing the wind, all four paws solidly on the ground.

It was familiar. He rubbed his forehead, trying to place it.

And then a scene lit his mind.

Of a freezing night and a tearful goodbye. Astrid kissing each of her family in turn, and blinking with surprise as the one she expected the least from handed her a gift.

His fingers tightened like bands of steel around the precious thing.

He leapt up, no clear plan of action in mind, just needing to move, and then collapsed to his knees, a scream frozen in his throat as his mind frantically sought a way around the wooden bear. Around what it meant.

Norga had hunted Astrid down. Had probably started the morning she took him from the mountain.

And here was the fruit of her labor. A slyly left message that his lady was dead.

He opened his fist and examined the bear in the pale light seeping beneath the door.

If Norga thought this would break him, she was wrong.

It enraged him.

It stripped him of his obligations in this bargain.

Stripped him almost of his humanity.

It made him want to kill.

He breathed—deep, uneven breaths—as he looked at the small thing lying gleaming on his open palm.

The sweet scent that had filled his nostrils earlier was gone. Instead he smelt the mold and must of his cell. The sharp evil stink of sweat and troll from the filthy sheets. The sour tang of crushed cliff spiders.

Norga thought to chain him to her with this bear. Instead she'd unleashed the bear in her own castle. Stripped of his magic and power, he could still teach her he was a force to be reckoned with, even if it meant using his bare hands.

He struggled to his feet, and walked to the locked door. Stood looking at it, his rage building in him until he could contain it no longer. He punched out with his free hand so hard the wood cracked like a tree in deep snow. A thin sliver of a gap appeared, a salve to the pain.

He felt an icy draft blow through it, sharp as a blade.

It blew in his face, reminding him of how the wind always seemed to hound him when he was with Astrid. Unfriendly as an older brother with their sister's lover.

He held his fist, knuckles dripping blood, up to the crack and the cold stream of air seemed to sooth them.

Not like with Astrid, then.

Now that she was gone . . .

He collapsed against the door, slid to the floor and threw back his head to howl in anguish.

"You make a better bear than you do a wolf, Mountain Prince."

Bjorn's howl died in his throat as the whisper chilled his ear.

"Who . . ."

A shape rose like mist off an ice-covered lake. A man his own size wavered into being. Wispy clouds formed a strong face and he stared into cruel, hawk-like eyes.

Unfriendly, and yet, not threatening.

"Who are you?" Bjorn kept his words to a whisper.

"The North Wind."

There was nothing to say to that. Bjorn stared at him in amazement.

"I serve the Wind Hag."

Bjorn thought of how the wind obeyed Astrid, how Jorgen had said the Wind Hag must have given it leave to serve her, and knew with gut-wrenching certainty why this emissary was here.

"Norga has already given me proof of her death," he said bitterly. He lifted up the little bear.

"You are mistaken." The North Wind sunk to the floor, and Bjorn thought he looked weary. Barely able to talk. "My mistress has spent the last two nights weeping at your side while you slept. It was she who left you the bear."

The air became even colder, and Bjorn's breath came out in puffs.

"Why would the Wind Hag come here? And if she has done as you say, how did I not know it?" He shook his head. "And how does she come to have this bear?"

The North Wind sunk lower. "Do not touch your food and drink today." He began to fade away, but on the last wisp of icy air he whispered, "Remember this favor I have done you when you are free, Mountain Prince. Remember it well."

Astrid did not know how long she sat on the beach, staring at the sea.

Too long.

Dekla had seen her message. She'd glanced too often at the table for there to be any doubt, and there had been fury in her eyes. She'd said nothing, though. Pretended all was well. And Astrid knew the moment she was out the castle, Dekla would go back and scrub it all away.

She'd been cautious, at least. She hadn't said who she was, just told Bjorn not to drink or eat the food that day. That he was being drugged. But that was all for nothing.

Which left only the bear.

And perhaps Dekla would discover that, too.

She rocked a little on the uneven pebbles of the beach, ignoring the cold and the stink of rotting kelp. A local village girl would not be giving carved bears to the Bear Prince. If Dekla found it, Astrid was no longer safe with the troll. Her secret was out.

Dekla would delight in showing no mercy.

In bringing her like a prize to her mother.

"I'm going to meet Dekla again." She stood, feeling truly like a hag; old, bent and stiff. Weighed down. She glanced at North, and started when she saw he wasn't there.

He'd been lying on his rock when she'd come down from the castle, the knowledge that her message was in vain hollowing her out. Her clever plan had failed, and Bjorn would be drugged again, if Dekla even agreed to one last bargain.

North had asked her what was wrong and she remembered trying to explain, her words slowly dying in her throat as she battled her pain. As she retreated deep into herself to look for strength.

He was a silent but comforting presence. Or so she thought.

She stared at his rock, a terrible, growing fear blossoming within that he'd somehow . . . expired. That carrying her all this way had been too much.

"North?" she called in a whisper, although in her

heart it was a shriek, a throat-wrenching scream.

A breath of wind eddied around her feet. And she felt a chill down her spine.

Wind? In this place?

"I wanted to test my strength."

"North?" She turned and found him standing behind her, upright for the first time since they'd arrived, his hawk-face etched deep with exhaustion. She held out her arms and stepped up to him, felt the strange wonder of hugging the wind. All quick air—cold and concentrated as a gale through the cracks in a glacier. She shivered.

"Rest. I need to get to the meadow before I miss Dekla."

"Even though she's destroyed your message and the Mountain Prince may sleep through the night?"

"I have no choice. I can only hope the bear is enough."

"Perhaps it is," North murmured as she slipped the flute out of the sack and into her pocket, and somehow, his words comforted her. Gave her strength all the way along the bottom of the cliffs, and helped her climb the steep rocks beside the waterfall.

Every step she took shook loose a shower of sparks within her.

She would never give up.

She chanted it in her head, every time she put her foot down. Her steps became quicker and quicker. She was running by the time she reached the meadow, her feet beating in time with her determination. No matter how slim the chance, she would take it.

She threw herself to the ground in the field and pulled out the flute, perspiration sliding through her hair and down her back, making her shiver as it cooled in the chill air.

She was breathing in gasps, and thought only to sound a whistle with the delicate instrument. But instead, her first blast of breath produced a mournful melody that seemed to wind itself around her. Glittering gold in the still air.

She blew again, more carefully this time. High notes, piercing and pure, wove around her head, touching something deep inside with its loveliness.

She got to her feet before she blew again. It seemed . . . disrespectful to play the flute sitting down. And when she did start playing, everything faded away. The world consisted only of her, the music, and the beautiful instrument in her hand.

When the last note sparkled away to nothing, she had to pull herself back to the meadow, to the now, as if waking from a deep sleep.

Dekla stood right before her, dark and looming as her mother's castle, and Astrid leapt back, her jerk of fear hardening the troll's expression.

"Very beautiful." The princess held out her hand, as if to examine the flute, and Astrid flexed her knees, ready to run. She could not give this to the troll. It was against the fabric of nature itself.

"Just to look," Dekla said, half-pleading, and Astrid shook her head. She clutched the flute to her chest and forced her feet to stay still.

She must not run. She needed to deal with Dekla again. It was her last chance.

"Same bargain as before?" Dekla's lying eyes shifted left as she spoke, and Astrid wanted to launch herself at the troll. For once, it was *her* fingers that twitched in their desire to do violence.

"I don't get anything out of the bargains, so no." Astrid had meant to sound unsure, but with the flute in her hand, her words held an ominous ring of finality. She made a show of putting it back in her pocket, her hands shaking. *What had she done?*

"If the prince pretends to sleep through your visits, it is nothing to do with me." Dekla sneered, contemptuous.

"He does not pretend. It is no natural sleep he sleeps."

"Do you call me a cheat, peasant?"

Even with the flute out of her hands and in her pocket, Astrid still stood longer than was wise, longer than was acceptable, thinking about her answer.

Too long.

Dekla moved her arm across her body, lifted it high and lashed out for a backhanded blow.

Winning was getting Bjorn, Astrid reminded herself, as Dekla's blow caught the top of her head as she ducked, throwing her back into the grass.

The pain in her head exploded across her eyes and her ears, for a moment making her blind and deaf, and she did not get up. She lifted a shaking hand to the lump, and winced as she felt the swelling.

Winning was walking out of here with Norga defeated.

Her pride. Her sense of outrage. They had no place here.

Slowly, feeling like a bent crone, she picked herself up, and stood with her head resting in her hands.

"I do not call you a cheat, Princess." Her voice came out faint, and she felt lightheaded. "But I have lost two precious things for no gain. Many would say I was beyond foolish to throw away the best of my possessions in the same way."

The troll princess lowered her fists. "I cannot promise you he won't be asleep again."

Of course not, as promises were binding, even for trolls, and Dekla intended to drug Bjorn again. Astrid gave a stumbling curtsey.

"I will be very disappointed if he is." She lifted her head and put her hand in her pocket, caressed the flute.

Dekla's eyes twitched as they followed the movement of her arm.

"Perhaps he will be recovered from whatever

afflicts him, but whether he is or not, tonight is your last chance." Dekla gave a bitter smile. "I'm marrying him tomorrow, and when I do, there will be no more bargains."

"I will try one last time then." Astrid curtsied again, and as she watched Dekla walk away, her hand crept up to fist over her heart. She knocked once in silent promise.

She would go to the castle tonight, and she would give up the flute. She would trust this was not a trap, that Dekla hadn't found the bear.

Because no matter how small the chance, she was willing to risk everything.

Chapter Thirty-three

Bjorn lay, back turned to the door of his cell, and heard the slap of Dekla's feet on the stone floor of the passage. The door creaked open, but Dekla did not even walk over to examine him.

Things looked as she expected them to.

Her grunt of satisfaction made him grit his teeth, furious that this had happened two nights in a row and he'd been none the wiser.

Her steps receded, echoing in the stone passageways.

Where was she going?

While he waited, Bjorn's heart beat in time with the water dripping from his ceiling. It calmed him, helped him release his anger and relax.

Time seemed to stretch out, and he couldn't say how much time had passed when she returned. There was a second set of footsteps with her, tense and hurried, and his scalp prickled with anticipation.

The Wind Hag?

Why else would the North Wind warn him against eating or drinking tonight, if his mistress did not intend to return?

"Remember, no noise," he heard Dekla whisper as the door opened again. It closed quickly and the lock turned.

Someone stood behind him, trapped with him in the cell. He could hear breathing, short, sharp gasps as if the visitor were frightened or panicked. Not what he expected from the Wind Hag.

"No."

The whisper chilled him, sent a shiver down his spine he had to fight to suppress. It was the sound of a heart breaking, and he rose up on his elbows and turned to see.

He looked at the bowed head of the woman weeping silently on her knees before him.

A roaring filled his ears.

"Astrid?"

He whispered her name so quietly, he was sure she could not have heard him, but her crying cut off and she raised her head, her eyes wide.

Shock ran through him, a lightning strike, freezing him in place.

It was Astrid, and yet, it was not.

The eyes of the woman before him were those of someone powerful. Someone who had struggled and faced death and dared. He blinked.

She stared back, and unease scuttled down his spine like a cliff spider.

What did she see in the depth of his eyes? A broken man? A defeated, powerless prince who had nothing left to give?

But her expression lit up with joy, not sadness or pity.

Her delight galvanized him. He stood, swept her up, held her, his hands smoothing down her shoulders, down her back, marveling at the feel of her in his arms again. She smelled of the sea, of outside air. Precious commodities in here.

He was distressing her, he could see, her joy diminishing, tears spilling onto her cheeks as she watched his face.

"You have haunted eyes." She tucked her head under his chin, and her tears wet his skin. "What has she done to you?"

"Shhhh." He rocked them both, tightly bound together. "I fear you have had a harder time than me. You look . . . changed."

"I am."

The way she said it, as if she meant it literally, forced him to focus, his mind to clear. He lifted back his head.

"How?"

"I discovered I *am* the Wind Hag, after all." She spoke in a rush, to get it over with. As if she were unsure of his reaction. And he remembered what he'd said to her many weeks ago. Remembered his fear, that, just like his father, he'd married a beauty to find she was a monster beneath.

"So that is why the North Wind warned me." He waited to feel the sense of outrage at having taken a lady who was far from what she seemed, but there was only happiness in his heart.

She had managed the impossible to find him, and her eyes showed the risks she'd taken to get here. If she was the Wind Hag, he didn't care. As long as she was still Astrid, she could be whatever else she pleased.

"North was here?" She frowned and his interest sharpened.

"This morning." They were still entwined and he felt her begin to pull back, to pace, no doubt, but he refused to let her go.

She looked startled, as if unused to anyone or anything restricting her, and he grinned down at her, his happiness spilling out and lighting the dark cell golden.

She smiled back, rubbed her soft cheek against the base of his neck. "I thought I'd be too late. So to be just in time . . ." She gave a sigh. "I can't believe North came to see you. What did he say?"

Bjorn shrugged, not nearly as interested in North as in the woman in his arms. "Just not to eat the food, and to remember the favor he'd done me when I was free."

A laugh exploded from Astrid, quickly subdued, and she shook her head. "He is a sly one."

There was something more to North's words than
he'd thought, Bjorn realized, but it was nothing to him.
He'd be anyone's fool or dupe, as long as Astrid was
with him.

"You sound . . ." his words died in his throat as
her expression changed, as if she had had a revelation.

"Bjorn?" Her voice shook. "With all the vedfe and
the yggren on your side, who would take Norga's part?"

"There are only a few, but they are powerful, and
with all the trolls, they would be a formidable force. We
might have a chance to triumph, if only I could be sure of
the yggren."

"You can be sure of the yggren." She sounded so
certain, he almost believed her.

"They've attacked twice."

Astrid was shaking her head. "They attacked, but
not on Norga's orders."

Bjorn thought about it. "If they have their own
reasons, I can trust them even less. At least as Norga's
minions, I can predict their actions."

"Bjorn, only two were turned. And it will not
happen again. The yggren swore loyalty to you and me
the morning Norga took you. They can be counted on."

"How do you know it won't happen again?" Bjorn
tried not to sound disbelieving, but he couldn't help it.
Astrid was naïve. She trusted too much.

"I know it won't happen again," she said, and
lifted a hand to his face, "because I now command the

one who turned them in the first place."

————◄✑►————

"The North Wind was trying to kill me?" Bjorn leant back against the wall and looked at Astrid, sitting on the bed beside him, in astonishment. "What have I done that he would try?"

"Took me." Astrid smiled. "My winds are jealous of my attention."

It made a strange, twisted sense.

"And the yggren are behind me?"

She nodded.

"Though I had my doubts, all the vedfe have proved they are loyal."

"So who does Norga have for her army? Besides her trolls?"

"Those who live in dark places, and would welcome more of them." Bjorn tapped his lips. "But—we are more than evenly matched with the yggren on our side. I never counted them into the fight, as they looked set to remain neutral. Norga was handed a boon the day they appeared to turn against me but now, with them actively against her, I would risk war."

"You will have the aid of the Wind Hag, as well." There was an edge to Astrid's voice, a hardness, he had never heard before. "My winds and I would stand beside you."

Bjorn thought for a moment what that would look

like. The four winds gathered together, Astrid raised up amongst them. The hair on his arms rose, and he shivered.

"But all this is just talk. Norga will kill you if you refuse to marry Dekla. You are at her mercy here. I doubt she would give you the option of war now." Astrid drew her knees up, hugged them against her.

It was true. But there was always a way. If Astrid could find him here, he could find a way out of the ceremony.

"The wedding is tomorrow," he said, his voice barely a whisper.

"I know," Astrid whispered back, and for the first time, she sounded afraid.

———❧———

Astrid stood facing the door as Dekla's footsteps approached. She did not dare look at Bjorn, even though he faced the wall, too terrified she would give herself away. Give him away.

She felt hollow-eyed with exhaustion, and energized at the same time.

They had not slept. They had talked and planned, and when their words ran out, they sat quietly, taking strength from each other.

Astrid let her shoulders droop in resignation, in defeat, as the door swung open, and she shuffled forward, her eyes on the floor.

"Looks like you were out of luck."

Dekla kept her voice even, but though Astrid didn't dare look up to see, she knew the troll's eyes would be triumphant.

She shuffled out the cell. Dekla swung the door closed with a crash, and turned the lock, a half-smile tugging at her lips.

Enjoy your triumph for now, Astrid thought as she put her hand in her pocket for the troll princess one last time. It didn't want to obey her, and her mouth filled with bitterness as she pulled out the golden flute.

Dekla's eyes widened in anticipation, the hot stone smell of her intensifying in her excitement.

"How do you play it?" Her words were greedy, impatient.

Astrid managed to hold the flute out, forced her fingers to relax as they tried to close in a vice-grip around the golden cylinder.

"You blow into it."

"That is all?" Dekla's tone sharpened, disbelieving, but Astrid shrugged.

"That's all."

"If you're lying . . ." Dekla snatched the flute up, blew into it, and a melody, darker, greener, than Astrid's high, golden tune, spiraled from the instrument. Dekla's eyes glazed over, and she walked away, down the corridor from which Norga had once come, as if she'd forgotten Astrid was even there.

They'd planned for Astrid to sneak back into the castle. She'd thought she'd have to climb the cliff wall again. But this was better. This was better by far.

She simply wouldn't leave.

Chapter Thirty-four

Astrid kept her head down, weaving through the crowd of servants standing on the edges of the courtyard like timid brown sparrows watching vultures.

The guests were not seated, but stood in loosely-formed groups, their manner one of curiosity rather than excitement. The way they turned their massive, mottled bodies away from the raised dais showed an uncertainty with this forced alliance.

Dekla stood on the stage alone, her eyes furtively sliding to the doorway from which Bjorn would emerge. The parody of a nervous bride.

Astrid bowed her head lower and stopped in the cluster of people nearest the platform. She could go no further. If she stepped out of the protection of the crowd, she'd be as exposed as a rabbit in a field, with a hawk circling above.

Dekla must not see her.

She tried to stand easily, naturally, with the others. Her clothes were as dirty and tattered as theirs, her face as grimy. Her downcast face and hunched shoulders blended in. It was as if an army of people were here, disguised, for some secret purpose, just as she was.

The thought made her glance at the nearest person, the woman she'd seen sweeping the courtyard yesterday. The woman's attention was fixed on the spectacle of the bower and the waiting troll bride, a defeated droop to her lips.

She turned as she felt Astrid's gaze on her, and a spark of interest flashed in her eyes.

She half-lifted a hand, almost beseeching, and Astrid fought down her instinctive recoil, forced herself to stare back with disinterest. She made her face blank and turned away, the depth of the woman's need frightening her.

She hunched her shoulders even more, made her body sag, gave the tiredness, the hunger and the cold battering her free reign, and looked at the woman again.

Slack-mouthed, the woman returned her attention to the wedding group.

Astrid edged away from her, but she had a feeling she needn't bother. She'd been forgotten.

She focused her own attention ahead. More was happening now. Norga had taken the dais, standing as if to officiate in the ceremony. But suddenly she raise her head and looked across the courtyard to the massive main entrance, and Astrid saw the other trolls had, too. They stood in silence, tense and waiting, and a strange expectancy crept through the crowd, making Astrid's arms tingle with nerves.

At last she heard what the trolls had heard long before—the rumble of cart wheels. The servants began to shift uneasily. More and more drifted closer to the inner castle wall, ready to bolt within to safety.

Astrid found herself suddenly abandoned, alone in no-mans-land, and she edged back to the new front line of spectators.

A troll came through the gates, a forerunner. He seemed surprised at the gathering of people, and he started visibly at the sight of the dais.

He came to a halt and stood as if lost, as if afraid of the news he brought with him, and Norga beckoned him with her finger.

Astrid watched him hesitate before he climbed up onto the platform. He bent his head close to Norga's, whispered his message.

Norga shrieked. Lifted her hand and hit him so hard he was thrown back, landing heavily on the cobbles.

"I told you there must be no second time."

The troll rubbed at the blood running from the corner of his mouth. "I lost three trolls. We never saw them again."

"So she's still out there." Norga turned, and Astrid knew she was facing the direction of the mountain. Knew her escape from the three trolls in the palace was the cause of this temper.

Trolls and humans stood quiet and subdued, waiting for the storm to blow over. Each afraid the smallest movement would make them Norga's next target.

Rumbling filled the silence and Astrid risked a look at Dekla, saw her mouth purse to a thin line. She seemed impatient. Bored with the added complication of the return of Norga's little army.

Two trolls, pushing against a massive wooden harness like oxen, rolled a covered cart through the massive doors. They looked battle worn, with gashes across their chests and arms, some half-healed over, some inflamed.

They had been traveling from the forest all this time, Astrid realized. It had taken them as long to get here as it had taken her to visit the four corners of the world.

They came to a shuddering stop in the center of the courtyard, directly before the dais, but the cart continued to rattle. There was someone caged within, under the covering, shaking the bars.

A place deep within Astrid grew still with shock.

"You cut things fine, Hedle. You're almost too late, but at least you got this right." Norga jumped down to the ground and strode forward, pulled the heavy curtain down. Beneath the rough canvas was a metal cage.

Astrid's heart was seized in her chest and squeezed by an unrelenting hand. She bent down, putting her hands on her knees, closing her eyes. Gasping for breath.

If she didn't look, perhaps it couldn't be true.

The few servants around her murmured in amazement, and Astrid felt an icy drop of fear hit the back of her neck and speed its way down her spine.

She forced herself to look up. Saw one strong, muscled arm—its deep brown gouged by trolls' claws—fade in and out of focus behind the iron bars.

She stepped closer, unable to help herself, and her movement caught the prisoner's attention. Jorgen lifted his eyes to hers.

He was a wounded oak. Trembling with pain, uprooted and dying. But his shock at seeing her, his blink of understanding at what her being in the crowd must mean, sent her reeling back.

She crouched down, a forest of legs around her, hugging her knees, breathing deep. This wasn't about her and Bjorn anymore. It was about Jorgen too. And if they managed to trick Norga, to get her to concede defeat, there was nothing to stop her killing Jorgen in the backlash of her spite and rage.

A shudder ran down her, almost unbalancing her on her haunches.

In all conscience, could they put their future happiness before Jorgen's life?

<hr />

The trolls who brought him down from the cell,

two gray slabs of rock, must have thought him too weak and subdued to escape or commit violence. They let go of his arms as they stepped into the courtyard, and he was forced to walk toward his bride himself.

The hiss and suck of the sea sounded as if it were miles away, instead of just beyond the wall, and Bjorn used the beat of its far-away rhythm as he made his way to the raised dais. Not a death march, but a march of humiliation.

He did not try to make out Astrid in the crowd. Too much rested on Norga never discovering she was here until it was too late—

He froze, a high-pitched buzz in his ears. Hazel eyes, cool as the deep forest, stared out at him from a cage, bracketed on either side by iron bars.

Bjorn lifted a hand toward him, then clenched it into a fist. He looked up to the dais, locked eyes with Norga.

She smiled. Her eyes glinting with the knowledge of how this must affect him.

"A witness from your kingdom," she said. "So it can never be said that this did not take place."

Jorgen slumped against the bars, and slid, half-faded, to the filthy floor of his cage.

"He will die this far from the forest. It's his lifeblood." He was stripped of his power, but if Astrid had not been there, if this wasn't about more than him, he would try to kill the troll queen right now.

He shuddered in a breath. Held himself still and calm.

"You are becoming more pragmatic as you get older." Norga moved forward to the steps, unaware how close she was to a wild animal. "It is time to pledge yourself, Mountain Prince."

Beside her, Dekla shuffled, her eyes darting between Jorgen, Bjorn and her mother.

Bjorn felt a thread of pity for her. A pawn of both sides.

"It looks as if your witness is dying, Mother."

At her bored tone, the pity he'd felt evaporated, and his chest contracted with pain as he spun back to Jorgen.

The vedfe lay, eyes closed, almost completely faded away.

"No!" Bjorn threw himself at the cage. Thrust his hand between the bars and touched hot, fevered flesh.

"He needs water. What good is he to you dead?"

Norga said nothing, but the calculation in her eyes told him everything.

"He will get water and a quick journey back to his forest once the ceremony is complete. My little way of making sure you behave today."

Bjorn walked to the dais but did not put his foot on the first step. The blood pounded so hard in his head, he felt lightheaded. His heart gave him such a stab of pain, he put his fist over it.

If he and Astrid went ahead with their plan, Jorgen would die. Either because he would never be returned to his forest, or because Norga would kill him in revenge.

He turned to face the crowd—searching, searching. This was not his decision alone.

He tried to swallow, and found he could not. A rock had lodged in his throat, hard and choking.

A small movement, someone standing from a crouch, drew his eye and suddenly there was Astrid amongst the servants. The tears glistening in her winter blue eyes made his knees give way, and he stumbled forward a step. She gave a tight nod, and stepped backwards, deeper into the crowd. Disappeared among the servants.

"We are waiting, Prince."

Bjorn turned to the dais, looked over his shoulder one last time, and placed his foot on the first step.

Chapter Thirty-five

A deathly cry, the final creaking scream of wild oak as it falls to the woodman's ax, silenced every voice.

Bjorn leapt from the top step back to the ground and gripped the cage's iron bars, straining to bend them with his bare hands.

Jorgen had faded away completely. Bjorn could see nothing of him.

"Give me the key," he screamed to Norga, so wild he touched the heart of the bear, that place he had never allowed himself to go in all the time he was enchanted. Too afraid it would seduce him into forgetting his responsibilities, offer him a half-life with no real purpose, but no pain, either.

He embraced that wildness now. Was able to remember it only too well. He'd lived with his mind rubbing side by side with the beast long enough.

He saw, through the red haze around his vision, that Dekla's eyes were wide, and Norga had taken a step back, her face twisted with shock.

She threw him the key, and expecting to have to

fight for it, to kill, he missed the catch and it bounced off his chest, fell at his feet.

He scrabbled for it, his fingers shaking, and he cursed as he fumbled with the lock. He ripped the door open, then moved carefully forward on his hands and knees, feeling his way.

His hand touched a shoulder, and he knelt closer, touched Jorgen's hot, dry face.

The lord of the vedfe was lifeless.

Bjorn sat back on his heels and looked across at the troll queen, murder in his eyes.

———— ·⦚· ————

Astrid pushed her way through the crowd that had frozen around her, and took a step away from the safety of the herd toward the cage. Like an unexpected slap, the open space between the servants and the trolls brought her to her senses.

She watched Bjorn throw open the cage door, crawl in and touch Jorgen's invisible body. Saw him sit back and look up at the dais, every muscle tensed, his lips drawn back over his teeth as if he planned to leap straight through the iron bars and rip Norga's throat out.

If he did attack, she would join him.

What did she have to lose?

But even as she braced to run forward, Bjorn jerked slightly, as if touched by an unexpected hand. She watched the rage drain out of him, his head and shoulders drooping over his chest, his fisted hands opening and rubbing his temple.

Norga's dark magic at work? Bringing Bjorn to heel?

Astrid trembled, hardly breathing, waiting for Bjorn to come back to his senses. To fight.

Instead, he stood, stooping slightly in the cage, and walked slowly, as if carrying a heavy weight on his back. He eased himself out of the cage door to the ground, rather than jumping down as she would have expected, and seemed to wander, puzzled, away from the dais, toward the measly center court fountain that trickled its water into a moss-stained bowl of stone. He stumbled as he got to it, slumped to the ground, and shook his head.

He put out a hand, caught a palm-full of water, and rubbed it over his face. It seemed to revive him, and he stood up, his face controlled again, his eyes hard.

Norga and Dekla watched him, their faces giving nothing away. But Astrid thought the way they stood since Bjorn was overcome in the cage was more relaxed. Their hands no longer clenched, their necks no longer straining forward.

They had been afraid of him.

As he walked back, Bjorn's step was normal, no longer slow and full of effort. He looked down at the first step up to the platform, but his feet remained firmly on the cobbles of the courtyard. "If this it to be a true marriage, I am entitled to ask my bride-to-be to prove herself. To do something for me."

As Norga hissed in a breath, Astrid's mouth dropped open. This was how it should have gone, had Jorgen not arrived. This is what they'd planned.

But she would never have chosen to do it over Jorgen's dead body.

Bjorn could see Norga had not thought of the groom's prerogative to ask a favor of his bride. Had forgotten it, perhaps, or never knew it. But his words hung silver in the air, the clear ring of truth to them.

"What would you have me do?" Dekla stepped forward, speaking—asserting herself—for the first time.

Bjorn looked into her eyes and saw nothing but hardness.

"I would have you wash my shirt." He lifted the fine cotton, gray and dull, off his chest as if its very touch offended him.

Norga frowned, and Bjorn could see her mind working, sure there was a devious trick behind the simple request.

"And when she does that, you will marry her?"

"I will marry whoever is able to make this shirt completely white again. If your daughter is the one to do it, then I will marry her."

"You wish to humiliate me. Make me to do the work of a servant, before you are forever under my thumb." Dekla spoke softly, and Bjorn had to strain forward to hear her. "You had better enjoy it, Mountain Prince, because it will cost you."

Bjorn shrugged. Stared up at her, defiant.

"Bring me warm water in a basin and some soap," she called into the crowd, and two women hurried off into the inner castle.

Under the guise of watching them go, Bjorn searched for Astrid, found her standing in the first rank of servants, close as she could to him. She was tense, waiting, and he could see her cheeks and eyes were red from weeping.

The two women stepped out of the kitchens, a large wooden tub between them. One stumbled in her nervousness as every eye turned on them, and they set it down with a thump, spilling water. It swirled over Bjorn's worn, scuffed boots.

Slowly, deliberately, he loosened the ties that held the top of his shirt together, and bent forward to pull it over his head. He straightened, holding the shirt like a rotting fish with the tips of his fingers, and looked up at Dekla.

Her eyes moved from the shirt to his bared torso, and she pursed her lips, her gaze refusing to meet his.

She walked down the steps to him and stopped just near his shoulder, at least a head taller than he.

"I can make myself beautiful, you know," she whispered. "Beyond my mother's lands. Where my power will not clash with hers."

Bjorn flinched.

She reached out and took the shirt, and for a moment, her eyes did meet his, blasting him with barely controlled emotion. Lust. Yearning. Greed.

"As she looked for your father, I could look for you. And I have things. Beautiful, golden things."

Bjorn stepped back, crossed his arms over his chest, and said nothing. He felt a muscle jump in his jaw, and realized he was grinding his teeth together.

Dekla watched him a moment longer, and did not find what she was looking for in his eyes.

"Never say I didn't give you a chance, Bearman. You could have had the illusion of beauty, but I will not try to make your life easier again."

"I have spent too long enchanted," he answered her, so quietly it was her turn to lean forward. "I am giving you the benefit of my experience. It is no way to live."

She reared back, her black-tipped fingers gripping the shirt as if she would tear it to shreds.

"Careful," Norga called from the dais. "He is a tricky one. We do not want to forfeit anything because of your temper."

Dekla shot her mother a look of loathing, but her grip loosened and she turned to the basin at her feet.

"I will make you wash everything in our palace every day, for this," she said to Bjorn, her voice sweet and light as Norga's had once been in her magical woman's body. "And I will turn myself into a beautiful woman each day, and tease you, and tease you, until you beg me to lie with you. And just as you get into my bed, I will take my true form again."

Bjorn dropped his hands to his side, cocked his head, considering.

"You and your mother keep confusing me with an animal, princess. I may have looked like one for a long time, but I never was one." He nodded toward the basin. "If you are able to do this task, and I am forced to marry you, there is nothing in heaven or earth that would make me beg for your body. You are chaining yourself to a life of unhappiness for your mother's greed. I feel sorry for you."

Dekla cried out. Whether in pain or anger, Bjorn could not tell.

"*You* prepare yourself for a life of unhappiness, Bearman. You are about to lose." And Dekla plunged the shirt into the soapy water.

Chapter Thirty-six

A strid held her breath. Bjorn was confident this would work, but they were in Norga's world here, and she didn't want to place her hopes on the magic woven into a linen shirt.

She saw Dekla smile as she bent over the tub, the clear water now murky as she pummeled the cloth with the bar of soap.

Triumphant, Dekla lifted the shirt out, streaming with water, and Astrid could see it was white.

"You missed a spot," Bjorn said, leaning forward and poking the left breast of the shirt with his finger.

Dekla frowned, and peered closer. She dipped the shirt back in again. When she lifted it out, her frown deepened.

"It looks like those three dark spots are spreading." Bjorn showed no sign of glee, his face serious under the scrutiny of Norga's suspicion, but Astrid felt a catch of triumph in her heart.

Dekla scrubbed again, harder, more viciously, and even some of the servants gasped at the black patch that spread from the left breast across the shirt.

"This is enchanted," she cried, lifting up the sleeve, which was now completely black. "The black tallow is spreading everywhere. I cannot clean it."

"Your mother stripped me of my power when she took me. If it is enchanted, it isn't enchanted by me." Bjorn braced his legs apart, and Astrid knew he thought Dekla's temper would not hold much longer.

"You knew." Norga leapt from the dais, and Astrid flinched, sure she was going to strike Bjorn. "You knew this was going to happen."

"All I asked was for her to complete a simple task any woman here could do. You," he pointed to Astrid, "come here."

Astrid stepped into the open, and hunched her shoulders, cringing like the other servants did. Norga, Dekla and Bjorn stood around the wash basin, and as she reached it, she heard Dekla draw her breath in surprise.

"This is a trick." Dekla's voice shook.

Her mother looked sharply at her, then back to Astrid, and Astrid felt her knees weaken at the power in her gaze. "How do you know it's a trick? Do you recognize this creature?"

Astrid looked up into Dekla's eyes, held her gaze for one long, cool beat, and Dekla hesitated, shook her head.

"I have never seen her before." Her eyes cut down and away.

Norga bent forward and examined Astrid,

grabbing her hair, looping it around her massive fingers and pulling Astrid's head back for a better look. Astrid balanced, her neck exposed, vulnerable. One jerk of Norga's hands and her neck would snap. There was no need for artifice here, her whole body quivered with fear, her heart hammering loud enough for Norga to hear it without leaning any closer.

Norga shoved her forward, her face sneering. "You think this pitiful, grubby thing can do what my daughter cannot?"

Bjorn gave a smile, icy as the plains North called home. "Let us see, shall we?"

What if she couldn't do it? Astrid held the wet shirt in her hands and stared down at the now-filthy water.

She dared a glance at Bjorn, and saw a brief gleam of delight and certainty in his eyes.

It gave her the strength to kneel before the basin and drop the shirt into it. She picked up the bar of soap, slippery and soft, and plunged her hands into the water.

It was hard to see. The water was so dirty, she at first had no idea whether she'd succeeded or not. But when she lifted up a sleeve, and it was white as pure snow, she knew she had.

"Has she got it completely clean?" Dekla asked, and her voice was hushed.

Norga grabbed the shirt, lifted it up against the sky, and her action had a touch of the marriage sheet ceremony about it, with her trolls and the servants as witness. This time, though, a lack of stain was the triumph, not the bloody mark of virginity lost.

"How did you do it?" Norga turned, her face darkening. She grabbed for Astrid, but Bjorn was there first, standing in front of her. He tugged the shirt from her hands and pulled it, wet and dripping, over his head.

"What do you care about her?" Norga looked over his shoulder at Astrid, her eyes narrowed, her long fingers flicking in irritation.

"She is my future wife, after all."

Norga's gaze left her and moved sharply back to Bjorn, and standing behind his broad back, Astrid realized Norga thought he was needling her. Her expression was annoyed, but not enraged.

"Let my daughter try again."

"There is nothing left to clean, and she was given plenty of chances." Bjorn widened his stance.

"They know each other."

Dekla's words cut through the air sharper than North through a thin coat. Norga turned to her slowly, and Astrid could see the rage building in her. She made short, jerky movements.

"What do you mean?"

Dekla's skin went a paler shade of green. "I think she is his lover. The one from the mountain."

"How do you know?" Norga took a threatening step toward her daughter, and Dekla cringed back.

"It doesn't matter. I just do."

Norga struck out, the sound of her slap like the crack of a whip. Dekla stumbled back, holding her cheek, and Astrid saw tears on her cheeks.

Norga spun back, and Astrid fought to stop herself cringing, even with Bjorn between them. She had never seen pure hatred before.

"Is she?" She spoke to Bjorn, but her eyes never left Astrid's face.

Bjorn said nothing, but Astrid saw him tense, the muscles on his back and arms bunching.

"You could not have tricked me so." She shook her head. "The original agreement still stands. You marry my daughter, and there is no war to keep the balance."

"I have found a new ally, and rediscovered my old ones." Bjorn crossed his arms over his chest. "There will be no ceremony. If we must to war, we must."

Norga stilled. "What new ally?"

"The Wind Hag, and her four winds."

There was a murmur from the trolls, and the one Norga had struck from the dais earlier stepped forward.

Astrid felt a grudging respect for his courage.

"The wind was our enemy, from the moment we entered the forest. It harried us all the while there and all the way back until we reached the Far Hills." He pointed to the peaks encircling Norga's peninsula.

"But it came no further?" Norga's voice was controlled.

The troll shook his head.

"You are lying, then." She turned to Bjorn and her eyes were narrow. "You have had no chance to make a new alliance. And the winds cannot reach here."

"I am not lying." Bjorn opened his arms and spoke without force.

The trolls murmured again, and Astrid saw they believed him.

"We shall see. To war it is, then, but it's a war that will be fought without you." Norga's face twisted, and she leapt forward, her arms coming out in attack, and Bjorn leapt to meet her.

Astrid swallowed a cry.

They grappled, locked against each other, the strain on both their faces.

Astrid saw Dekla watching the fight, the strangest expression on her face. Her hand was still to her cheek, as she watched Bjorn take her mother on. Astrid could see it excited her. The open hunger in her eyes made Astrid feel sick to her stomach.

Norga may want to vent her rage personally on Bjorn, but if she lost to him, there were fifty or more trolls to do her bidding. To kill him or capture him.

Astrid edged backward. They needed reinforcements. The odds were too stacked against them. And there was only one who could come to their aid.

She turned and dived into the crowd.

Chapter Thirty-seven

A strid ran up the open stairs of the inner wall to the parapet, lifting her dress so she did not trip on the uneven stonework.

Halfway up, she heard another set of footsteps pounding behind her, and turned.

Dekla.

For a single moment, they looked into each other's eyes, and Astrid saw hatred burn bright in the troll princess. Dekla was chasing after her to kill her, not stop her.

She spun, carried on. Faster. Faster. *Faster.*

She used the words as a rhythm to climb to. She burst out on top of the wall, her lungs heaving, and raced across to the place she'd come up from the cliffs that first day here.

"North." Her scream echoed down the rock, with no wind to snatch it away. She looked down, but nothing stirred. "North!" She thought his name over and over in her head. Concentrated on calling him.

"You have a companion?" Dekla leaned against the wall of the parapet, drawing in gulping breaths.

"How can they help you?"

Astrid looked uneasily behind her, at the parapet guard house with its closed door. It was a dead end.

"North!" The shrieks of the swimming gulls and the swish and rattle of the waves on the pebbles were her only answer from below.

"You tricked me." Dekla's voice quivered with rage. "He was supposed to be mine."

Astrid blinked at the fury, the darkness, in her face.

"He is not. And never will be. Even if you win." Astrid stood taller.

Dekla threw her arm forward in a chopping motion. A child having a tantrum. "You think he should be yours because you are both beautiful?"

"No, he should not be mine because of that." Astrid risked another glance over the wall. Could North really not have heard her? "He is mine because he has chosen to be mine. And I have chosen to be his."

Dekla always unsettled her. She was forever torn between pity and revulsion for the troll. She caught a fleeting impression of pain on Dekla's face. "If you have also chosen to be his, then I am sorry."

Dekla's eyes flickered, a lightning fast change of mood to sly and calculating, and then she bent her head into her hands, and sobbed.

Astrid watched her, knowing Dekla was about to strike. Where was North?

"But you didn't chose him, did you?" she said suddenly. "Your mother did. And you want him only because your mother had one like him. You don't want him for himself."

She'd hoped her words would provoke a response from Dekla, give North a little more time to drag himself off his rock, but instead, Dekla dropped her hands from her face and pounced. She grabbed Astrid up as if she weighed nothing, pinning her arms to her sides, her grip cruel. Biting.

She turned to the inner courtyard and held Astrid up like a trophy. Looking at her feet dangling out over the edge, Astrid was gripped with the certainty Dekla would simply let go. Drop her two floors into the crowd below.

"Bearman," Dekla called down, and Astrid saw Bjorn and Norga freeze mid-wrestle. They were on the ground, grunting as they fought against each other's hold.

Bjorn let go of Norga, pushed himself off her and stood, his face a mask of horror.

"Dekla . . ." His voice was pleading, and he held out a hand, a begging motion.

"I told you I'd make your life a living hell," Dekla called down. "Say goodbye."

"No!" Bjorn's shout echoed through the courtyard.

"You won't even have her body." Dekla turned to the cliff side, lifted Astrid over her head, and the world tilted topsy-turvy. "Farewell, golden girl."

Fear closed Astrid's throat, and she could not respond. Dekla swung her back and then forward, hurling her over the parapet like a javelin.

Bjorn sunk to his knees, Norga forgotten. Everything forgotten but Astrid's scream as she was thrown from the castle wall.

"Well done." Norga's call up to her daughter bounced against the walls of a courtyard otherwise still as the grave. A stunned silence clung like mist to the servants, an uneasy one swirled about the trolls.

Bjorn struggled to his feet, forcing his body to move, though he could barely draw breath. Dekla had taken his air when she'd thrown Astrid over the parapet. He looked for a weapon, anything that would inflict pain, and as if sensing his intent, Dekla hesitated in her descent of the stairs.

"Come." Her mother's dismissive, almost contemptuous, tone at her pause made her flounced down, defiant.

That's right. Come to me.

"There is nothing left for you now." Norga unclipped the ax from her belt and hefted it, and he could see in her eyes she was weighing up the consequences of killing him.

Before he could move, two trolls pounced, each grabbing one of his arms, holding him in place for their mistress. Forcing him back to his knees.

"Either pledge to my daughter or die, and as the blood drains from your throat, think of your precious kingdom. Of how they will curse your name as I cut them down."

"Pledge to your daughter?" Bjorn looked at her, incredulous.

"You heard me." The ax dipped up and down in Norga's hand, like a child bouncing on its parent's knee.

"I will never pledge to that murderess." Bjorn spoke in words so controlled, even Norga peered closer at him. If he lost to his rage now, he would never regain himself. He would become a mad thing.

Norga nodded. A short, sharp movement, decision made. She lifted the ax.

"No." Dekla took the last step into the courtyard. "I want him."

"He doesn't want you." Norga shrugged. "He's too tricky, anyway. It's better this way."

She lifted the ax over her head and stepped back to balance her huge swing.

———⟨✦⟩———

Astrid fell head first, screaming as the pebble beach rushed toward her.

At the last moment, a freezing hand reached out of the air and snatched her up, pulling her to an icy chest. Tiny sparkles of frost dusted her arms and face, and Astrid breathed out in relief, her breath hanging white and wispy as North himself in the air.

"That was close." Her voice wobbled, and she cleared her throat.

North drew her under the lee of the cliff, and put her down.

"The troll who threw you is looking down, trying to see your body."

Astrid brushed the icicles off her skin. "We need to help Bjorn. Are you able?"

"I am well rested." North's face glittered cold and hard, a freezing fog poured into the shape of a man, and Astrid thought she saw vengeance in his changeable eyes.

"Then let's go."

North did not argue. He expanded, and she jumped onto his giant hand, felt the air flow over her face as they shot up from the beach. They raced over the parapet and hovered above the courtyard.

Their arrival went unnoticed.

All eyes were on Bjorn, held on his knees in the courtyard. And on the ax in Norga's hand.

Norga lifted the ax, and brought it up past her head. Stepped back.

"Down." Astrid choked out the order, and North

swooped. They were too late, too far. They would never get there . . .

Before she could bring the ax down, Norga went over, arms windmilling, ax flying, a scream of fury ripping from her mouth. North caught the ax as it spun through the air, turning it sparkling white with frost. Then he crushed it in his fist, into tiny pieces of wood and steel.

Norga lay on her back, kicking out at something, and Astrid heard a cry of pain.

Jorgen?

She saw a flash of brown. Felt her heart lift. He was alive and fighting to the last. Tripping up the troll queen.

But the moment Norga saw North, she ceased her kicking and leapt to her feet, breathing heavily.

"You." She pointed a shaking finger at North. "You helped me, once." She finally seemed to see Astrid. "Who are you, who kills my trolls and flies with the wind?"

"The Mountain Prince's new ally." Being in North's grasp, air swirled around her, teasing her hair out above her head, and snapping her dress.

"The Wind Hag?" Norga staggered back, her mouth slack with shock.

"And neither you nor your daughter will kill my mistress again." North whispered the words, but they swept through the courtyard with a whistle, an implacable, icy promise.

A small movement caught Astrid's eye, and she saw the trolls holding Bjorn release him and step back, staring at North with terror-filled eyes.

Before she could blink, Bjorn had grabbed an ax from one of them and was running forward.

"Norga." His cry was a battle challenge, and the troll queen turned eagerly to meet him. She looked down at her hand and realized her ax was gone and jerked her club off her belt, instead. They met with a crack of wood, Bjorn's ax slicing into the club and sending splinters in every direction.

She jerked the club free of the blade, swung it, but Bjorn ducked and came up right in front of her, ax raised to strike her heart.

She slammed her forehead into his, and he staggered back, shaking his head and blinking his eyes. Norga gave him no moment to recover, she started forward, swinging the club before her, aiming at head height.

Astrid turned to North, eyes wide, a cry on her lips, but the wind shook his head.

"His fight," he said in her ear.

The crack of the club hitting Bjorn's ax handle jerked her back to the battle. Bjorn had raised it, two handed, just in time, and she saw the blow had sent vibrations shuddering through his arms.

Norga swung again, but this time Bjorn didn't

block, he threw himself on his knees and brought the ax over his head, buried it deep into Norga's chest.

She let the club go and it spun through the air and slammed into the wall, splitting down the middle. Her hands came up to the head of the ax, almost completely embedded in her heart, and looked down at it in surprise.

"I . . ." She toppled and fell dead to the floor.

Bjorn looked down on her, a mere flick of his eyes, and then up to Astrid. She blinked.

"Whatever you did before, for saving my lady from her fall, the slate is wiped clean and I am in your debt, North Wind," he said, and he did not take his eyes from her.

"The slate was already wiped clean when I warned you of the troll's tricks yesterday," North said, his voice chill and dry, but approving. Bjorn had avenged them all.

"Then I owe you two debts." Bjorn moved toward them, toward her.

"And what of me?" Dekla thumped her chest on the last word, striding through the cowering servants, the dumb-struck trolls. "What of *me*?"

Astrid saw her grab an ax from the belt of a troll just as Bjorn had, gripping it two-handed.

"Enough." North's roar was the rumble of an iceberg crashing into the sea. He tossed Astrid down into Bjorn's arms and stretched out his hand, grabbing the troll princess by the neck like a rat. "You are the one who threw my mistress from the castle walls."

It was as if Dekla only just realized who and what she was dealing with. She cried out, dropping the ax as North flew straight up, dragging her behind him.

When her last screams faded to nothing, the silence in the courtyard still lingered.

"Where has he taken her?" Bjorn asked at last, gently setting Astrid on the ground.

She shuddered, still in the circle of his arms, remembering the place where the sky met nothing. "A place from which she can never return."

There was a murmur from the crowd at her words and she suddenly realized they stood, without weapons, without North, in a courtyard full of trolls. And they had the undivided attention of every single one.

Chapter Thirty-eight

Bjorn dropped his arms from her shoulders and took half a step in front of her as the first troll moved forward.

A flash of dark brown winked in and then out of sight at Astrid's feet.

"Jorgen?" Her throat felt as if it held a stone. She ignored the trolls, and crouched down, her hand out, patting the air. "Jorgen?"

"I am trying to be an invisible aide, my lady," he answered dryly. "Except now the enemy knows where I am."

Astrid stood hastily, her face flushed. "I thought . . ."

"No time." Bjorn tried to push her further behind him, but she resisted. Looked up into the sky for North.

Another troll stepped forward, and then another, then they were running, not at them, but around them. Dividing like a river around an immoveable rock and racing out the castle entrance.

"We will not challenge you again, Mountain Prince. Leave us be and we will keep to ourselves." The troll who called out was the one Norga had hit on the dais. He stood still a moment in the surging crowd, and Astrid saw Bjorn nod to him, and with an almost imperceptible bob of his body, the most minimal of bows, the troll followed his new subjects out of the castle gates.

With them gone, the courtyard seemed huge and empty, save for the servants huddled near the kitchen doors.

"You are free," Bjorn called to them, and Astrid saw they looked dazed, like birds too long kept caged. They did not know how to respond to the open door.

She walked toward them. "You can return to your homes."

The woman she'd exchanged glances with earlier shrank back, afraid of her. They were all afraid of her. The woman edged toward the gate, past Astrid and Bjorn, keeping the wall to her back. When she reached the huge open doors, she scuttled through them. It started a stampede. Men and women jostled for place as they ran. None looked back.

"I don't blame them for their haste," a voice said at Astrid's feet. Weak, but sardonic. "This place could kill you."

Bjorn crouched and put out a hand. Felt the air. "Give me a clue, Jorgen," he said, and Jorgen winked into sight.

He lay, dry and shriveled, curled up on himself.

Astrid forced down a cry. He looked near death.

"As bad as you look, you saved my neck when Norga tried to ax me, didn't you?" Bjorn knelt beside him, and felt his forehead. Lifted worried eyes to Astrid, and she came to kneel on Jorgen's other side.

Bjorn frowned in concentration and before Astrid's eyes, Jorgen seemed to improve, to uncurl.

"You have your powers back?"

"Norga is dead." He spoke with no emotion.

"So is her poisonous daughter." Chill air descended from above, enveloping them, and Astrid's skirts danced around her ankles.

"Thank you." She rose and turned to where she knew North stood, lifted a hand to his cheek, and he shimmered into being. "Can I ask another thing of you?"

"Take the vedfe back to the forest?" North's head was cocked to one side, his eyes on Jorgen.

"Yes. Return the vedfe to his forest. There are some things I need to find in this castle and give back to their owners, and I don't know how long it will take me."

"What things?" Bjorn lifted his hand from Jorgen's brow and frowned.

"Magical things," Astrid told him. "The price of your rescue."

Bjorn looked up at the grim, black battlements and she could see the distaste on his face. "I have many treasures, let us rather leave now with the North Wind. I will compensate those who helped you."

Astrid shook her head. "You go then, with Jorgen.

These treasures are special, and I realized long after they were given to me that the owners expect them back if it is in my power to do so. Otherwise I will not be their equal."

Bjorn stood, and they faced each other with Jorgen lying between them.

"Who are they, these people you are in debt to over me?"

"They are . . . women like me."

Bjorn looked down at Jorgen. Astrid saw already some of the healing power he'd used earlier had been leeched out of the vedfe this far from the forest.

"If it is something you must do, of course I will stay and help you."

A lightness enveloped her, and it felt to Astrid as if a wind sprite had taken up residence here. That there was the tiny possibility of an air platform. "North will be back for us when he has rested enough."

North nodded, short and sharp, as he lifted Jorgen gently into his palm.

"Go well." Jorgen waved as North arced up and away, and suddenly, Astrid and Bjorn were alone.

"Let us find your treasures and be gone," Bjorn told her, holding her close a moment.

She rested her forehead against his chest and nodded. Drew back. "I think I know where to look."

"There is something here." Bjorn called from the next room, and Astrid looked toward the door as he came in. He had a small sack in his hands, and when Astrid looked inside, she found her three treasures.

"The room where you found them must be Dekla's chamber."

"This one is probably Norga's, then."

Astrid agreed. The room, though untidy and dank, was well-furnished.

"We can go now. These were all I came for."

"One moment." Bjorn had flipped open the lid of a chest and was tossing things from it. "This looks like the treasure you gave Dekla." He held up a golden knife, and as her gaze fell upon it, Astrid knew with certainty it was *hers*.

The old Wind Hag's.

Stolen from her dead body by her murderess.

She reached out and took it from Bjorn, and strength flowed through her, crackled along her arm and up, making her hair stand out with static. As if she'd been wrapped in layer upon layer of padding and it had finally been stripped away. She could suddenly feel properly.

She could feel each of her winds. Knew they could feel her. There was a connection between them and she could command them from anywhere.

She felt a tingle down her spine, and almost heard the click deep within her, two parts of a whole finally fitting smoothly together. Where they belonged.

She perceived with wonder what the gifts she'd been given had cost their givers.

Understood that had she not sought out the treasures to return them, she would forever have lost a part of herself. Of her power. She shivered at the thought.

"What is it?" Bjorn asked, looking at her with a strange expression.

She ran her fingers down the golden hilt, engraved with wavy lines, and something made her throw the knife upwards, glittering end over end, to hear the singing sound it made as it turned in the air. She reached out and grabbed it in mid-spin, slipped it into her pocket.

"It is mine." And, if it should one day be necessary, may she give it with as much generosity and grace as her gifts had been given to her.

"Good." Bjorn flicked the chest lid closed and held out his hand. "Let's go."

Astrid smiled and slipped her hand into his. And they walked out of the door together.

ABOUT THE AUTHOR

Michelle Diener was born in London, grew up in South Africa and now lives in Australia with her family. She was bitten by the travel bug at a young age and has managed to feed her addiction with numerous trips to exciting places all over the world. She writes historical fiction and fantasy, and loves traveling to other times as well as places through the pages of a good book.

If you enjoyed Mistress of the Wind, read on for an excerpt of the first book in *The Dark Forest Series*, The Golden Apple, based on the fairy tale The Princess on the Glass Hill. The Golden Apple is followed by its sequel, The Silver Pear.

THE GOLDEN APPLE

Chapter One

The laughter rising from the festivities below was not at her, although it felt like it was.

Kayla threaded her fingers together on her knees and closed her eyes anyway, trying to block out the sounds of merriment.

She was part of the entertainment, and her father's subjects were throwing themselves wholeheartedly into the spirit of the occasion.

Whereas she . . . if she had been clamped naked into the stocks, she could not have felt more exposed, more vulnerable. More disrespected.

Even knowing today was coming had not prepared her for sitting high above a shouting, laughing crowd, merry with holiday fever, in a gilded chair on top of a glass mountain.

She opened her eyes again and watched the fair-goers move below her, skirting the mountain as they talked, ate and drank. More a mystery than how a glass mountain came to be in the jousting field was their acceptance of the mountain at all. It had appeared in the night a few days ago, and now it glittered and flashed in the early morning sun, blinding the unwary.

Was she the only one who wondered at the power it would take to create something like this?

It stood perhaps three stories high, almost as high as the castle itself, but although its peak did not reach the height of the castle towers, it squatted malevolently beside her family home, dominating it.

But if the mountain made no sense, what made the least sense of all was that her father would do this to her.

Auction her off to the boldest adventurer to try his luck here today.

And yet he had.

He'd stuck her up on this crystal monstrosity like the cherry on top of a cake. Her dress wasn't red, though. It was virginal white.

And that color was no longer appropriate for her. Not after last night.

The breeze blowing the sounds of the fair and the aroma of cooking pies up to her suddenly felt cool against her heated cheeks.

As if it could sense her thoughts, the golden apple in her lap throbbed, heating the skin of her thighs through her thin skirts.

She looked down at it with loathing. A distorted image of her face looked back at her through the shine. As distorted as her world had become since her father embarked on this mad course.

She lifted her hand, hovered it over the apple. Her father had worn gloves when he placed it in her lap, just before she was lifted up the glass hill.

"Don't touch it," he'd said. Then he'd walked away, her obedience a foregone conclusion.

She wanted—wanted so badly—to toss it. To throw it, as far and as hard as she could, away from her.

She hesitated, just a moment, then closed her hand over it. And cried out. A light leapt from the apple to her palm, the pain hot, intense. She let go, and immediately the light disappeared. The pain lingered, a throbbing reminder, and then faded away.

She stiffened her spine against the tears clogging her throat and pricking her eyes. She had given away her innocence last night, so pride was the only thing she had left.

No, that was wrong.

Her mouth lifted in the corners. She'd given nothing away, only gained something. Some power. Some control. She had exercised a deeply personal right. To choose her first lover. Before one was chosen for her.

Did she regret it?

She pressed her thighs together, the movement causing the apple to wobble, and thought of the gentle caresses, the soft sighs, as natural and calming as the falling night rain.

The sight of her lover, tall, broad-shouldered, filling her vision as he held himself levered above her. The hot, heady smell of his skin. The contrast of her pale hand against the bronze of his hard-muscled arm.

She shivered.

No. She did not regret it.

She looked out over the arena, at the crowds filing into the stalls for a good seat to the spectacle. Above her, a bird cried, the sound haunting, and she shaded her eyes and searched the skies for it. Yearned to leap from the glass peak and fly to join it, leave the crowds and her fate behind her.

As if on cue with her thoughts of fate, one by one the knights arrived. They were a rainbow swirl of blue, green, yellow and red plumes and banners, polished metal shining almost as much at the glass mountain.

They paraded, playing the crowd, racing in a loop down the length of the course and around the mountain. Getting the measure of what they were up against.

She recognized a few of them. Some were her father's own men—men she'd known since they were boys come as knights-in-training—some were in service to other kings, princes and lords. All were here for one thing.

Power.

Winning her was the means to get it.

They intended to use her, to take this opportunity offered by her father and exploit it, and by dint of taking part in this contest at all, they had her unreserved contempt.

They obviously felt the same way about her, as not one so much as glanced her way. She was but a means to an end, and for her father to put her in this position was unsupportable. Incredible.

She'd thought she'd managed to control the bands of steel that tightened across her chest when she thought about what he'd done to her, but she'd been wrong.

Kayla gasped for air, every gulp like breathing the poisonous smoke of a tanner's fire, burning her throat, all the way down to her lungs.

The trumpet sounded, and Kayla saw her father standing in his box, dressed in rich red robes, his crown in place. He lifted a hand.

Silence fell, rippling out from the crowd until the only sound was the creak of leather saddles and the huff of horse breath.

"Welcome, gentlemen. The rules are simple. You will each have a chance to ride your horse up the glass mountain, and pluck the golden apple from my daughter's lap. Whoever succeeds will have my daughter's hand and become the heir to my kingdom."

The knights let out a cheer—dogs barking as their master threw them a bone. Kayla wondered how happy they'd be to know the bone had been tasted already. Her lips curved. Oh, she did not regret last night for even a moment.

"Is every competitor present?" the herald called out.

There was a murmur of assent, and then a shuffle of horses near the gates. A late-comer?

Kayla almost deigned not to look. What did she care how many and who? But the murmurs of the crowd piqued her curiosity, and she raised a hand to shield her eyes and saw him.

A knight all in black, on a black horse.

Her heart gave a traitorous lurch at the figure he cut, his mount dancing through the crowd, moving towards her shimmering perch.

He was the first to approach her. Acknowledge her.

And when he was close enough, he raised his visor.

The breath caught in Kayla's throat. Her heart stuttered.

Bright blue eyes looked up at her. No longer warm and laughing as they had been last night, but cold with purpose.

He turned with a salute and rode back to the waiting pack, and she clenched her skirts with white-knuckled fists.

Whatever she had to do, she would make sure he was the one.

"What in hell is that thing?" Jasper stood with Rane in the knights' holding pen and eyed the glass monstrosity with dislike. Rane knew it was an unwelcome obstacle to Jasper's plans.

Usually anything that was a problem to Jasper was cause for celebration in Rane's view, but in this instance, Jasper's goal was his own. For the last time, though.

"A glass mountain."

"I can see that, but where'd the king get it?" Jasper's plump face was unusually pale.

"Dark magic," Rane answered shortly. He could feel magic coming off the thing. Crackling the air around it. Snapping at him. And Kayla sat on top of it, her face blank and white. At its mercy.

As she was at yours just last night, his conscience whispered. And did you not take from her her only bargaining chip?

He fisted his reins in the heavy black gloves and his mount moved uneasily beneath him, sensitive to his mood.

Of all the stains on his soul, letting Kayla of Gaynor think she was seducing him while he reeled her in as finely as any master would be the hardest to wash clean.

She'd been determined to give away her virginity last night and oh, she was sweet.

He had no excuse.

He could have walked away, but he did not. Even as she whispered her joy at the taking, moaned his name, knifes of disgust tore through his heart.

Why had he not walked away?

He'd meant only to gain her favor. Become her favorite, even while she thought he was not participating in the contest. So when he did appear, it would seem as if he'd come to save her.

He'd been here days before the others, and he knew full well the task set was impossible. The only way to succeed was with help.

And who could help him more in this than the princess herself?

"Rane? Are you listening?"

He jerked his head down, saw Jasper's impatience in his stiff bearing. "Yes?"

"You said dark magic. Who would oblige the King so?"

It wasn't impatience making Jasper so tense, Rane realized—it was fear.

He shrugged. What did he care whose power the king made use of for his strange husband-choosing?

"I've heard whispers that a few of the kings in the Middleland have a sorcerer obliging them, these days. Now the King of Gaynor?" Jasper rubbed the side of his face, and Rane noticed his fingers trembled."You suspect some plot?" Rane controlled his expression as Jasper flinched at his words. He'd never seen Jasper this rattled.

The sheer size and magnificence of the mountain, the strangeness and the power of it, pointed to someone of immense power. And Jasper was in the business of power. Rane knew Jasper thought he had an edge with a sorcerer for a brother, but if the King of Gaynor had a sorcerer of this calibre on his side, there were few who could stand in his way.

"No . . . No. I wonder who the sorcerer is, that's all."

"The question should rather be, why is the King making the trial so difficult? Why does he want a fighter and a madman for his daughter?"

Jasper's eyes widened. "You think he wants a bodyguard for her?"

Rane had not, but it was a good point. One to ponder. "I thought he might have a further quest in mind. One that would take more than a spoilt prince to accomplish. A quest he could trust only to his future heir."

"With this trial he can sidestep the rules of royal marriage, and find the best man for the job, even if he is a commoner." Jasper nodded his head slowly.

"Only a theory." Rane's eyes swung back to the magic hill, back to the woman in her white gown, her dark hair woven with tiny white flowers and flowing over her shoulders. Hair he'd grabbed in fistfuls, felt like silk between his fingers as he exposed her throat to his mouth. Hair that twined round his arms as he'd taken them both to a better place for a while.

Jasper's gaze turned curious, and Rane regretted

his thoughts. Regretted what must have passed across his face.

"Just get me the apple, and you can have your brother back, and all the pleasures that come with marriage to the royal house. Or not." Jasper shrugged. "Walk away from it all if you choose, if the king has a more dangerous job in mind for you than impregnating his daughter. I don't care."

Rane didn't clamp down on his hatred fast enough. Some of it must have flashed across his face for Jasper's eyes to narrow.

"Any hint of a double-cross, Rane, and you'll never see your good-for-nothing brother again." Jasper paused and his face hardened. "Except maybe in little pieces."

CPSIA information can be obtained
at www.ICGtesting.com
Printed in the USA
FSOW02n1257210416
19529FS